The Shepherd
Of
Spring Hollow

Aubret H. White

The Shepherd
Of
Spring Hollow

Aubret H. White

PUBLISHED BY:
BRENTWOOD CHRISTIAN PRESS
4000 BEALLWOOD AVENUE
COLUMBUS, GEORGIA 31904

A Gift Presentation to

Clyde

My friend in Christ

In Honor of

Date

July 12, 2001

Comments

Keep Clean & Pure

Christ White

Ps. 139: 23-4

3

Table of Contents

Acknowledgment

Friendship and professional helps are two attributes of great value a person receives when attempting to write a book. Without the help of talented persons communications would break down and the end would come prematurely.

I thank my wife Florence, who has tolerated my various moods and work habits while writing this manuscript. Also for her willingness to read, correct, offer information and constructive criticism. She has been my helpmate and sweetheart for fifty three years. Florence is retired from teaching elementary education in public schools after forty two years.

I deeply appreciate Cathy Karst for her dedication in typing the rough draft of this manuscript. She willingly gave of her time to make *The Shepherd of Spring Hollow* readable for editing. Her ability to understand and decipher my script was amazing.

I thank Carol McDonald for her pencil art work for this manuscript. Carol is a Senior High Student at the Prattville High School, Prattville, Alabama. Her willingness to read the manuscript and select the art suitable for several events is deeply appreciated. Her giftedness and recommendation is highly praised by her art teacher and many other acquaintances. Also her dedication and attendance to her Lord and church is praiseworthy.

Without the Divine Love of my Father in heaven, ministered to me by the Holy Spirit, I could not have had a thought or lifted my pen to write. Through tears of joy and praise to Him, my prayers were answered. With all my being I say, "Thank you, Father."

The names of persons and placed contained in *The Shepherd of Spring Hollow* are purely fictional. If there is a similarity, it is totally coincidental and no harm or plagiarism is meant.

My prayer is that the inspiration offered herein will generate into lives of all ages who read. In the Lord's Church, all have a responsibility to grow and serve Him with dedication. Jesus gives the gifts, we deploy their content in service to His glory.

May your heart be warmed in the joy of Jesus as you read.

Foreword

The community of Willow Bend consisted of about 150 native residents. On special days, such as Church Homecoming, Decoration Day at the cemetery, the population would double, and then some. It was common knowledge that everyone claimed kin to a lot of folk scattered from here to yon. Scattered among the small community were a few folk whom no one could trust, nor would they trust the good folk. People just called it bad blood. There seemed to be no cure for these social ills. Most times, when social ills trouble the community, a spiritual void is evident and that generally leads to immoral acts. When the spiritual dilemma goes unchecked or neglected, the community gets sick and folk begin to blame someone else for this trouble. Blame turns to suspicions, and suspicions to hate. Unless hate is corrected, it turns to violence. All violence has its beginnings in neglect and non-application of love. When persons of a community, whether by individuals or by family, turn their attentions inward to deal with problems, their spiritual security system is neglected and friendships destroyed as trusts are questioned, where love and mutual help were once strong and dependent.

Timothy Karr was about the most common young man any community could produce. He was plain, a little awkward in his walk, only talked when first spoken to, honest as the day is long, non sociable, but respected by youth as well as grownups. No one expected Timothy to amount to anything. Everyone thought him to be too polite and vulnerable. Timothy respected people of all walks of life. His obedient respect for his teachers, both public school and church leaders, brought him honors that others had to work for.

Timothy's presence seemed to bring security and a sense of peace to any gathering. Many times his opinion was asked for to settle questions. Even in that, he did not push himself on anyone. He would use bits and pieces of others' comments and intertwine them so as to make them feel they were not left out and actually were a part of the equation. He was indeed a friend and a great blessing to all.

Timothy was born in Willow Bend. The commonness of this small town was inbred in him. His mother, Karen, was twenty-three years of age when she gave birth to her first child, a son. Timothy's father was twenty-six. Rance Karr was tall, skinny built, mild mannered, hard working, and a good provider for his family. Both parents were committed Christians who accepted their church responsibilities faithfully. There was never a question as to where the family would be on Sunday morning. The activities of Willow Bend Baptist Church were as natural and important as was any daily meal. Mr.& Mrs. Karr believed spiritual maturity was vital to character growth for mature adulthood. For this reason, their children were never neglected.

Spring Hollow community is representative of hundreds of others across our land. These communities are filled with people who care deeply for their families. However, there are elements within these communities, families and groups, who are willing to sacrifice less fortunate ones, not like themselves as non-sociable. These are people left to themselves without friendships of the whole community. They must make their way the best they can. Such communities are not spiritually healthy. It is void of love, God's love, even though Christians live there and a church house is present.

Spring Hollow Baptist Church is typical of many other churches of all denominations. It is "there" and whoever wishes to attend, may do so. There is no effort to extend an invitation. This is not God's way. If any, or all who live in the community should visit on any Sunday, chaos would abound.

One problem is that people attach themselves to a name for their spiritual endearment, or a cause for their own selfish desires. They make themselves comfortable in their choices. The "old time religion," not Christian, is lived out to the end without ever experiencing rebirth from God through Jesus Christ.

A church or community within the confines of such spiritual attributes is sick. Revival is needed and must happen, or death will occur. Self-centeredness and complacency are spiritual diseases which will kill its victims. Holy Spirit revival is a tough

7

love medicine from God. His medicine for cure of the illness is very powerful. It is known to cast out devils, forgive sin, cleanse from sin, restore relationships of friendship and marriage. It has been known to heal many other illnesses. God's medicine literally restores life from death. Anyone who accepts God's medicine becomes a new creation.

Spring Hollow Baptist Church chose to repent and be restored to Christ Jesus. The Holy Spirit began working His will in people's lives and they became a living organism, rather than an organization with a lifeless cause.

The Shepherd of Spring Hollow, the book title, is not about a dynamic personality of its pastor. Nor is it about his ability to preach. It is not about his high educational attributes. The pastor doesn't have either of these. Neither is it about wealthy and powerful community tycoons. It is about a small church repenting of sins against their Savior; then obeying the leadership of the Holy Spirit. The results were a whole host of spiritually dead being raised to new life in Christ Jesus. The Spring Hollow experience is not something new from God. It is the new birth He sent His Son to accomplish in whomever accepts Him.

The Old Testament record of numbering people by the command of God was for His purpose and honor. Numbering people by man for his purpose and glory was sinful. The act by man minimized the trust in, and dependence, upon God. It was an attempt to transfer power from God to man. Immediately the plague from God was instituted and the community suffered death. The plague stopped when God heard repentance.

Spring Hollow Baptist Church, through repentance, stopped numbering people and magnifying their growth successes. The church stopped bragging about the amount of money flowing into its bank account. It renewed vows appropriate with God's salvation, no more or no less as He required. The plague of accusing, bickering, slandering and pride stopped. God's promised blessings came immediately. The people of Spring Hollow began working out from the abundance of their salvation what God put in for His glory.

Within the community of Spring Hollow lived people and families ostracized by church people. The church folk did not believe such trash measured up to their social status. Spring Hollow Baptist Church was sin sick, but did not know they were.

Most people, or churches, construct their own background mirror filled with contempt, malice, lovelessness, selfishness and other sins. It takes the Holy Spirit to reveal these truths to them for change. God's holiness reveals the sinner's errors. God did just that to the membership of Spring Hollow Baptist church.

God's amazing grace began its healing in Spring Hollow. His healing became evident in the church's acceptance of ostracized families. One family was Choctaw Indian, and another a drunkard's family. God's grace restored a couple from malice. He restored peace and unity in public school problems. He replaced suspicion and loneliness with solace and comfort of the Holy Spirit.

Chapter 1

The Announcement - The Call to Preach

The Sunday morning worship service seemed filled with unusual expectations. No one knew why. The same people were present. The Sunday School attendance was the same. The pastor was wearing his only Sunday suit. All five deacons were present as they always were, along with their families. The piano didn't sound anything out of the ordinary. The two keys, B & G, were dead. No piano tuner lived in Willow Bend, but Willow Bend Baptist Church had no money for the repair anyhow. Most people didn't know one note from the other, so odd sounds from the piano didn't make any difference.

The same number of people was in the choir, five men and eleven women. Mrs. Zanerly was in her choir place, and her flat alto voice never changed. Mr. Alex was still singing all the words of every song one note behind everyone else. No one reported any serious gossip. There were no groups with their heads all pointing together. Three tiny babies were crying as usual; their mothers trying to keep them quiet, without advertising their method of feeding.

The preacher delivered a good sermon. He was evangelistic as usual. He stressed giving and mission support. However, there was a sense of expectancy in his manner that fired the spirit of the church family. Something was being prepared to be disclosed at the end of the worship service. Was he resigning? There had been no pulpit committee present for several years. And, there was not one present today. His leaving was practically ruled out, at least for today. Perhaps a young couple was going to announce their marriage. A mental inventory was taken, and that was ruled out because no one was seriously dating.

The pastor ended his sermon with a prayer of gratitude and deep compassionate feeling. He particularly thanked God for His bountiful mercy and grace that was evident today in worship. He thanked Jesus for the families and hoped for more to commit themselves to the Lords work. He challenged the church through a moving invitation. Tears were being shed by many, but there was no public response.

The pastor concluded the invitation by asking the congregation to be seated for an announcement and presentation. Many looked around to see if someone was there who might be the object of the pastor's comment. All seemed to be home folks.

The pastor broke the brief silence by announcing that God had visited Willow Bend Baptist Church and called to Himself a young man to preach His gospel. The congregation was excited! Who? They all knew that no one had volunteered for any full-time Christian work during the last twenty-five years. The announcement was electrifying to the congregation.

With a big smile and his voice clear and commanding, the pastor asked Timothy Karr to come forward and stand by his side. He announced clearly and convincingly, Timothy Karr has heard Jesus calling him to the task of preaching and pastoring. He is one of our own, reared in this church and nurtured by you. Now he is going wherever Jesus Christ sends, to be what you have trained him to be. Do I hear an amen to this call? The church literally roared approval! People praised the Lord publicly who had never done so before. Someone was heard saying, "Maybe the drought is broken and we will have many more Godly visits in Willow Bend."

Timothy was asked to say whatever he wished to express. He commented:

"I am proud to preach the gospel of Jesus Christ. Thank you for being my church family. If you have doubts about God calling me, you will have to ask Him about His decision. All I can say, and know, is that He did speak to my heart and I said yes."

Engineering had been Timothy's choice vocation. He was just beginning his second semester of his second year at the University. He was home for a week of needed rest before completing his second year of studies. Timothy's decision for the ministry did not come suddenly while home on vacation. He had been heavily burdened about the commitment for more than a year. In fact, he knew that serious church work would always be a part of his life; even in engineering work. However, God intervened, and Timothy was obedient to His choice life style.

Timothy had written to his pastor about six months prior to his decision of commitment. In his letter, he expressed with deep concern the burden the Lord had laid upon him. He wanted help for understanding. Timothy knew his pastor would give the best counseling and guidance he needed.

Two days after arriving home from the University, he chanced to meet his pastor at a local service station. It was at this meeting that they made plans to meet on Saturday morning at a neighbors fish lake. There, they knew no one would disturb their talk. This meeting was an experience Timothy would never forget. He knew his pastor was intelligent and a good pastor and preacher. But, he did not know his pastor was so prophetic, particularly as it was related to him. The pastor told Timothy how he believed God was planning his life. When Timothy was a young teenager, his pastor witnessed the Lord's hand upon him and believed that not long in the future God would reveal His call. These revelations fascinated Timothy as he weighed the evidence for this day. Timothy felt so humbled as the pastor spoke of God's call for him to be His special witness. During this quiet time with his pastor, Timothy learned things about himself and what God was doing in his life, that had never occurred to his mind. It was an experience he would never forget.

They discussed the shift of college interest from engineering at the University, to ministerial student religion major, and a change to the Baptist College. This somewhat frightened Timothy, but he knew that God's will must be followed. The change would be from building things for people to that of leading and building people for God.

During his last year at Baptist College, Timothy registered to enter the seminary in the fall. He was a dedicated worker. Not only was his mind in good shape, but also his slim, strong body as well. He availed himself for job openings so that support from home would be minimal. He knew that Dad and Mom needed for themselves what they were sending him. Timothy owned no car. He was not tempted to be going here and there, neglecting vital study time. Occasionally, a friend would ask if he cared to go off campus for an evening meal. Other than that, he attended to his part-time job and studies.

During the first year at Seminary, Timothy managed to go home about once a month. He would hitch a ride with another student who was going beyond where he lived, or, sometimes within fifty miles. In the cases of not quite making it home by fifty miles, his parents would come for him and return him to the pick up area. This was an inconvenience to his parents. Parents are always glad to see their children. They were especially proud when the pastor gave Timothy an opportunity to preach. Though inexperienced, Timothy was showing good signs of spiritual growth. His sincerity overshadowed his lack of training.

The community of Willow Bend loved Timothy. Many non-Baptist and lost people attended the worship services on the days he preached. Some of the quarreling, unhappy folk of Willow Bend were made welcome. The folk of Willow Bend began to note that God had indeed visited them and picked one of their young men to preach the gospel. Due to this great Godly visitation, several adults, young people, and children were saved. Several whole families were included in their number. These decisions did not happen just when Timothy came home and preached. People began to expect public professions of faith every Sunday. The small Methodist Church became alive, and revival broke out. Serious prayer time began to happen in many homes. People would weep openly in Sunday School classes and worship services. The Sunday night and Wednesday night prayer service increased tremendously in attendance. Why all this? People of Willow Bend began repenting of their sins and let the Holy Spirit work His will in their lives. Timothy's decision was just a very late work of God that He wanted to do all along. But,

He couldn't because of hardened hearts. The Lord wants to do in every community what He was doing in Willow Bend. God may use Jill, Alice, Mae, Tom, John, Joe or any others in your community to bring about an awakening to His will. It also can be an event. The challenge is to look for it. Expect God to fulfill your prayer request. Out of these many spiritual experiences Timothy went through, at home and at Seminary, he learned and developed the greatest gift for the ministry. He became a soul-winner for Jesus Christ.

Chapter 2

Invitation to Preach

Timothy was a good student of God's Word. The more he searched God's great truths, the more he loved the Lord for calling him. The old hymn, "What a Friend We Have In Jesus," became a reality and he put it into practice.

Unknown to Timothy, the word about what was happening in Willow Bend, came to the ears of a small church and community about a hundred miles away. The people there were about the same as those in Willow Bend. The most important fact, there were people who needed Jesus Christ. There were church folk who needed commitment to Jesus Christ. Spring Hollow Baptist Church needed a change. Two deacons of the six serving Spring Hollow Baptist Church became convinced that such an awakening was sorely needed. The other four were not so sure that anything worthwhile could happen at Spring Hollow. However, all six agreed that something was wrong and whatever could be done would help this problem. It was agreed upon that the three deacons who were employed in the city where the Baptist Seminary was located would contact the young preacher, Timothy Karr. Spring Hollow Baptist Church had been without a pastor for five months. Retired preachers and laymen had kept the church going. However, the "going" of the church had just about "gone," and desperation had set in. Fair attendance had fallen off to low attendance. The offering was going the way of attendance. The lack of giving was effecting the overall missions gifts. The spiritual fervor was suffering. Most church folk fell into a spiritual lull, and problems were coming from every direction.

These three deacons agreed to stop by the Seminary after work on Tuesday afternoon. They hardly knew what to say to a young man whom they had never met. Before getting out of the car, one suggested that they pray and ask the Holy Spirit for directions. After praying, they walked inside the administration building and inquired as to the whereabouts of Timothy Karr. They also informed the person to whom they talked, why they were there. With directions in hand, they drove to the dorm where Timothy lived on the campus.

Timothy was working on a research paper to be turned in the following week when he heard a gentle knock on the door. He opened the door to face three strangers.

"Yes sir, May I help you?"

"Are you Reverend Timothy Karr?" the deacon spokesman said.

"I don't know about the Reverend, but I am Timothy Karr. Will you come in?"

"We don't have much time as we are on our way home from work. And, we do not want to take your time from studies. Brother Timothy, you have been recommended to us, the Spring Hollow Baptist Church, as a possibility of becoming our pastor. We want to know if you might come to Spring Hollow Sunday week and preach, that is, if you don't already have a commitment."

A warm friendly feeling came over Timothy as he bowed his head in a moment of silence. The deacons became aware of this young man's deep appreciation for their being there. Timothy slowly raised his head. His eyes were filling with tears.

"I'm deeply obliged for your thoughtfulness that I am invited to your church. No, I have no other obligations for that Sunday. I am glad you asked me. This will be an unusual experience for me, as well as for Spring Hollow. However, there is a little problem. I have no transportation. My parents have not been able to buy another car that I might use. Neither the part time job I have offers such help. I ride the city bus to work. However, I'll talk to some student pastors who drive in the direction of your church. Perhaps I can hitch a ride. I will need directions and perhaps a location where someone might meet me on my arrival. It will be necessary for me to come on Saturday as that is the day student pastors go to their church field. And, another thing, they return to the campus on Monday. We have no classes on

17

Monday. So, the problem, if it is a problem, is that I would be at Spring Hollow for two nights. Is there a motel nearby or a home who offers overnight lodging?"

One of the deacons, Josh White, seemed restless, glancing at the others as if he had a solution to Timothy's problem. Indeed he did, and with joy he presented it with certainty.

"Brother Timothy, you do not have a problem anymore. I've just settled it. I have a very dependable pick-up truck that I use only on weekends. I ride to work with these fellows and pay my fare. This is what I'll do. I can drive my truck on Friday and leave it with you on our way home. You can drive to Spring Hollow on Saturday. It will be full of fuel so that there will not be an expense on your part. How about that deal? Then on Monday, you can ride in with us, back to the Seminary."

Timothy began to laugh. The deacons joined in the laughter and, when the meeting was over, everyone was weeping unashamedly.

The youngest deacon of the three said with a choking somber voice, "I don't ever remember a time in my life that I've experienced such joy in Christ as I've felt in this short meeting. Before, I expressed doubt that anything of value could happen at Spring Hollow, but after this meeting, I'm expecting God to work wonders among us. How do you feel, brother deacons?" With a hardy "amen," they agreed.

"We must be on our way home, Brother Timothy We will see you Friday week to leave the truck with you. Will you lead us in prayer?"

"I'll be most honored," Timothy said.

Timothy prayed for these men and the church. He prayed for all concerned in preparation for the visit to Spring Hollow. Goodbyes were said and the deacons left. Timothy returned to his studies with a joy of glorious expectations toward Spring Hollow.

On the way back to Spring Hollow the three brother deacons were oddly silent for about half an hour. Their thoughts were about God's will for their church and community. John was the first to speak.

"I can hardly wait until prayer meeting tomorrow evening. Josh, how about you telling the church what we have experienced. I'll join in somewhere and tell how you volunteered your truck for Brother Timothy's use."

"O.K., I'll do it," Josh committed. "But, my emotions might get the best of me. Come to think of it that might be the best thing to happen. Some of us need our dry eyes wet with tears of joy and repentance. Yeah, that will be good for us."

"Lay it on us Josh; we all need what Jesus has for us. I hope some barriers will be broken down, because, my brothers, I've already been revived."

Wiley spoke up. "Fellows, I'm not one to butt in, however, I would like to challenge our church to prepare themselves for what the Holy Spirit is about to do in Spring Hollow. Something is going to happen and we are not prepared. So I want to tell us to be confessing our sins and praying for ourselves and each other during the next two weeks."

"We'll say amen to that, eh Josh," John said. Josh nodded his head in agreement.

That evening at supper, John, Wiley, and Josh told their families about the meeting with Timothy Karr. They asked their wives to spread the word tomorrow that Wednesday night would be an informative prayer meeting. With these plans completed and their other chores settled for the day, these three families rested and slept; the best they had been able to do for many months. Peace is a profitable element in life when we surrender all to the Holy Spirit for management.

Upon arriving home from work on Wednesday afternoon, Jake Dawson was the first to be called. His interest was if the young preacher man in question could lead a congregation like Spring Hollow, since most of the membership was more than 50 years of age. John confessed that he did not know. However, he assured it would be a two-way street. This was an opportunity for their church to grow and for them to grow a preacher for God, by loving and supporting His work and preaching. Jake was satisfied.

John called Larry Willoby next. He was concerned about salary. Since this young man would be in school during the week and actually on the church field for two, maybe three days. Would the salary be determined for the two or three days? Since he was in his early twenties and single, would the church be satisfied to consider a salary based on a minimum wage for the time spent on the church field? John assured Larry that all this would be openly and prayerfully discussed by all. We are a Baptist church and every member has a right to know how his or her tithes and gifts are spent. But, we should not consider a pastor's salary regardless of age, on an hourly basis. We must wait until after the church makes it decision about the call. Larry seemed at ease about his question.

John called Rufus Dean. He was deeply disturbed that a young man with no experience at all in dealing with people might cater to the misfits of Spring Hollow. He believed that some folk were too low down and community outcasts to become associated with Spring Hollow Baptist Church. In the not too distant past, Rufus had a serious conflict with one family in the outlying area of Spring Hollow. Since there were others who showed signs of poverty and sometimes a nonsocial attitude, Rufus thought all were bad, doomed, and couldn't be trusted.

John assured Rufus that he was aware of his problem and that all the deacons would work closely with their pastor in witnessing and doing the right thing for all.

The Wednesday evening prayer service was well above expectations in attendance. This should not have been a surprise to anyone, since the news was over all the entire church field that a very young preacher was coming to preach. This was unusual news in that all past pastors and supply preachers had been older men about fifty years.

Deacon John Canton opened the service with prayer. The prayer was simply asking Jesus to direct their thoughts and attitudes to the glory of our heavenly Father. A hymn was sung with unusual fervor. Deacon Larry Willoby led the congregation in a short scripture devotional and ended it with prayer. The Holy Spirit was definitely in charge of the meeting. A sense of peace prevailed within the congregation. The folk were not there to criticize someone's action or cast doubt upon the church's new direction. All knew something never before tried had to happen if Spring Hollow Baptist Church would survive. The congregation was anxious to hear about young Timothy Karr.

Deacon Canton reviewed with the church the initial meeting with Timothy Karr. He told of the unusual presence of the Holy Spirit in the meeting and then feelings about it on the way home. While Brother John was talking, sighs and whispers could be heard. Some folk bowed their heads and covered their eyes with hands or handkerchiefs. It was an emotional time. Nothing like this had ever occurred at Spring Hollow Baptist Church before.

When Brother John told about Deacon Josh White's promise to let Brother Timothy drive his truck to the church on Saturday before he was to preach, a strong "Thank You Lord" was voiced by someone and others followed. Questions were asked for, but no one responded.

Brother John asked that anyone who would pray do so to close the meeting. Brother Rufus Dean began praying in an attitude no one had ever heard before. It was as if he had lifted from his heart a very heavy burden. Others - women, young people, and even some children, prayed to their heart's content. Bart Dean, the thirteen-year old son of Deacon Rufus Dean prayed, "Lord Jesus, send preacher Timothy to us soon. Let him love us younger people and the old people. Let him know that everybody is important to you. amen." Bart's prayer stung the hearts of all. This reserved young man was not one to say much in public. What he said and how he prayed brought the church to tears. After much sobbing, blowing of noses, and mumbles of "Thank You Lord," Brother John said "amen." The following Sunday, Sunday School attendance was high, almost to the record. Everyone agreed that the prior Wednesday night prayer meeting was the cause of the good attendance. Sunday visitors were recorded in attendance also. This was a very good sign of renewal.

For this Sunday's worship service speaker, the deacons had met and decided that Brother Josh White would speak at the morning and Brother Jake Dawson would speak at the evening service. Both men had led the worship services before, the church knew they were capable. Both their messages emphasized what was needed in Spring Hollow and how each thought the church should help. Several hardy amens were heard in agreement.

No one knew if Brother Timothy Karr would come to Spring Hollow as their pastor. In fact, the deacons had not made a suggestion to this fact. They had asked him to come preach for Spring Hollow, stating that the church was looking for a pastor. They knew the church would make the decision to offer the call to Brother Timothy if it was the Holy Spirit's will. What all had heard, he surely was an excellent prospect. Only three deacons had seen him. They had not discussed his age. No one had even asked. No one had asked if he were married. This information had not been held from the church intentionally. His age, appearance, and marital status seemed unimportant. The next Wednesday night prayer meeting attendance was an all time high. The church was in an attitude of prayer. A lot of repenting and weeping seemed to be what the church needed. Everyone was excited about Sunday. No one was ashamed to testify that Jesus was more real to them now than at any other time in memory. All believed that revival had come.

Friday morning found Josh White up early checking his pickup truck. Everything seemed to be O.K. He gave John Canton a quick telephone call stating he would see them on the job. The trip to work seemed very pleasant. He had never lent his truck to anyone before. This was different and made him feel good. Lending his truck to Brother Timothy was like giving it to Jesus. It was just the right thing to do. If he had not let his truck be used, the cost of a bus ticket, someone meeting Timothy, and other inconveniences would have cost more and no one would have been blessed as he was right now. "Thank You Jesus for working all this out to your glory." Josh whispered to himself.

22

Timothy was expecting Brother White as he arrived at his dorm apartment around 4:30 p.m. Five minutes later Bros. Canton and Steale arrived to pick up Brother White.

"Good afternoon, Brother Timothy How has the school week been?"

"It couldn't have been better Brother Steale, I mean, White. "Forgive me for not remembering your name Brother White. How could I ever forget someone's name who was trusting me with his truck.? Sorry I didn't remember."

"That's O.K. with me, Brother Timothy." Brother John Canton and Wiley Steale were getting out of their car to greet Brother Timothy. Timothy walked briskly toward them with his hand extended to greet them.

"Good afternoon, gentlemen. It's good to see you fellows." He shook hands with both men as they returned pleasantries.

Specific directions were given Brother Timothy to the Spring Hollow Baptist Church. Then from the church he would go to Brother Steale's home and be their guest for the time he was at Spring Hollow. Everything seemed to be clear as to directions and about the time of arrival. They had prayer together and said so long until tomorrow.

Another student came to Timothy's room and asked if he would like to go off campus for dinner. There were four or five others planning on eating out. The fellowship would be good.

"About how long will we be gone?" asked Timothy, knowing that he had some loose ends to tie up on what he thought to be a sermon.

"Oh." mused his friend, "Perhaps an hour and a half."

"OK, I'll go. I hope it is not to be an expensive place. My money is short and I'm going out of town tomorrow," said Timothy.

"It will be just right," said his friend, "if you like Wendy's. We're eating salad."

"Sounds good to me," Timothy replied. "We should eat more of that raw green stuff. What time?"

"Six on the dot."

"I'll be ready."

23

The five friends were very jovial as they ate their fellowship meal. Various classroom topics were discussed. No definite conclusions were reached. It was Friday night, and it would not hurt too much if school would be put aside for a bit of other conversation.

"Say, Timothy, did you say you were going out of town tomorrow?"

"Yes, to a place I've never been nor heard of before last week."

"All I know," said Timothy, "is that a church is located there. Whether there is a town, school, or what else, I do not know. However, the name is Spring Hollow. Sounds refreshing, doesn't it?"

"Are you going there to preach? If so, will it be in view of a call to the pastorate there? Anyhow, why didn't you tell us sooner?"

"Well, I'll try to answer your questions by saying, I don't know to the first and to the second, I had to do a lot of praying about my going at all. So I was not sure until Thursday."

"Do you want us to go along and say amen to your sermon's strong points?" chimed in another of his friends. "I'm just trying to be funny. Really, I do hope the best for you. We will pray for you and the folk in Spring Hollow."

"I know you will. I am convinced of the Lord that Sunday will be a good experience," said Timothy.

"Just think," chimed yet another of his friends, "If we had not asked Timothy out for a Wendy's dinner, we would not have known where this bright young preacher went off to on Saturday. You made our day, Timothy. Thanks."

The last swallow of Coke was noisily gulped from the bottom of the glasses. The five friends returned to the Seminary campus. Timothy finished his sermon comments. By now it was time for sleep. Timothy really wanted a good night's sleep for Saturday would be a full day, he hoped. From the Seminary to Spring Hollow was about 60 miles. However, it was not the easiest place to get to. It was off the beaten path. Those who lived there had no problem, but to newcomers or visitors it was a different matter. It required four different turns onto four different state and county roads to Spring Hollow.

Timothy left the Seminary around 10:00 a.m. with his road map and penciled-in turns, etc., lying on the pickup truck dashboard. With a prayer in his heart and a very good feeling, he hoped to arrive around 11:30 a.m. He was assured of a good Saturday noon meal and a thorough tour of the community in the afternoon.

Well, it sometimes happens to most of us, and it did to Timothy. At the third turn, which should have been to the left, he turned to the right. The county road was through forest, with no houses, for about 15 miles. Timothy finally came to a small farm with no visible evidence that anyone was at home. He felt that a wrong turn was made, but wasn't sure. So he decided to ask for information from the occupants of the small farmhouse. He blew the truck horn, for fear that a protective dog might be nearby. To his surprise, a young boy about thirteen or fourteen came out on the porch. They spoke and Timothy asked for the information he wanted about Spring Hollow.

"Yes, I know where Spring Hollow is. You turned the wrong way on this road. If you go back the way you came and cross the road you turned off, from there you will not have any trouble finding Spring Hollow. Why are you going to Spring Hollow? I've never seen you around here before."

"Well, I'm from another part of the state, about a hundred miles from here. This is my first time in this part of the state. I am to preach at the Spring Hollow Baptist Church tomorrow. I probably don't look like a preacher to you, but I am. I am a student preacher at the Seminary. If the Lord Jesus wants me to, I hope I'll be back in these parts a lot in the future. Where do you and your family go to church?"

"Oh, we sometimes go to the little church on down the road about five miles." the young man responded.

"Tell you what, said Timothy, why don't you all come over to Spring Hollow tomorrow. It's not too far, is it?"

25

"No, about thirty minutes from here. I've been to church at Spring Hollow when they had revival. They are really good people, very friendly. I go to school with most of the young people from there. I might see you tomorrow morning."

"Thanks for the directions. I think the Lord let me turn wrong so that we could meet. I hope to see you tomorrow. So long."

Timothy finally found his way to Spring Hollow and to Mr. Steale's home. He was about forty-five minutes later than expected. But, his meeting with a new friend was worth the time.

Wiley Steale's fourteen year old daughter, Pat, first saw the truck approaching their house. She had been watching intently for Brother Timothy's arrival. She ran to the kitchen where her mother was finishing the noon meal.

"Mother, Brother Timothy is here. Do you want me to invite him in? Gee! Wow! He is not fat at all! We'll have to feed him a lot of corn bread and beans."

"Daughter, be sensible," the mother mildly scolded, after all he is a very young man. We will set before him what God has blessed us with and it will be up to Brother Timothy how much he eats. Let's be polite and hospitable."

"Oh, shucks, there comes Daddy from around the house. He must have heard the truck as Brother Timothy drove into the driveway. I was hoping to meet him first. Oh, well, it's all right. It was best for Dad to meet him, anyway."

"I believe you are right, daughter." Wiley Steale helped Timothy with his luggage into the house. As they entered the front door, Wiley said, "Welcome to our home, Brother Timothy You make yourself at home and enjoy what we are blessed with every day."

Mrs. Steale came from the kitchen, along with Pat. "Katie and Pat, This is Brother Timothy Karr."

"Welcome, Brother Timothy, we have been expecting you for over a week. It's been a pleasure waiting for you and preparing for your stay with us."

"Hi, I'm Pat. Thanks for coming to our house."

Timothy was profoundly pleased with the reception of these new Christian friends.

"I'm delighted to be here. I could tell through the Christian Spirit of Brother Wiley that your home would be as I'd dreamed. Thanks, deeply, for inviting me to stay with you. But, please, don't go to any special trouble. I'm just a plain country boy from Willow Bend. It is very similar to Spring Hollow. I'm sorry that I am a little late. I took the wrong turn and lost several minutes. However, there was a bit of good to come from it. When I stopped to inquire about my predicament, I met a young man who directed me right. He might be in church tomorrow. At least I invited him and his family."

"I'll take you to your room, Brother Timothy, while the wife and daughter fill the table with good old country cooking. Soon as you get freshened up, we will eat."

"Thanks, Brother Steale, I'm hungry."

At the table, the Lord was thanked for the food. "We were hoping that Mark would be home from State College. He is in his first year, and as you would understand, pressure mounts at the end of the school year. Perhaps you will meet him at another visit."

Mrs. Steale, you have my special thanks for a wonderful meal. Someone must have tipped you off that I was tall, slim, and in need of a lot of food."

"No, not at all. I just wanted you to eat your fill and be content. I've been cooking for Wiley and the children for a number of years. Sometimes they are hard to fill up. However, it is always a joy to cook for my family. Since you are with us today, it is a pleasure to add you to our number."

"Brother Timothy, I've asked Brother Rufus Dean to give you a tour of our community this afternoon. He will be over about 2:30 p.m. His son, Bart, might be with him. He is about twelve or thirteen. I believe you will enjoy meeting these folk and will like what you see in our community. I have some chores to do this afternoon. Had it not been for them, I would have given you the tour."

27

"I'm looking forward to seeing Spring Hollow. If the rest is as interesting as the part I've already seen, my afternoon will be spent well and with good company."

Timothy excused himself from the table as Wiley left. Mrs. Steale was again thanked for a good meal.

Pat looked at her mother to get a little recognition for the meal. After all, she did peel the potatoes and make the salad. She remembered that the boiled eggs were her doings also. And, she made the tea. If she did say so herself, it was the best sweet tea to ever be poured over ice cubes. In fact, she noticed that Brother Timothy drank four glasses.

"Mrs. Steale, I'm going to enjoy the porch swing awhile before Brother Rufus comes. You don't mind, do you?"

"Not at all, Brother Timothy Make yourself at home."

Timothy strolled his tall lanky body to the swing. A cool breeze was blowing and the swing felt comfortable. He really wanted to prop his feet up in the swing as he did at home, and take a nap. But that would not be proper here, he reasoned.

The front door opened and Pat appeared with a glass of ice and a pitcher of her good sweet tea.

"Brother Timothy, a glass of ice tea goes good with swinging. My Dad and I like to swing and drink ice tea. I'm a good tea maker. I made the tea we drank at dinner, and I made this. Have some."

"You bet, I will. If I had known you made the tea for dinner, I would have drunk six glasses. Can't say that I've ever had better. Why don't you sit here with me and drink your tea? You can tell me about your friends and how much you love Jesus. Do you mind?"

Pat was more than willing to stay and talk with Brother Timothy. This conversation was interesting to say the least. She told about her asking Jesus to save her and how Jesus had changed her plans for the future. She also told Brother Timothy that many of the youth of the community were not Christians, and there were many parents who did not believe.

Pat did not realize it, but she had given Timothy a lot to think about in deciding his acceptance of the pastorate if it was offered. Somehow the tea tasted better as their conversation was about the Lord's work. The experience with Pat would make the tour far more meaningful.

"Pat, you have been very kind to help me understand what I must do in the near future. Let's pray now and ask Jesus to bless this afternoon and tomorrow." Timothy prayed that Jesus would reveal His will and purpose for him. When he said "amen," Brother Rufus and his son Bart were driving up.

"Get out and come in Mr. Rufus. Hey, Bart." Pat invited them into her home. "Brother Timothy, this is Mr. Rufus Dean and son Bart."

"Hello my brother. I'm proud to meet you. I've been looking forward to this meeting and spending the afternoon with you."

They all shook hands warmly. "I'm really glad to meet you Brother Timothy. We have heard a lot of good things about you." Bart spoke to Brother Timothy as he shook his hand. "I prayed for you, Brother Timothy I believe Jesus is going to help us through you. I'm not old enough to do much, nearly fourteen, but I can help Jesus at school. We need a lot of things to happen here in Spring Hollow. I've got two friends coming to church tomorrow. They don't attend anywhere."

"That's great, Bart. You know, it might just happen that Jesus is going to do something in Spring Hollow that has never been done before. Wouldn't that be great!"

Pat chimed in with a big smile; "I'll help too, Brother Timothy."

Brother Rufus spoke up beaming with a laugh; "If my son is going to help to bring about revival, I better join in now. Brother Timothy, these children are right; there are lots to be done and a lot of people to be told about Christ Jesus. Right here and now, I commit myself to the Lord for whatever He wants of me." At that, Bart gave his Dad a big hug.

Timothy was teary eyed with joy. He thought to himself; "Why am I hearing these things?" Why me, Lord? I'm not their pastor—yet. Are You, Lord making plans for me here? Isn't it enough that these good people are burdened about their community's spiritual condition? Timothy thought he heard the word, "Perhaps—pray about it."

Mrs. Steale came out onto the porch and greeted the Deans. She was listening to the conversation, and she liked what she heard.

"I hate to break up these good revival plans, said Brother Rufus, but if you get to see our community, we better be on our way."

Timothy agreed, and as they were walking off the porch, Pat turned to her mother and asked: "Mother, let me go along. Bart and I know where all school age children live who are not in Sunday School. We both will be good help for Mr. Dean and Brother Timothy. Can I?"

"Yes you may, agreed her mother, but be nice and not talkative. Rufus, make sure she behaves."

"I'll do that, Katie." Replied Rufus.

Bart and Pat occupied the back seat. "I'm glad you could come with us Pat," said Bart. "You know our Sunday School class had been praying a long time that God would help us. We will have something to tell our class tomorrow. I can hardly wait."

Rufus had driven about three miles down the road when the first house came into view.

Pat said, "That's my uncle's house, Brother Timothy He is my mother's brother. They don't come to church."

Bart and Pat described the families as Rufus drove down road after road. Many were old couples or old widows. Many were young and middle aged. Some worked outside the community. Others lived on farms from 60 acres to 200 acres. A small country store was at one crossroads. Several vehicles were parked in front. There was never a big volume of grocery buying here. Most folk traveled about 30 to 50 miles to super stores. It depended on the direction, north or west. The owner of the country store, Mike Brannon, had been accused of bootlegging hard liquor a couple of times. No one had ever caught him. He was a very kind and gentle man. His family was well liked and his children, two girls, ages eight and thirteen, and one boy, age ten, attended church regularly. Neither of the children had made a profession of faith in Christ. Pat and Bart knew the children and spoke highly of their conduct. Susie, the 13-year-old, was very smart in her school studies.

Rufus had driven down one road, which he seldom traveled. He actually didn't want to bring Brother Timothy down this road. But, he was compelled to do so. He couldn't understand why. He felt very uncomfortable as he drove along.

They came upon a house, which was quite rundown, and the yards were unkempt. A teenage boy and girl and two smaller children were playing in the front yard, if it could be called a yard. Bart yelled; "There's Joe! Daddy, stop a minute and let me speak to Joe. My Sunday School class has been praying for him and his whole family. I want to ask him to come to church tomorrow."

By the time Bart had voiced his interest in Joe, his Dad had come to a stop at the yard gate. Bart opened the car door and jumped out.

"Hi, Joe. Whatcha been doing lately? Ya'll have moved, haven't you? The last time I saw you, you were living over near Clay Pit Pond."

"Hello, Bart. Good to see you. What are ya'll doing out this way?"

"We're showing Brother Timothy, our preacher for tomorrow, our community. We hope he will become our pastor."

"Callie, you know Pat." Bart wanted Pat and Callie to talk while he talked with Joe.

"Yes, I do. Hi Pat. Get out a bit." Pat jumped out as quickly as a flash and gave Callie a little hug.

"Callie, we don't have long to visit, but I want ya'll to try hard to come to church tomorrow."

"Pat, you know our parents are strict and don't want us to associate with folk not like us. But, I'll try to convince them. We've been friends at school a long time. I wish that everybody at church would act toward us like you and Bart."

"Well, we have to go. Hope to see you and Joe tomorrow. That's Brother Timothy Karr in the car. Brother Timothy, say hello to Joe, Callie, Beth, and Agnes Sims."

"Hi, boys and girls."

Timothy had been listening to some of the conversation going on between these children. He liked what he heard. Timothy surmised that the Sims were kind of community outcasts and he knew why. The Sims were Indians. He did not know what tribe, but he would guess them to be Choctaw. As they were leaving, Timothy turned toward Rufus and saw tears in his eyes. He wondered why.

"Bart, Joe's family is Indian, aren't they?" asked Timothy.

"Yes, they are. They are Choctaw. They are really good people."

Pat spoke: "Callie is very smart. She is a straight "A" student. Callie is friendly to everyone. But, there are a few students who don't like her. It's their fault, not Callie's."

Bart spoke: "It's the same with Joe. He is a good guy. Boy, is he a good baseball pitcher. He can play first base too. What we need to do at our church is to win this family to the Lord and make them as welcome as anyone else."

"I can say amen to that, Bart." Timothy chimed. "That's what the church is all about."

Rufus was very quiet as he drove back toward the Steale's house. The tour was over for now, but a serious burden was lingering in his heart. He knew, after what he had witnessed this afternoon, that the problem between him and Mr. Sims had to be resolved. The sin in his heart had hurt him long enough. The devil has had his way long enough. This afternoon, he promised Jesus that he would ask Carl Sims to forgive him of his terrible sin. He had lived five years in misery.

Meanwhile, in another part of the Spring Hollow Church field, another visit was being made by two deacons, Jake Dawson, and Josh White. Both men were unaware of the blessing God was about to give them. An old retired couple had become embittered about what they thought was neglect by the church. They were partly to blame for the incident, along with two widows who had shown a jealous spirit toward Millie and Frank Stewart, the retired couple. Frank had retired from the railroad about six years ago. Millie was a retired rural mail carrier. They had no children. Frank had served the Spring Hollow Church for several years as the 45-

up Men's Sunday School teacher. He was a capable teacher and seldom absent from his duty. The church planned a recognition service for several of its faithful workers. Such a recognition service was long overdue, not because the workers wanted it, but because the church should do it in recognition for how those special members had blessed them. One of the widows was on the planning committee. The other widow was her neighbor. They were not included in the group being recognized. Angry spirits erupted and caused bad feelings. To justify their dislike, false accusations were leveled at Millie and Frank. The outcome was the resignation by Frank and a departure from all church activities. Frank and Millie stopped going to church anywhere. They were hurt and bitter. They were hardly seen in the community. The Spring Hollow Baptist Church was tagged by them as non-caring.

Jake and Josh had a difficult mission to perform. After much prayer for more than two months, they knew this visit had to be made. Jake and Josh were concerned about the physical health of Millie and Frank also. Upon their arrival they found them both not feeling well, and had not been for several days. But, due to the past circumstances, Frank was adamant about not alerting the church folk. A casual welcome was offered to Jake and Josh who did not allow it to stifle their purpose of being there.

"Frank, Millie, it's been a long time, too long, since we have visited your home."

"Yes, it has. It has not been your fault, nor do we blame you. I guess it's been mostly us. We let some things happen to us that we can only attribute to the devil. It is his business to hurt God's people and we let him do it. I've been too ashamed to own up to my sin of leaving the church fellowship. Millie and I have prayed about it, but could not muster the courage to come back. But, to see you two good men here and showing concern for us is enough for me to kick the devil out of our business. Thanks, fellows, for coming."

"Praise the Lord." laughed Jake. "I feel like a ton of weight has been lifted off me. This visit should have come about a long time ago, Brother Frank. I'm making you a promise. Frank and

Millie, I'm going back home and kick the devil out of my family's business too, as you say."

"I'll say the same for me." chimed in Josh. "What we came for was to pray with you two dear friends and to tell you we care. We promise that the church will never neglect you again, ever. What we have heard is answered prayer of the church. Thank Jesus for leading us to your house today."

"Brother Frank and Millie, last Wednesday night at prayer meeting, a thirteen-year old boy volunteered a prayer that shook our church. It was short and from the heart. He simply asked the Lord Jesus to send us a pastor who would love and help the old folks and the young people. He was really pleading with Jesus. Because of his prayer, we are here in your home this afternoon," Jake said, as his eyes filled with tears.

"Tomorrow morning we will hear a very young preacher. He is in the Seminary. His name is Timothy Karr, and he is from Willow Bend, a community about 100 miles from here. We have heard a lot about him. He has never held a pastorate before. Brother Timothy had planned to become an engineer. He is from a fine home and church. It is our prayer that you, Frank and Millie, come hear him. I'm convinced God is planning a great revival in Spring Hollow. The Lord knows how terribly bad we need revival."

"Brother Jake and Josh" said Millie, "I'm very sorry for all the bad feelings we've caused in this community. I know it's not all our fault, but we have let it be ours. Many nights I've wept since the death of the widows. Not for them, but that I did not make peace with them before their deaths. However, I've asked my Lord Jesus to forgive me. I believe He has. Your visit with us today assures me of my Lord's forgiveness."

"Will we see you tomorrow at church?" Jake asked.

"I'm sure you will, Brother Jake," replied Millie.

Josh and Jake left Frank and Millie feeling a lot happier than before their visit. On their way home, Josh spoke about "church" problems which are not church problems at all. Really, they are individual sin problems.

"Jake, do you remember the Christmas program we had about six years ago?" A large number of Christmas baskets were prepared and decorated. Even a personal Christmas card was placed in each basket. All the senior citizens of the church were to get one. It was a very good idea."

"Yes, Josh, I remember the incident well. What happened on Saturday afternoon, the day the baskets were to be delivered, was a disgrace. All the deacons were to help the pastor with the delivery. But, not one of us came to help."

"Yeah, what happened on Sunday night was something no church should experience."

"I know, Jake. Our pastor had to deliver all those baskets by himself. You remember one of the cards got lost and the pastor did not know for whom it was meant. Instead of bringing the basket back to the church, he gave it to Aunt Gracey, that dear old colored woman. She was about 89 or 90 years old then. It made her so happy, the pastor said, that he wished the church would have made Christmas baskets for the colored seniors also. But, what happened at church on that Sunday night was totally un-Christian and uncalled for. It was a mess! Deacon Mike Hasting's wife accused the pastor of deliberately giving her mother's Christmas basket to an old black lady. She did it right in front of everyone. I remember how the pastor just bowed his head in shame that any one of the church members would conduct themselves in such a way."

"Both the Hastings are dead. But, I do not believe either ever asked the pastor's forgiveness," remembered Josh.

"We've had a good afternoon, Josh. Thanks for letting me go with you. I'll see you tomorrow in Sunday School, O.K.?"

Jake dropped Josh off at his home. Mrs. White was just completing supper as Josh walked into the house.

"Hi, sweetie. What's for supper? I'm hungry. I hope it is not sandwiches."

"No, it's not sandwiches. I have pork chops, mashed potatoes, brown gravy, fresh green beans, biscuits, and apple cobbler. Does that suit your appetite?"

"Yes, it sure does. Where are the children?"

Before Mrs. White could answer, two rambunctious five and seven-year-olds came bounding into the kitchen.

"Daddy, Daddy, I talked to Grandma on the telephone. She said she loves me a whole bunch. I told her I loved her as much as the world. She laughed and gave me a kiss over the telephone. Where have you been, Daddy? Did you know we have a preacher at our church tomorrow. His name is Timothy. Is he the same one in the Bible? Mommy said he's young. Could he be the same one? Preacher Paul said Timothy was his son."

Josh laughed as he picked up his five-year-old son Mark and gave him a good hug. He knew that Mark was sincere in his questioning.

"I'm glad you talked with Grandma. Yes, our preacher's name is Timothy, but he is not the same one in the Bible. You will meet him tomorrow and I bet you will like him. He is tall like Brother Jake, but not as fat. I want you to shake Timothy's hand and tell him who you are. Will you do that?"

"You bet, Daddy."

"Daddy," said Jeremy, "Will Brother Timothy be our regular preacher? We need one badly. Our Sunday School class has been praying for a pastor. It seems that our church does not go as well when we don't have a preacher. Why is that?"

"Jeremy, we will have to wait and see if our church folk like Brother Timothy. It might be that he will not like us. I should have said that God might not lead Brother Timothy to our church. It could be that He has another place for him. I hope Brother Timothy will be led to our church. I'll agree, when we do not have a pastor things aren't the same. Let's pray, tonight, that Jesus will bless us real good tomorrow. O.K.? Let's eat before Mommy decides to put this good food in the refrigerator. Now, bow your heads as we ask Jesus to bless our meal. Jeremy, will you thank Jesus?"

"Lord Jesus, thank You for this food. I thank you for our home. We love You. Bless us tomorrow at church. Give us Brother Timothy to be our pastor. amen."

Chapter 3

Preparing for Sunday

Willow Bend Baptist Church was aware of Timothy's visit to the community of Spring Hollow. Since Timothy was the first preacher to come out of the Willow Bend Baptist Church for the past twenty-five years, a few faithful thought it might be proper for a special prayer meeting on Saturday night at the church. This was announced at prayer meeting on Wednesday night. They were very proud of Timothy and his call of the Lord. Since his announcement, a little more than three years ago, the Willow Bend Baptist Church had taken on a fresh, vibrant mission spirit. The pastor seemed to be a new person. His preaching was more Biblical and powerfully delivered. Several people had been saved and many of the old church membership had recommitted themselves to the Lord Jesus. Many new tithers had resulted in larger offerings and mission gifts. The church debt, which was not too large, had been paid off and new padded pews had been installed. A new air- conditioning system had been purchased along with a speaker system to the nursery.

Because of several young couples committing themselves to Christ's cause, and for the benefit of their young children, the church had employed a full-time nursery worker. Within this three-year period, due to the nursery growth, a new wing on the church was already planned for a new nursery department. It would be ready for use within ten months. Many other growths were happening at Willow Bend Baptist Church. Who would ever believe that what had happened would happen, looking back to four years ago. Willow Bend had learned a vital lesson in trusting the Holy Spirit. All that had happened was a miracle, yes, a miracle.

They came to the prayer meeting on Saturday night to pray. This prayer was to God in thanksgiving for Willow Bend Baptist Church, for Timothy, for Spring Hollow, and specifically for Sunday at Spring Hollow.

No one from the Willow Bend community had ever visited the Spring Hollow community. But, they were excited for the Christian friends there. It was like they were praying for a special mission program. Indeed it was! Willow Bend had a son there and that was reason enough for them to pray. It would be at next Wednesday nights prayer meeting before a general report would be heard about Timothy's experience at Spring Hollow. Until then, they were trusting the Lord Jesus for His work to be done well in Spring Hollow.

Jim Tilley, the Sunday School Director for Spring Hollow Baptist Church, was optimistic about Sunday. If all the people who had been contacted during the week would be present, a new record in attendance would be made. He and the teachers had made an all out effort to contact members, absentees, and new prospects for this day. The excitement generated about high attendance seemed to radiate everywhere. Why was this all happening? No revival was planned. It was not homecoming. No associational or statewide emphasis was involved. Everything was centered within the Spring Hollow community. All had agreed that God wanted His "something" to happen and He was getting them ready for it.

Jim called the teacher of the young married couples class. "Alice, this is Jim. Are you expecting your class to respond to our high attendance emphasis?"

"Oh, yes. Brother Jim. I've already had every couple stating they would be present. But, let me tell you some better news. Do you remember the four young couples whom we've worked to enlist for so long? Two lives on Pine Lane Creek Road. That's a way out, about ten miles from the church. Well, two couples from my class visited them this week. One man, about 28, made a profession of faith right there in his home. His wife is a member of a Baptist church in another state. They have three children, 2, 5 and 8. They will be in Sunday School and Church tomorrow. The other couple, the same class members visited on Pine Lane Creek Road are coming also. They are both Baptists from another community, but out of fellowship with Jesus and other Christians. They have two children, ages 8 months and 3."

"Two other couples from my class visited two young couples up on Cherry Hill Road. If you remember during our last church community survey seven years ago, there were no homes up that way, except for the old Lackey place. All this has changed. Several houses are there now, spread out over about 50 acres. We found out about them from a friend in the next county. Well, our class members had a wonderful visit with them this week. Both couples have two children, each about 4 to 5. They promised to be present in Sunday School tomorrow. In fact, they told our class visitors that they hoped someone would come by and tell them about this Church. Brother Jim, I do believe Jesus had them prepared and waiting. So, that looks about what my class will be doing tomorrow. With all these children, several classes will be effected."

Jim Tilley made several more calls. All teachers seemed highly optimistic. Jim was deeply pleased with all these good reports. When he had made and received the last report, he bowed in prayer, thanking Jesus for tomorrow. Something wonderful was going to happen! He just knew it.

Saturday had been an eventful day in Spring Hollow. Most people of Spring Hollow Baptist Church had shown interest toward plans for the worship services on Sunday. All knew the need of change, but none knew what effect it would have on their community. All agreed that God was offering them a reprieve from their sins of complacency. Surely, Jesus was showing mercy and offering forgiveness.

Down at the Steale home, supper had been enjoyed and, for a very short time, the family sat on the front porch talking about the days events. Timothy was impressed with the hospitality he had received from the Steale family. But, he was a bit weary from the long day. Soon, he asked permission to retire to his room. He wanted to brief over his sermon notes and perhaps go to sleep early. He also knew that Mrs. Steale had gone all out to make him welcome and comfortable. She seemed tired and needed early rest. Before leaving the family, Timothy asked that they pray together. This request pleased Pat because she knew that she would participate.

"A great time for prayer." said Wiley, as he began thanking God for the days events. "Lord Jesus, my Savior, You have been very kind to us today. Accept our thanks for Your gifts of love. I know you are aware of our needs here in Spring Hollow. Let tomorrow be an unusual day of worship and fellowship. Thank you for sending Brother Timothy to us at this time. Use him for Your glory and purpose. amen."

Before anyone spoke, Pat began to pray. "Jesus, remember what a group of us young people asked you for, about six weeks ago? I remember, Jesus, when Sabrina asked to be forgiven of her sins and how she wept so long. I didn't think she would ever stop crying. You remember how we all wept with her. She caused us to see our mistakes and sins and repent. Remember, Jesus, how good and clean we felt after that prayer time. We didn't know what would come of it then, but I believe you have answered our prayer by making all us in Spring Hollow, feel that You are planning something tomorrow which is great. Thank you for sending Brother Timothy to preach for us. I believe he is the kind of pastor we need. amen."

Mrs. Steale was weeping from joy listening to her daughter pray. She did not know that such a sincere prayer meeting had occurred among the youth. How thankful she was for this church and their concern for change. She prayed:

"Father, my Lord and Savior, I'm not worthy for such blessings I've received today and to be a part of this thanksgiving time. Oh, my Lord Jesus, I'm proud of my praying family. I'm proud for Your glory. Please forgive my sins and failures of today. Thank You for Brother Karr. He has brought joy to us. We expect You to use him to Your glory tomorrow. Let him be humble and submissive. We need a fresh word from You and many hearts changed. We entrust our lives to You, tonight, for rest and protection. Keep us from the evil one, In Jesus' Name. amen."

Timothy cleared his throat because he had been sobbing. What he had heard, he needed to hear. The humble attitude of this family had moved his spirit like he had never experienced before. He was very pleased. He prayed:

"Jesus, My Savior. How compassionate You are. How understanding and revealing of our needs You are. How wonderful and pleasant to be in Your presence. You have allowed it and we are grateful. Thank you, Lord, for this family. They have opened their hearts and home to me, Your servant. Surely You, Oh Lord, have made provisions for this community. You have already revealed Your concern for Spring Hollow through this family. I ask, humbly, that You do Your great work as will please and honor Your great Name. Thank You, Lord, for allowing me a bit of Your fresh and mighty Spirit for my part tomorrow. You are so gracious and kind. Accept our thanks and bless us in rest in body, mind, and spirit tonight. Bring us together tomorrow in Your will and power. In Jesus Sweet Name. amen."

Timothy rose from the porch swing where he had been enjoying the evening. As he left the Steale family, he said, "Good night dear friends. I'll see you at breakfast. Rest well."

"Good night, Brother Timothy," the three spoke simultaneously.

Spring Hollow rested Saturday night. Many families prayed for God's will to be done on Sunday. Many sins had been confessed and the Lord's forgiveness received. All this was evident by what happened on this bright, spring, sunny Sunday at Spring Hollow Baptist Church.

Chapter 4

The Wimples

Dan Wimple put down the daily paper, adjusted his lounge chair, and walked over to Marsha, where she was looking over her favorite cookbook.

"Marsha, I've come to a decision about our problems of constant bickering. I'll accept all the blame, because it is my responsibility. I brought you two hundred miles from your home to a lonely piece of land not close to anyone. I know it has been difficult for you to adjust to this situation. However, this is not all our problem. I feel that we have grossly neglected our spiritual responsibilities, which makes everything else seem worse than it is."

"Today, I happened to meet Mr. Henry Nobles in the hardware store. I had not seen him for two years or more. He inquired about you and our welfare in general. Then he asked me about our church attendance and where we were involved. Remember, we have not visited Spring Hollow for a long time. Mr. Nobles asked to visit us this Friday evening. His wife, Jean, will be coming too. She has a present for you, something she canned from their garden. I told him it would be O.K. I hope you don't mind. If you object, I'll call and cancel the visit. However, I believe we will benefit greatly from their visit."

"It's O.K., honey. I just hope I am in a good mood. I'll cook some of my favorite cookies and will have coffee with them, or tea, which ever they prefer."

"I'm glad, dear. It had worried me a lot, that I did not ask you first."

At 6:45 p.m., Dan and Jean Nobles drove into the driveway of the Wimple's home. Just before they arrived at the Wimple's, Jean led in a short prayer, asking the Lord's guidance during this visit.

Marsha opened her front door and walked across the porch and into the front yard, greeting the Nobles with a warm hug.

"You dear folks do not know just how much seeing you means to us. We've been hungry for a visit from someone like you. Welcome to our home."

Dan came out with a dishtowel over his shoulder and with another was drying his hands.

"Welcome, Brother Henry and Mrs. Jean. My, I'm glad to see you. Excuse my kitchen looks. I've just started to dry the dishes. That's my job when I'm around the house. Come in, come in."

"Marsha, you look terrific! You are so trim and so very pretty. It's good to see you and Dan," said Jean.

"Indeed, it is, chimed Henry. I'll O.K. what Jean said about you, Marsha."

Dan beamed a big smile because he knew Marsha needed the compliments of these two friends. She accepted them in her graceful good manners and welcomed the Nobles into her home. Petty talk about many things took their time for about thirty minutes. Jean had forgotten to give Marsha her gift until she looked down beside her chair where her purse had been placed.

"Oh, my, I clearly forgot your present, Marsha. Here, honey, these are two jars of different kinds of preserves. I just know you and Dan will like them. Both are my own recipes. Henry likes them, and if he likes what I've made, I know you will." As Jean was talking, she presented Marsha with a small brown bag.

"Thanks, Mrs. Nobles. I'm sure we will enjoy your special preserves. As long as they last, we will be reminded of your wonderful friendship. You and Mr. Henry are very kind. Now, let's have a nice hot cup of coffee and some of my special cookies I've made. Will you come and sit at the table? I believe we will enjoy the refreshments there better than sitting on the couch."

From the tasting of the cookies and sipping of coffee, the conversation led from one thing to another. Finally, Dan mentioned that he had heard about a young preacher coming to Spring Hollow Baptist Church, Sunday.

"Yes, Henry spoke up. We haven't met him yet, but the ones who have, highly recommend him. His name is Timothy Karr from Willow Bend. Jean and I are in high hopes that you and Marsha will visit our church Sunday. We are planning high attendance in Sunday School. How about being a part of our group? It would bless our hearts to see you in church again."

"Yes, it has been too long, said Dan. "We've let other things keep us away. Both our backgrounds have been for strong church attendance. But, the past two or three years, we've let it slip, and we've been the worse off for it. However, we do feel we have one legitimate excuse. We feel that we were never accepted into the fellowship. Actions by some gave us reason to believe we were outsiders. It might not have been that way at all. We might be the trouble. We were never asked by our age group to participate in any of their plans. So, we dropped out. From this until now, no one of that age group has ever called or visited us. It hurts when you are excluded."

While Dan was talking, Marsha began to weep. She had felt so lonely. Her friends, and Dan's, were those who worked with them. They needed Christian friends. Dan and Marsha were both 26 years of age. They had no children, yet. Marsha had often talked to Dan about moving back near their home and beginning their family. Dan agreed they needed to start their family, but his job would not support them if Marsha quit work. He had worked so hard to keep payments going on the 25 acres and a house. It was a good investment, and he would hate to sell. Marsha wanted a child, the church seemed no longer friendly, and she was homesick. All this was a big problem for them both.

Henry and Jean took up their battle for them. They, too, were childless and in their mid-40s. Jean used her experience to calm Marsha's fears. She asked Marsha and Dan to do something beyond their power.

"Marsha and Dan, you are our friends. I'm ashamed that Henry and I have not kept in close contact with you. Even though I've prayed for you often, I should have made my way to your house for fellowship. Forgive Henry and me for this negligent sin. Now, I want you to do something we did a long time ago. It worked for us and it will work for you. God is involved in this. Please, please, right now, while we are here, place this burden that you have carried for so long, before God. Leave it there. Walk away from it. Don't look back. Trust God! Jesus said in Matthew 11:28-30, "And fear not them which kill the body, but are not able to kill the soul: but rather fear him which is able to destroy both soul and body in hell. Are not two sparrows sold for a farthing? and one of them shall not fall on the ground without your Father." "Marsha and Dan, Jesus said those very words for you. You need to bring your burdens to Him now, not later on at some more convenient time. Will you do this, as I lead us in prayer?"

Marsha and Dan were weeping. Henry was praying silently. Jean began praying:

"Oh, Jesus, my Lord, no one has felt the loneliness, rejection, and many burdens that Dan and Marsha are bound with, more than Henry and I. We took them to you, believing your promises and left them there. You, Lord, did what you said you would. Thank you, dear Jesus. Please, Jesus, for Your Name's sake, release Brother Dan and Sister Marsha from their guilt, loneliness, rejection, and many other burdens. They are Your children. You love them. Help them to respond to your love. amen."

Immediately after Jean prayed, Marsha asked Jesus to take this burden:

"Jesus, my Lord, I've always thought my petty problems were too personal to ask for Your help. But, now, my Lord, please accept them as I can't bear them any longer. Please forgive me for my lack of faith. I'm sorry for my sins. Help Dan and I to overcome our spiritual problems too. Lord, I promise to return to your fold and again begin growing in your grace. Thank you for Brother and Mrs. Nobles. We know this is your visit to us through them. Dan and I recommit our lives to You now. Thank you, Jesus, for Your forgiveness. amen."

When Marsha ended her prayer, Dan and Henry were on their knees, each weeping and praising God for the renewed spirit that had come to this house. The conversation between the

Nobles and Wimples took on a new attitude. They talked about what each could do for the other and about a new involvement at church. Dan and Marsha assured the Nobles that they would move their church membership to Spring Hollow Baptist. No one expected such a change to come over both families. The Nobles agreed God had sent them on this mission. The Wimples agreed that Jesus had sent them to their home for spiritual restoration. The visit had been wonderful.

The Nobles left for their home, about 9:00 p.m. They could never have spent a more blessed time with anyone than they had experienced tonight. The Wimples went to bed more peaceful and hopeful than they ever had.

Chapter 5

Sunday In Spring Hollow

"I hope I'm not guilty, like Peter, of denying You glory and honor today. The crowing of the rooster reminded me, Lord, of my weakness. Make me strong for Your task today. Let my mind be alert and my spirit strong. Give me wisdom for these good people in Spring Hollow. I've needed what You, Lord, have already allowed me to experience. Bless us all today for Your Name's sake."

Timothy got out of bed, picked up his Bible and sat in the chair next to the window. He turned to his devotional Scriptures and asked Jesus to bless His Word to his needs. For forty-five minutes, he meditated on what he had read. Laying the Bible aside, he eased to his knees and prayed for Spring Hollow people, that God's will would be revealed and done today. He was still on his knees when he heard movement about the Steale home and heard the coffeepot being prepared. A good fresh cup of coffee would be a blessing. I'll just shave and shower while I have time, before that good cup of coffee. Soon after the shower, there was a gentle knock on his door.

"Brother Timothy, coffee is ready and breakfast is not too far off. See you in a minute."

"O.K." answered Timothy "I'll be there pronto."

Timothy sat down at the small kitchen table, after being greeted by Wiley and Mrs. Steale. Wiley poured three cups of coffee, and they began their chat about things of the day.

"Mrs. Steale, you make a good cup of coffee," Timothy complimented.

"Can't accept the compliment, Brother Timothy This is Wiley's specialty. He always brews the coffee. It is good, isn't it?"

"You bet," said Timothy "I think I'll warm mine up a bit with the Wiley touch. Just kidding, my brother."

"That's O.K. Brother Timothy I know my coffee is good. That is, if I accept what Katie says about it."

Pat entered the kitchen in her curls and pajamas and a lot of sleep still in her eyes. "Hi, Brother Timothy It's early, isn't it? Did you sleep well?"

"Did I ever!" responded Timothy, hoping to make his hosts feel good. "I awoke about an hour and half ago. Had to get my sermon ready, you know. Not really, I'm just joking. I am an early riser. It's something my parents drilled into all of us children."

"It's a good thing," Wiley said. "But, we do have a little problem sometimes with Pat. Besides that, she is a very sweet peach eh, honey?"

"Brother Timothy, how do you want your eggs cooked?" Katie asked.

"Sunny side up. Is there any other way to cook eggs?" They all laughed at Timothy's remark. "I like them sunny side up," said Timothy, "so that I can mix them with my grits. Do ya'll mind if I do that?"

"You fix and eat your eggs and grits any way you please. Wiley does the same thing. Pat does not like eggs unless they are cooked in an omelet. Pat dear, do you want an omelet for breakfast?"

"No, Mom, I'll stick with a bowl of cereal. I want to be real hungry for dinner. Mom, do you remember the dream I told you about, that I had about going to a foreign country? Well, last night I dreamed that I was a nurse or doctor and I was teaching poor people how to keep clean and eat the right food. Much of it doesn't make sense, this morning. Somehow Bart was involved. He was helping people to get across a muddy stream of water. The place they were coming from was dark and ugly. But, the other side was pretty green farmland. What do you think, Brother Timothy? Do you think, maybe, that Jesus is saying something to me about being a missionary?"

"Yes, Pat, I believe He is. You will have to trust Him for a clear call. However, you just leave the doing to Him. He holds the time and the place for your life. And, Pat, He will not make a mistake."

"Thank you, Brother Timothy"

"Pat, honey, mother and I will pray with you about the Lord's place of service in your life."

"Let's all get to the table," ordered Katie Steale. Breakfast is ready. Look at these pretty brown biscuits. If they taste as good as they look; everything is going to be yummy. Pat, why don't you say the blessing for us."

"Dear Jesus, thank You for a good night's sleep and rest. I thank you for my family. I thank You for today and our worship experience. I thank You for this good food Mom has prepared. Bless it and our lives to Your glory. amen."

After breakfast, Wiley stated that he would leave home early for a prayer meeting with the deacons.

"Brother Timothy, six months ago, the deacons convened together to pray daily for our church. We also formed our prayer time each Sunday morning at 9:15 a.m. This gives us thirty minutes to share and pray before Sunday School time. We haven't broken this promise. But, we have been vitally strengthened by it. Would you wish to join us today? If so, be ready to leave at 9:00 sharp. You will be blessed."

Yes, I do want to join you. I'll be ready and waiting. This will give me an opportunity to meet the other deacons whom I haven't met."

"See you later," said Wiley.

Sharing began at 9:15. Every deacon expressed concerns of the spirit relative to Spring Hollow Baptist. They mentioned no personal request. It was apparent they were burdened about a spiritual revival in their church. They were not ashamed to shed tears. Two of them wept openly as they poured out their soul to the Father. Since Timothy was visiting, he was asked to close the prayer time. His heart was touched and strengthened. He believed God was going to do something wonderful today.

Sunday School started promptly at 9:45 a.m. People were going and coming from every direction. Timothy got stuck in a hallway where people of all ages were introducing themselves to him. He was not expected to remember all their names, but he was impressed by their enthusiasm. They all welcomed him to their church.

About three months prior, the church had organized a singles class of young career and college age adults. They had started out with four members. After two months the membership had increased to eight. Today, several prospects were present. Timothy was asked to meet with them during Sunday School, since he was a single young adult.

"I'll be proud to be a part of your class Bible study. Thanks for asking me."

As he and the young woman who had invited him walked into the class, she announced, "Class, this is Brother Timothy Karr. He is our preacher for today. I've asked him to visit with us for our Bible Study."

"Hi, Brother Timothy," they all chimed in.

"Hello to all you. I'm privileged to be here," replied Timothy.

"Brother Timothy, will you lead our Bible study?" said the teacher.

"Oh, no, never. You are prepared to teach, I'm not. I'm afraid if I tried, I would chase rabbits too far and lose your interest. I'll listen and promise you that I will learn and enjoy the study."

"Thank you Brother Timothy"

The bell rang for Sunday School to end. The bell also signaled that the morning worship service would be starting in a few minutes. The classrooms emptied quickly, and people flocked to the rest rooms and auditorium. Just about every class had visitors today.

The piano was already playing old familiar hymns that call people to worship. The choir was in rehearsal in the fellowship hall where the only other piano was located. No church bulletins were put out, simply because Spring Hollow had never used them.

Timothy met John Canton outside a small office and inquired if the congregation might sing his favorite hymn, "What a Friend We Have in Jesus".

"Let's ask our song leader about it." said John. They both stepped inside the fellowship hall and waited for the choir to finish its special.

"Brother Timothy, this is Dick Reveere, our song leader. Dick, Brother Timothy would like to request, "What a Friend" as one of our songs. Would this change upset the program?"

"No, not at all. That's one of my favorites. Brother Timothy, I've heard a lot about you. I'm looking forward to our worship service. Do you have a special time you want "What a Friend?"

"Yes, maybe just before the choir sings their special. Is that O.K.?"

"Sure," said Dick.

"I'll be praying for you folk as you lead our singing," said Timothy.

John and Timothy walked into the auditorium, took their seats on the pulpit platform and waited for the choir to enter. The house was full. Several people were milling around greeting visitors and regulars. There was a good spirit in the church. John whispered to Timothy:

"We have not had a crowd this large in years. I see folk here who have not been in Spring Hollow Church in years. Praise the Lord, this makes me feel good."

"Well, I don't know how to respond to that, but I like what I see. Do you think our Lord is saying a word to us?" Timothy whispered.

The choir began to file in and the congregation became quiet. When they were all in their places, Brother John Canton stepped to the pulpit and asked the congregation to rise for prayer. His voice was firm and strong as he led the congregation in prayer.

"Oh, Lord our God, You know our hearts. We ask forgiveness for our sins and cleansing from all unrighteousness. We are sorry that we have offended you by our sinning. Have mercy upon us all. Take what we are in this assembly and mold us into the purpose of Thy will. Let the glory of this hour be Yours. Spring Hollow needs a renewed image of Thy Self. Overshadow Brother Timothy with Your love and power. Give us a victory. amen." During the prayer there were several amens throughout the congregation.

"Now, Brother Dick, come lead us in singing. Let's all join right in and be happy," said Brother John.

"Thanks, Brother John. Will you open your hymnals to the hymn, "Amazing Grace." There is nothing more glorious to sing about than God's Grace. Express your heart feelings through your voice as we sing," encouraged Brother Dick.

The congregation began singing with great joy. By the middle of the third stanza, Dick became so overjoyed that he stopped singing and lifted up his hands and tear filled eyes, and blessed the Lord. Timothy thought the windows would crack as the people sang, "When we've been there ten thousand years." Truly, the Holy Spirit was present. The singing was a joyous experience for all. People wept openly and unashamedly.

John whispered to Timothy, "I've never experienced such joy as there is here today. This truly is revival."

"I couldn't hear the choir for you. What singing! Let's do it again. "Amazing Grace!" "Our neighbors in the next county might hear us and rejoice with us." said Dick.

The people did sing, and they did worship God. Truly, it was a time of rejoicing. Brother John made several announcements about the week's church activities and comments about plans for the summer. Then he introduced Brother Timothy to the congregation.

"I'm proud to introduce to you this young preacher from Willow Bend, Brother Timothy Karr. He is a graduate of Baptist College and nearing the end of his second year at the Seminary. Many of you will want to meet him after the worship service and tonight. Let's be in prayer for ourselves and Brother Timothy. Brother Timothy, after the choir sings, you are free to preach whatever God has said for you to preach."

Timothy nodded his head in approval.

The choir had chosen an old hymn that had not been sung at Spring Hollow for several years. It was very appropriate for today. Timothy seemed to agree. The hymn special was "Give of Your Best to the Master."

The congregation was feeling the impact of this great hymn. God used it to help bring His people to a oneness of attitude in spirit. Brother Dick was very pleased with the choir's response. Several strong amens were sounded from both men and women.

Brother Timothy arose and walked slowly to the pulpit. He stood tall and thin, but his voice was strong and clear.

"I'm deeply indebted to Spring Hollow Baptist for this privilege to worship our Lord with you today. What I have witnessed today makes me feel at home and welcome. In fact, I had rather be here in Spring Hollow than anywhere else in all this world. I feel wonderful being in God's will right now. amen. The choir led us to God's throne in singing didn't they? And, how you, the church sang my favorite hymn, "What a friend We Have in Jesus."

"The message I had prepared, prayed over, and asked Jesus' blessing upon, is not to be preached. Yesterday, afternoon, the Lord said, "No." He said to me, "Timothy, you know a great deal about the people in Spring Hollow. The deacons and others have told you about their spiritual needs and how they hoped God would visit Spring Hollow. But, they do not know you. I want you to tell them who you are. Your sermon can wait."

"Now, don't ya'll be disappointed. It's the Lord's will. He won't let us down. We have already witnessed His presence. At the close of this service, I believe He will do other miracles. Trust Him."

At this, Timothy stepped aside from the pulpit and began deliberately to unfold his life to Spring Hollow.

"I am not a preacher by my choice. It was in all my plans to get an engineering degree from State University. I have always been fascinated by machines that make things work for us. In my second year of college work toward that degree, the Lord Jesus spoke to me and changed my vocation. His call to me was as plain and sure as my voice is to you now. I've known Christ Jesus as my Savior since I was ten years of age. His saving me then was as real as His call to preach His gospel. I am the first person to be called to preach from my home church in Willow Bend, for the past twenty-five years. My home church had gone through a long spiritual drought. Not one soul had been called out from the church. Everyone may have his or her opinion, but God knows the reason. Sin, serious rebellion toward Gods divine grace is the problem my home church faced. Now, there is a revival going on, and has been going on for four years. I'm

53

not the reason this revival is happening. Several members and families became convicted of their spiritual complacency. Repentance was God's choice for them. They did, and God began to work His will in our community. Out of this experience God called me to preach. Only my pastor was aware that Jesus was dealing with me. The only awareness I had was that I wanted to serve my Lord Jesus in any way He chose to do. But, I had made that promise and committed to Jesus when He saved me at ten years of age."

"I am not a hypocrite. What you see and hear is what I am. I never have been, nor will I ever be, one person in public and another in private. I am a Christian. Wherever I go, I'll always be a Christian. I will act like a Christian should act, to the lost as well as to the saved. I'm a friend to the old, and I'm a friend to the young and children. I am Timothy Karr, saved from my sins by Christ Jesus. I have no reason to be otherwise."

"I do not know if Jesus will ever call me to be your pastor. If he does, what you hear of me in the community, you will hear and see of me in the pulpit. I will forever present Jesus to the people, but never myself. What I am at church, I will be in your home, hospital, school, or jobs."

"I am single. I am twenty four years of age. God has not yet chose a wife for me, at least He has not yet told me who she is. At this the congregation roared in laughter. I believe Jesus is preparing me for a mate and preparing a mate for me. Many responded with hearty amens.

"I believe in witnessing to the spiritually lost, to present Christ Jesus. I believe in training Christians to be witnesses to Jesus' saving grace. I believe in training Christians to be servants to others in church and elsewhere. I believe that others, besides the preacher, have a message that should be heard from the pulpit. I will never be afraid of losing my call to preach. God owns the whole world. He might send me to any place to preach. Or, He might leave me here. I belong to Him, totally."

"I believe in missions. The entire church business is missions. I believe in the support of our worldwide missions program as well as all the mission work at home. I believe in preparing and sending those whom God calls. I believe in tithing and offering as Gods material way of growing His children to support His work. I would be a hypocrite if I did not practice what I preach. I am a friend, and I believe in a good, alive fellowship. It is evidence that we are alive in Christ, reborn to a new life of joy. We have experienced that here today."

"I will not seek publicity. Neither will I glory in no one but my Lord Jesus. I ask you to honor Him too."

"Today must be a first for you; it surely is for me. I would have never done what I did, had it not been for Christ's Word to me. When I began to weigh the matter of telling you who and what I am, I thought it proper to do so. To preach a sermon tells very little about a man. Now you know enough about me to make your right decision. I'll preach tonight if it is the Lord's will." This brought other laughs.

"In closing and before the invitation to anyone who wishes to make your decision for Christ, I want you to know that I am absolutely sure that the Bible is God's inspired Word. I will preach it only, and not anther's philosophy. Several loud praises were voiced. It is the power of God, to everyone who believes. Will you bow your heads in honor to God and ask His will to be done here, now?"

"Jesus, my Lord and Savior, thank you for allowing us to come into Your presence today. You have heard our words, prayers, and seen our tears. We ask for your mercy and grace. You are so wonderfully good. amen."

Brother Dick stood and announced the invitation hymn, "Just As I Am." On the first stanza, Frank and Millie Stewart walked down the isle, arm in arm, and weeping. They were greeted by both Brother Timothy and Brother John Canton. Joe and Callie Sims came confessing Jesus Christ as Savior and Lord of their lives. They were the oldest brother and sister of the Sims family. Dan and Marsha Wimple came rededicating their lives and for the transfer of church membership.

Many people were weeping so that they could not sing. By the time the invitation closed, Brother Dick was about the only one singing. The people wept and prayed. Joy in Christ abounded. It was indeed a time of rejoicing. During the welcome and fellowship time, the people greeted each other with hearty handshakes and hugs. God had blessed His people because they repented of their sins. He always blesses because He loves us. There was no benediction said. One was not needed. The people were rejoicing and there was no reason for them to stop doing so. Jake Dawson had been trying to get a word with Timothy For someone who was always a bit cautious about new preachers, Jake was anxious to talk with this young man.

"Brother Timothy" Jake's voice was a little above the others, "May I have a word with you?"

Timothy moved back down the isle to the front pew. Everyone else was moving outside, slowly, as the worship service was over.

"What a worship experience we've had today, Brother Jake!"

"Yes, my good friend, our Lord did bless us. He knew just how much I needed what I've heard today. I want to tell you, Brother Timothy, I've never heard a more powerful sermon that was not supposed to be a sermon, than you preached today. I'm convinced Jesus was right when He told you to tell us about yourself. Now, I understand. I believe He told us all, individually, who we are. At least, I know more about me, now, than I did before our worship experience. Brother Timothy, you really don't know just how much Jesus has used you for our benefit today. I have been a member of Spring Hollow Baptist for many years, but we have never experienced the presence of Jesus before as we have during the last three weeks and today. I know you will not take any credit, but you have been His instrument and humble servant. Thank God!"

"I'm going to agree with all that you have said, Brother Jake. Only God can bless His people, and He has today."

At that, the two walked outside the church where many people were still in fellowship. Very few had left the church grounds. Someone was overheard saying, "Wouldn't this be a wonderful time for dinner on the ground?"

Others chimed in saying, "Yeah, boy, we could carry this on for hours."

A young couple approached Timothy, whom he had not met before. They were all smiles.

"Hey, Brother Jake."

"Howdy, Pete, Sandy. Brother Timothy, I think I'll leave you with these two good folk. They will treat you well."

With that, Jake walked away and began another conversation with two other deacons.

"Brother Timothy, we're Pete and Sandy Carter."

"Hello, I'm proud to meet you. I thought I saw you, Mrs. Carter, in the choir."

"You did, but, I doubt if you heard me. Wasn't that singing great?"

"Brother Timothy, you are our guest for dinner today." said Pete. "And, what I smelled from the kitchen this morning, you are in for a treat. Sandy is an excellent cook. By the looks of you, meaning how slim you are, you need a lot of her cooking. You can see what it has done for me." Pete pulled in his chest and raised himself about another two inches. He was six feet, one inch tall and weighs 190 pounds. He laughed as he put on his demonstration.

"I'll accept your invitation and challenge. When do we eat? I'm hungry."

"That a boy." said Pete. "I like this young man better already. Your sermon made me like you, but you wanting to eat our food makes me like you a lot more. Let's go home and feast."

"You must permit me to catch a ride with you. I have no transportation."

"We wouldn't have it any other way, Brother Timothy Sandy does most of the driving around here. She is a good driver too. I'm a lucky man to get all this goodness in the woman God caused me to fall in love with five years ago."

They were off to the Carter house. Dinner was delicious. Pete spoke words of truth about Sandy's cooking. To be a young woman, she was an expert on cooking any style. She had prepared turnip greens, butter beans, corn, fried okra, chicken and dumplings, hot fresh biscuits, and fried country sausage. For desert; coconut cake, pound cake, and ice cream.

Timothy ate his portion. Pete joked with him that he could not detect any difference after the meal, than before. They laughed about the quantity of food consumed. Timothy said it may take four or five more meals like this to make any difference with him. And, jokingly said that if that sounds like a revisit, it is.

"I like your cooking, Sandy. It's no wonder Pete is healthy and, aah, big." Laughing, Timothy said, "I mean that, Pete, with the best of friendship."

"That's alright, Brother Timothy If you hang around this community in the future, I'll see to it that you get a chance to be my size. However, it's not likely you will ever get to my size. I hope we will see you more than four or five times."

"That goes for me too Brother Timothy" said Sandy. "We need your youth, commitment, leadership and personality in our church and community. Do you feel that you might come share the Lord's gospel here? What we heard about you today is the type life that needs to be demonstrated in Spring Hollow. Please pray hard for us and you serving Jesus here."

"Sandy and Pete, I promise you before my Lord that I will do what ever Jesus says. His work is important anywhere. Spring Hollow is no exception. What I've seen of this community, I like very much. Ya'll will pray with me, too."

"Let's move to the den for our cup of coffee." said Sandy. "We can talk about other matters also. Pete will help me with the food and dishes later."

As the afternoon passed, conversation about many things, the church, community, and their lives were discussed.

"Brother Timothy, remember the elderly couple, Mr. & Mrs. Stewart, who came for rededication? Well, they are a very fine Christian couple. They have no children, but are truly devoted to each other and to the Lord. You might have, by now, heard mention of the two widows. Well, the widows, who by the way were not kin, and the Stewarts had some hard words between them several years ago. It had to do with land lines. Their properties joined and still do. It hurt the Stewarts a great deal. Both the widows were in the wrong, but wouldn't admit it. The widows died about two years ago, not making things right with the Stewarts. Since then, everything has been corrected. You see, one of the widows was my mother. The other was Sandy's mother. We could not do anything about the problem until the wills were probated. We are the only children of each. The Stewarts have never held any bad feelings toward Sandy or me. We both admit that our mothers were stubborn. Sandy agrees with all I've said, because we have discussed it many times. Everything is O.K. now. I was so proud for the Stewarts today. Their burden has been lifted."

The afternoon passed, and then it was time for the evening service at Spring Hollow Baptist Church. Training Union was well attended, which was unusual. Baptist Training Unions have taken its toll of low attendance for some years. This is tragic because out of this noble Christian training organization designed to teach us what we believe and practice of our faith, Christian stewardship and character building come to fruition. Mike Owens, the Director of Training, was pleased with tonight's attendance. In fact, the attendance was a record. He voiced his pleasure in seeing old and new attendees, with the hope that tonight's participation would only be the beginning of continuous growth.

After the evening offering, which was far above average, Brother Josh White introduced Brother Timothy Karr to the congregation. The choir generally did not sing at Sunday evening worship service. The reason was the lack of attendance and spiritual value of the evening worship service. However, tonight the choir seats were full. Dick Reveere was greatly pleased. The choir sang, "We're Marching to Zion."

As they did for the morning worship, as now, the choir sang unusually well, with deep feeling. Some in the congregation sang softly, along with the choir. Many voiced their approval by saying, "amen."

Before Brother Timothy got out of his chair, Brother Larry Willoby stood and asked for permission to speak. This was very unusual for Larry, since he was not known to say hardly anything in public meetings. All knew him to be a very dedicated man, but speaking like this was not like him.

"Brother John, since you are the chairman of the deacons, I'll first say to you, Bros. Steale and White, that I am deeply indebted to you and to our Lord Jesus for finding and sending Brother Timothy Karr our way. I've been a member of Spring Hollow for many years. I've witnessed deep valley experiences, and a few hilltop experiences, but never have I, or our church, witnessed what has been our lot for the past three weeks and today. As Brother Timothy said this morning about his home church going through a spiritual drought, so has Spring Hollow been in a long, deep spiritual drought. But, today, our wonderful Lord Jesus has led us to the mountain peak." Several amens and praises interrupted him. Larry began to weep and, for several minutes, could not continue. Sniffles and nose blowing from tears were heard throughout the congregation. People seemed free to weep and praise God. Finally, Brother Larry continued his testimony.

"Brother Timothy, you might think us strange, but we are not. We have allowed sin in our hearts and lives here in Spring Hollow, which brought us to our knees. When we began confessing our sins, the Lord began blessing us; and, today is really a hallelujah time for our church. You did not bring this blessing, but you are the Lords messenger to reveal what He wants us to do. I thank God for you. Now, I'll hush. I didn't intend to say all I've said, anyhow."

There were many hearty laughs and "amens."

Timothy moved to get up from his chair, but again he was interrupted by Mrs. Jean Nobles.

"I'm a bit bashful in a public meeting like this, but I had to say something about my feelings of the day, or bust. Thank you Brother Larry. You voiced a lot of our feelings and spiritual needs. I have never witnessed a personal testimony from a preacher, instead of a sermon, that fit me and our church needs as was that given by Brother Timothy this morning. I don't outwardly physically shout, but I've been shouting to the Lord ever since this morning worship service. This is the first time I've ever stood up and given a testimony in our church. I just had to do it." many people were weeping.

Before Timothy made an effort to get up from his chair, he looked about the congregation for someone else to stand. Before he could' say, "Is there anyone else?" Young Bart Dean stood up.

"Well, I'm young and most times I just sit back and listen. That's O.K. too, but I've been so blessed for the last week or so, and especially today, that I wanted to say how much Jesus means to my family and me. Us young people are going through terrible testing and trying times. I decided for myself that no one could help me, and all us, but the Holy Spirit." Amens came from everyone; the loudest was from Bart's Dad, Rufus Dean.

"Brother Timothy, I have asked Jesus to send us a preacher like you, even though we haven't heard you preach yet. Joyous laughs came from everywhere. I know you will care for us, as a pastor should. Our children need you as well as the old folks. You told us this morning how Jesus touched your life. Let Jesus touch us through you. I've asked Him to send you back. I believe He will. amen."

Clara Lucas, a teacher of 8 and 9 year olds in Sunday School stood to give her testimony about what was happening in Spring Hollow.

"I'm proud of my Christian fellowship here in Spring Hollow. I've known Jesus as my Savior since I was the age of these boys and girls of 8 and 9 years old. For the last two Sundays, Jesus has blessed our class with a number of requests for prayer and information about how to be saved. I've laid aside my prepared lesson material to teach how the Lord desires us to come to Him for salvation. Our class attitude is completely different. God is working in these young lives, and I'm convinced He will bring forth fruit from these labors. After all, this is what we are to be doing. Jesus has provided us a field that is white for harvest. I, for one, have committed to be about the work of the church in witnessing and harvesting souls for Jesus." Many, 'And Me too' came from the congregation.

Brother John Canton stood and walked to the pulpit. He was notably moved by what the church had witnessed tonight. As he spoke, his voice was shaking and tender.

"Brethren, we have come to the cross road at Spring Hollow and passed the crisis of testing by the Lord Jesus. We have overcome the power of Satan, with which he has hurt us so terribly bad. I'm convinced that God has given us the visit we've asked for in prayer. Now, it is time for us to move forward under the leadership of the Holy Spirit to greater heights." Amen.

"Well now, Brother Timothy, this is the first time we have ever invited a preacher to our church and he did not preach, but a revival broke out anyhow. I believe the Lord planned all these events. What we have heard tonight are four or five good sermons anyway. Don't we all agree? We believe you can preach, and we believe God has called you to do so, but tonight it is getting late. God has honored us with your presence today. Will you consent to come back next Sunday?" Timothy nodded, yes. "We will listen to you preach two sermons then, we promise. How about it folks?" The congregation agreed.

"Brother John, I'm bursting to say one word, may I?" said Brother Timothy.

"Why, yes, you may say two if you wish." The congregation applauded.

"Folks, you have blessed me more than I've ever been blessed before. Thank you. Now, we do need to close with an invitation to Jesus. Someone has been touched today. Will you come to Christ for salvation?"

Brother Dick announced the hymn: "I Surrender All."

Immediately, at the beginning of the first stanza, Beth and Agnes Sims came forward confessing their faith in Christ Jesus. Tammy Reveere, the twelve-year-old daughter of Dick and Louise Reveere, came confessing her faith in Jesus. Dan and Marsha Wimple, came rededicating their marriage and lives to God. Laird Dubose, husband of Alice Dubose, came on promise of transfer of church letter and rededication of his life to Jesus.

Brother Dick led the singing on the last stanza. No one else responded. Brother Timothy turned the closing of the worship back to Brother John. Brother John announced the decision of each one who had responded to the invitation and asked the church for its decision. The congregation responded with a loud "amen."

The pianist played during the church welcome and fellowship time. Finally, the benediction was prayed by Brother Mike Owens. The time was 9:00 p.m.

"What a day!" someone said. "Could we have several days like this?" said another. "Why don't we come back tomorrow night and let the revival continue." said someone else. "Mommy", a little child said, "Can we keep Brother Timothy forever?"

Pat Steale slowly made her way to where Timothy was encouraging youth to be faithful to Jesus wherever they were in the company of unbelievers. Pat knew this to be so, because school environment was very testing of her faith. Slowly, Pat edged herself near Timothy and whispered that they had to be going home. Timothy said so long to the group until next week.

When the Steales and Timothy arrived at home, Timothy asked for a cool glass of water.

"Make yourself at home, Brother Timothy There are dinner leftovers in the refrigerator. Help yourself to what's there." said Mrs. Steale.

"I'm not hungry. I'm just very thirsty. It's late and I know Brother Wiley needs to retire for the night. He works tomorrow, but I only go back to school." Timothy laughs.

"That's right, Brother Timothy We leave at 6:00 a.m. It will take about ten minutes to run you by the Seminary. Traffic is heavy at that time of day."

"I'll be ready to leave when you are, Brother Wiley. Let's pray together and go to bed, OK?" Wiley led the prayer.

"Jesus, our wonderful Savior, thank You for Your gifts of grace today. None of us deserve such love. But, You Lord want us to be blessed and cared for as we have been today. Let our minds and bodies rest well tonight. Keep us safe now and guide our actions tomorrow. Forgive us our sins and mistakes. We love You very much. In Jesus Name and for His glory, I ask this prayer. amen."

Chapter 6

At The Seminary

The trip to the city was not boring today. Conversation was about yesterday. When Timothy was dropped off at the Seminary, he was encouraged for the week. He thanked his good deacon friends for their hospitality and hoped they too would have a good week.

"We will see you Friday afternoon. You have the use of my truck again, Brother Timothy," Josh reminded him.

The three deacons; John Canton, Wiley Steale, and Josh White continued on to their jobs. This week was to be profitable for them as well as that for Timothy. God blessed Spring Hollow to His glory.

As Timothy walked into the dorm, he was about to open his room door when two of his friends heard him and dashed out to hear about his trip to the country.

"Hey, friend. How's the tired old preacher after a grueling day yesterday? We just know you have some great news to tell us, eh?"

"Well, yes I have, but not now. Could you fellows wait till lunch? I'll tell you all about it over a hamburger, that is, if you will buy. What I've got to tell is worth far more than a hamburger. OK?"

"What if we decide it is not worth the price of a hamburger, what then? Will you refund our money?"

"What I've got to say, you will be offering me several hamburgers all week."

"We'll see. However, you sound very confident. It's good to see you back. We are only teasing. However, we will buy your lunch. You don't eat much anyhow. If it were the other way around, you would lose. You know how much I can eat," said Junior Clark, the larger of the two.

Timothy sat at his desk for the next three hours, preparing lesson materials for tomorrow. Part of the time was put on a fifteen-page mission paper on "The Basic Philosophy of Starting Mission Work in Difficult Areas", in states where Baptist presence is weak.

Ralph Gates gently knocked on Timothy's room door. "Your friends are ready to buy that expensive hamburger. Can you break away from your studies? We are hungry."

"Coming, Ralph, I'm hungry also."

The three went to the nearest Arbys. They decided an Arbys roast beef would be O.K. for today's lunch, and a green salad on the side.

"Now that we are comfortably set, lets hear about your experience in the country," said Junior.

They knew already about the good deal with the pickup truck Mr. White was so gracious to lend Timothy.

"I left the Seminary while you guys were still asleep on Saturday. I made a wrong turn after I got within ten miles of Spring Hollow. However, a young boy, at whose house I stopped gave me the right directions. From there I had no trouble finding the Spring Hollow Baptist Church and the home of Mr. Wiley Steale. They were my hosts for the time spent in Spring Hollow. Boy, oh boy, what fine people! Their son, whom I didn't meet, was away in college. I believe it was his first year. Pat, oh pretty little Pat! She was fourteen and going on fifteen, she informed me. She is a dynamic Christian young woman. Someday we will hear more about her."

"Mr. Rufus Dean and his son Bart gave me a tour of the church field. It is large, some twelve or more miles square. We met a couple of families. One family was Choctaw Indian."

"We returned to the Steale home and I settled in for the evening and night. After supper, the family sat on the front porch for about an hour and a half. We had prayer, and I went to my room to review my sermon notes for Sunday. Have you ever had a feeling that something unusual was going to happen? Well, that's the way I felt Sunday morning. It was not only I, but also the whole community. Spring Hollow Baptist Church had been repenting and praying for months".

"Now, before I tell you more about my visit to Spring Hollow, I want to say that I did not preach either sermon I had labored over for two weeks. In fact, I did not preach at all."

"You didn't preach after they went to all the trouble of getting you out there to this church?" What happened?" Timothy's friends asked.

"Well, late Saturday afternoon the Lord informed me that I was not to preach on Sunday morning. But, I was to give my testimony. I was convinced about this, and when I was introduced as the preacher and stepped to the pulpit, I announced about what Jesus had said I should do."

"Wow! Hallelujah!" Ralph said.

"I walked slowly back and forth on the platform, telling my life's story. Often times I was interrupted by praises to the Lord. As I finished, I called for the invitational hymn. The first to come forward was an old couple rededicating their lives to Jesus. People were weeping freely. Then a young man and girl, he about seventeen and she about fifteen, came confirming Jesus as Savior. Then a young married couple came rededicating their lives to Jesus and transferring their church membership. Praise God! We had a good morning worship service."

"Man! I wish we could have been there with you. But, we did pray for you and all those folk. Maybe the Lord did let us be a little part of what happened," said Junior.

"Oh, I'm sure our wonderful Savior will give you blessings for your support in prayer. After all, we are one in Christ," said Timothy.

"Yeah, I feel good about your experience in Spring Hollow Baptist Church, Timothy. Jesus uses all his children to help perform His will. I'll remember this from now on. "What happened Sunday night, Timothy?" said Ralph.

"Both song services were very good. I thought the windows would shatter from such good singing. Those good people in Spring Hollow really know how to sing to the glory of God. I was told that the church had not had a choir on Sunday night for several years. After the choir sang Sunday night, I was introduced again. As the deacon sat down and I started to get up to the pulpit, another deacon, by the name of Larry Willoby, stood and asked to speak. What he said brought joy to our hearts. As he sat down, a young woman stood and gave a good testimony. People were crying and praising God. The Holy Spirit was doing what we needed done to us."

"A young man about fourteen by the name of Bart Dean, who by the way, went with us on the tour of Spring Hollow, told of his praying for a time like this in the church. He had prayed for a pastor who would care for the old and children alike and all ages in between. He thanked God for his family. Barts Dad said "amen" so loud that every one laughed of joy."

"Lord have mercy, Timothy How did you endure all this? Were you worried about not preaching?" Junior asked.

"Not at all, Junior. This was Gods will and He had allowed me to be there. But, there is more. The teacher of the 8 and 9 year old Sunday School class was the next and last to give a testimony. She told of the Holy Spirits work among her class age group. Most of the class was present. Well, Brother John Canton, the chairman of the deacons and spokesman for the day, closed the service after no one else wished to speak. He did not say, "We're sorry Brother Timothy for you not having an opportunity to preach. But we have heard from the Lord and this is His will. Brother Timothy, if you will come be with us next Sunday, we will let you preach then. Will you come back?"

"Yes, Ill be glad to. But I would like to say one word, if I may."

"You may say two if you wish," John said. A lot of laughs roared over the congregation.

"You folk have blessed me so much today. I'm glad God sent me to Spring Hollow Baptist. Now we should close the service with an invitation to Jesus. The invitational hymn was "I Surrender All." The two smaller children of Choctaw descent came immediately confessing Jesus as Lord and Savior. The song leaders daughter came confessing Jesus as her Savior. The husband of the teacher of the young adult couples Sunday School class came rededicating his life to Christ and the transfer of his church letter."

"What a glorious day at Spring Hollow. Timothy, you might just have you a good church to pastor. It sounds so good, do you think they might need an assistant pastor, like me?" ask Junior.

"It might come to that in the future. I don't know anyone better that I would like to work with than you two friends. But you know right well, this is the Lords work. It is amazing to look back on yesterday and reflect on the power of the Holy Spirit. No sermon, how well planned, could have produced the results we witnessed. Only the Holy Spirit can move people to the glory of Christ. He must get all the credit and honor. amen.?"

"Now, my friends, what you have heard; is it worth you paying for my dinner?" chided Timothy.

"Oh, yes, my friend. Your day has made my week. I'll dream about Spring Hollow many times. Perhaps some day we can go along with you. I would like to met people who love the Lord as do the people of Spring Hollow Baptist," said Ralph.

At six thirty, the phone rang at the Karr home.

"Hello," said Rance Karr.

"Hi Dad. This is your number one son. I only mean that as your first born. Is everyone there OK?"

"Yes, we are doing just fine. We had a good day at church yesterday. Many asked about you. They were anxious to hear about your trip to Spring Hollow. What can you tell me?"

"I can tell you more than a telephone call. For all the experience I'll have to write to you or wait until I can come home. However, the day was a most unusual experience. I did not preach at either service. Many things happened to change the preaching. At the morning service, I gave my testimony. At the evening service, we had church folk testify that really did all of us good. All of this was the work and will of the Holy Spirit."

"There were confessions of faith in Jesus, rededications of lives, and transfers of church membership in both services. I've never witnessed such power of God before. Dad, you would have loved being there and witnessing the work of God. I'll never be the same again."

"Tell the folk at Willow Bend about this, and thank them for their prayers. Tell Mom and the siblings hello and that I love ya'll. I'm going back Sunday and preach, I hope."

"Goodbye son. God bless you. We will pray for another great day for you and Spring Hollow."

Chapter 7

Back To Spring Hollow

Friday afternoon was rainy and a bit chilly. John and Wiley arrived a few minutes before Josh. Timothy was waiting for them and saw the car before it came to a stop. He came to meet them and to ask about the week in Spring Hollow. He was anxious to see them.

"Hey, Brother Timothy," called Wiley. "How are you? How's the week been with you?"

"Fine, just great," responded Timothy "How's been the week with you fellows? I see Brother Josh arriving."

"We've been doing very well. The weather has been good up until this afternoon. Everyone back in Spring Hollow is looking forward to Sunday. Maybe the weather won't be a hindrance," said John.

Josh had joined them in the meantime. "Hello, Brother Josh. Are you doing OK?"

"Just fine, Brother Timothy. I thought you could use a pickup truck this weekend. Since you didn't get to preach last Sunday, we figured you would be loaded down and would need a truck to haul it all up our way." A good laugh was shared.

"Thanks Brother. While I'm preaching, I'll look right at you and unload it all on you."

"I wish now I had not mentioned your need for a truck. You will have the last word. But, I'll tell you what; I'll just share some of the load with my friends here. They need it as much as I. How about you pointing a finger or two at them." They all laughed heartily.

"Well, we better stop this nonsense and get on home before dark," said John. "See you tomorrow Brother Timothy. Don't get lost."

The three deacons were on their way home, and Timothy secured the pickup truck and went inside his room. He felt real good from having had a brief happy fellowship with friends from Spring Hollow. To go back to Spring Hollow Baptist church was like a dream come true.

Meanwhile the Carl Sims family underwent an unusual transformation during the week. Carl and Cynthia loved their four children very much. The children loved their parents and were always privileged to discuss matters with them. This was one of those weeks where a brand new topic was foremost in importance - that of the four children accepting Jesus Christ as Savior.

Cynthia Sims professed being a believer. Her experience happened years ago, even before Joe was born. But, she had not practiced her belief in Christ through these years, as she should have. To her it was only a claim to be something, but not having any proof.

The conversation going on in her house this week brought back memories. But, these memories brought sadness and guilt about herself as a failure. She should have taken the lead in her family's religious upbringing. That part of her life was not good. Being a mother and seeing after the physical welfare of her family was good. That, she was proud of, and being a good wife to her husband.

Carl Sims was not a professed believer. He had shown tolerance toward religion, but it made no difference with him. He was not a mean man, but did lack traits of kindness towards others, sometimes. He loved his family and provided as well as he could for them. In particular, he was proud of his children's achievements in school.

This week in the life of the Sims family was a miracle. Joe and Callie made professions of their faith in Christ at the morning worship service. Beth and Agnes made their professions in Christ at the evening worship service. Their mother Cynthia attended the evening service. She witnessed her children's public decisions, weeping as she remembered her own years ago. Their father Carl did not attend either service. This had bothered him, somewhat, when his four children told him what they had done. He did not object, but was ashamed and felt guilty as if he had neglected something very important in his children's lives.

After Sunday dinner, Joe said, "Daddy, will you walk with me down the road aways. I've something to talk with you about."

"Yes, son. It must be pretty good and private."

"It is very good, Daddy. It's something that happened to me and Callie."

Dad and son stepped from the porch and started their casual stroll down the road. Joe was anxious to tell his beloved Dad about his experience with Jesus. Dad wondered what was on Joe's mind that was so private. Carl respected his son and let him say what was on his mind. He would listen carefully.

"Daddy, I did something today at Spring Hollow Baptist Church that I have wanted to do for several weeks. I made a profession of faith in Jesus Christ as my Savior. I'm saved from my sins, Daddy. I'm a brand new Christian. I don't know what all this means yet, but I know it is the best thing I will ever do. I have never in all my memory felt as I do now. The Bible calls it a rebirth. It happened to me. I am reborn by Jesus Christ."

"Joe, you are seventeen years old. You are your own man. You know what you want and what you think is best for you. I won't scold you for what you've done. Did Callie follow you in this?"

"No, Daddy. She told me about her decision before we went to church. We have talked it over between us for about a week. Daddy, Callie is a smart, solid young woman. You can be proud of her."

"I am proud of all my children, Joe. I'm glad you are the oldest. You have a good head on you. The other children look to you for help many times. I'm proud of you for that. I trust you and Callie. She is a beauty, isn't she?"

"Daddy, we have prayed for you that you too would let Jesus save you as He has saved us. It is very simple. All you have to do is ask Jesus to forgive your sins. All of us have sinned. You are no different from all the rest of the people. Jesus will save you, forgive you, like He has all others who repent and ask His forgiveness. He won't treat you any differently than He has treated me."

72

Carl felt the impact of his sons witness upon his sinful soul. He knew Joe was wanting him to experience the joy and assurance he now had. He also knew that what he was hearing from his son was the deep compassionate love for his Dad. At this moment, he was having feelings deep inside that had never disturbed him before. He had always wanted the best for his family. Could this be what Joe experienced, the very best? If so, he wanted that for his family also.

"Joe" - for two or three minutes, he was silent - - "Joe," his voice quivering, "I don't know how to pray. I would like to have the experience you've had. But, I don't know how to ask God for anything."

"I'll help you, Daddy. I don't know much about praying either, but I know what you should do now. Will you trust me to help?"

"Yes, Joe, I will."

Carl stopped, turned toward Joe, and embraced his son and began weeping like a little child. Joe had never witnessed his Daddy crying. He knew this was the work of the Holy Spirit on his Dad. Joe wept with him for sometime. For several minutes, neither spoke.

Then Joe said, "Daddy will you say what I said to Jesus when I asked Him to forgive my sins and come into my heart?"

"Will you help me, Joe?"

"Yes, Daddy, repeat what I say." As they were still embraced, Joe said, "Jesus, please forgive me of my sins. I'm sorry that I've sinned against you. Come into my heart now. Save me by your wonderful love. I accept your forgiveness and salvation now. Thank you, Jesus, for saving me from my sins."

"Daddy, if you were truthful to Jesus, He saved you as He did me. Did you?"

"Yes, my son. Jesus did forgive my sins and save me. I feel fresh and new inside. As you said before, I feel reborn. Isn't it a good feeling to know you are saved from your sins? Now I've got to do something about this."

"Daddy, lets thank Jesus for this experience." They embraced again, and with stammering words, Carl voiced his thanks to Jesus for His salvation. Joe said "amen".

When Carl and Joe arrived back at home, the other members were on the front porch waiting for them. As Carl and Joe came through the gate, Cynthia walked down the steps and met Carl. He had been crying, but she noticed, as did the children, his whole countenance had changed, and he was smiling with joy.

Cynthia embraced her husband and, weeping herself, said, "My dear Carl, I'm proud of you. I'm glad you accepted Jesus as your Savior. Now we all can be a big wonderful Christian family."

"Yes, Cynthia. I am happy. What I am experiencing now, I should have done a long time ago. I'm proud of Joe. He wanted me to experience what he had. Jesus has done a wonderful thing for our family, Cynthia."

All four children gathered around their parents and hugged them with all the love they knew how to express. Joy at its best had come to the Sims' home.

Carl told his family that he would not be able to attend church that night. The reason was; he had to leave in about an hour to visit his very sick Daddy. It would be about 11:00 p.m. before his return. He promised his family that next Sunday he would make whatever decision his children had. That promise was good enough for them.

Personally Carl wanted to tell his old and ill Daddy what Jesus had done in his life. His Dad was a long time Christian and had often prayed for and witnessed to Carl. However, Carl would always find a way around or out of the conversation with his Dad. Now he had this good news he wanted to tell himself. The trip to his old Dad's home was one of joy.

Meanwhile, John Canton had called the deacons for a meeting Monday night at 7:30 p.m. The purpose was to discuss their decision of recommending Timothy Karr to Spring Hollow Baptist Church as pastor.

"Gentlemen." said John, "It is our duty, placed upon us by the church two months ago, that when we had carefully examined a prospective pastor and all deacons agreed, we would present that person to the church for their decision. We have not heard Brother Karr preach yet, but we do know his personal characteristics that are needed for our church and community. You are free to state your thoughts about him."

"Brethren, said Rufus Dean, I'm deeply impressed about this young man. His commitment to Christ was given to us unashamed. I believe young Timothy Karr is going to be used mightily of the Lord. We will be most fortunate to have the Lords blessings bestowed on us through Brother Timothy. My convictions are positive toward his purpose in serving the Lord."

"I can say amen to what Brother Rufus has said," spoke Wiley Steale. "It is true that I saw him in a more homely setting, as he was our house guest. However, that situation only added to what I already knew. I'm impressed with his commitment to missions support. He is not just interested in the financial support of missions, but that people will surrender themselves to be used of the Lord. After all, that is the heart of the church work. Take that away, and the church will die. Brethren, you well know that our church has been sliding downward fast in this matter. I believe God is offering us a turnaround through His choice of Brother Karr. If we bypass this opportunity of spiritual awakening, we might not get another."

"Hear, hear, I concur," said Jake Dawson. "The whole church has felt the reality of need and awakening by the Holy Spirit. What Spring Hollow needs is a leader with a shepherd's heart. I believe he is, and will become, a good preacher. We heard him say that wherever the Lord sends, he would be a friend and pastor to all alike. I like that commitment in a pastor."

"I'm agreeing to all that has been said," spoke Larry Willoby. "We have discussed his spiritual qualities and agree they are God sent. Now, lets discuss a salary and a place for him to live when among us. As you know, our offerings have been above average and budget requirement for the past two months. This too, is a sure sign that the Lord Jesus is preparing for us according to His will. Let's offer him a salary somewhat above what he is earning now. In this way, if we need him during the week, when he would otherwise be on his job, he could respond without loss of time. And, he will not have to worry about interruption of his

75

studies to attend his job. This summer and the next, Brother Timothy can live on the church field. Especially, do we want to honor our Lord Jesus in support of Brother Karr?"

"Thank you, Brother Larry," said Josh White. "I believe we are headed in the right direction. Our church is a well-informed intelligent people. We know our needs and what we want. We will do the right thing. I believe Brother Timothy fits all the requirements for our pastor. I make the motion to us deacons that we strongly recommend Timothy Karr to Spring Hollow Baptist Church as our pastor."

"All agree?" said John.

"Amen," all the deacons said in unison. So it was that the deacons would make the recommendation to the Spring Hollow Baptist Church on Sunday morning, after the worship service.

All other deacons, who were not serving on the finance and budget committee, met with the committee to prepare a salary for Brother Timothy, if the church called and, if he accepted the call. After good frank discussions and prayer about the salary, the committee prepared the statement for the church. Everyone seemed very satisfied that no problems should be forthcoming. The committee report would be given to the church Wednesday night, with the vote on Sunday.

The place for the pastor to stay on weekends was a problem. Brother Steale said they could not offer the accommodation because his son would be home shortly. Brother Timothy had occupied his son's room the week before. Since no particular home could be settled upon, the deacons decided to pray about it and wait Sunday for further development.

Meanwhile, Monday morning found several lives changed at the public school. Friends of students attending Spring Hollow Baptist Church had heard about the spiritual revival. Joe Sims was very open to witness of Jesus about what had taken place in his life. The baseball seemed lighter as he threw more strikes. His friends asked many questions about his newfound faith in Christ. Some had expressed bad attitudes toward Joe. But, now a new friendship emerged, and it was positive. Several promised to visit Spring Hollow Baptist. Joe assured them all that they would be welcome.

Pat Steale took on a new and strong commitment to witness of Christ. Her classmates were anxious to hear about Spring Hollow Baptist revival. Several of her close friends were not Christians. With boldness she never knew she possessed, her witness began bearing fruit. This was God's good grace that what was happening in their school; He wanted this to happen in other schools across the State. Pat was proud of her newfound spiritual strength in her Lord.

Callie Sims was a quiet, modest person. She had never been forward in any situation. But, her attitude was always positive and contagious. She was intelligent, but never let smarts get in the way of friendships. This week was a challenge for her. She wanted her friends to know Jesus and what Jesus had done in her life. All that knew Callie were assured of her trustworthiness. In her very private way, her witness of Jesus began bearing fruit.

Many other students and school officials would be affected during the next several weeks. School days were coming to an end. Many people would not be seen again until the next school year. The Holy Spirit's influence upon many would touch every community of the school system. Several life changes would be affected during the summer months. At this time, no one could have predicted the impact of four or five committed Christian young people upon this entire school. The Lord Jesus was working His wonders to His glory.

Friday night was busy for Timothy. He was making final sermon preparations and he was anxious to start his trip to Spring Hollow early Saturday morning. He planned to make two visits before arriving at the Steale home. The first was to the home of the young man who gave the directions to Spring Hollow church. The other was to stop by the country store and visit with Mike Brannon.

Josh White's pickup 'purred like a kitten' after Timothy had driven out of the city and onto the highway leading toward Spring Hollow. The weather was cool and overcast from the last evening and night of rain. He thought of his sermons he had prepared to preach. To him, they were suited to the community of Spring Hollow. Many times during this week, he had asked Jesus to bless these messages. Even his two friends had been asked to give their opinions. They, too, seemed to agree that something good would come from his sermons.

Timothy turned onto the county road that led to the young boy's house. This was his second time on this road, and he paid close attention to distance and objects to guide him. Soon, after a few miles, he recognized the house where he had stopped for directions. He slowed his speed and turned into the driveway. To his surprise, the young boy and a middle-aged woman were sitting in their swing on the porch.

"Mama, look. That is the same man who was lost last week. Do you suppose he is lost again? He is the man who preached at Spring Hollow Baptist Church. You know mama, he don't look like a preacher."

"Go out and invite him in, Sam. He looks hungry." Timothy was getting out of the pickup truck as Mrs. Matthews was making her observation of the slim form of Timothy.

"Hey preacher," said Sam Matthews. "Are you lost again? Come in and meet my mother."

"Howdy, young man. No, I'm not lost this time. I came by to visit with you and your family. Is it O.K. that I do?"

"Sure is. Mama, meet the preacher of Spring Hollow Baptist Church. What's your name, preacher?"

"Timothy Karr."

"I'm Nancy Matthews, Rev. Karr. "Come on in and sit a spell with us. I'll call Bob, my husband. He's out back feeding hogs."

Nancy walked around the house and, in a moment, she was heard calling Bob.

"Bob, Oh Bob."

"Yeah, honey,"

"We have a visitor. Can you leave off what you are doing for a few minutes?"

"Yeah, I'll be there in a moment."

Nancy walked back to the front and sat down in the swing with Sam.

"Rev. Karr," said Nancy.

"Please mam, I'd rather not be called Reverend. Just Timothy is O.K. That's what most folk call me. Reverend sounds too high collar. I'm just a country boy from Willow Bend."

"Willow Bend? That's where I'm from. My maiden name was Kimpsley. But, I have not been in Willow Bend for several years, actually, since I was fourteen years of age."

Bob appeared from around the corner of the house with a bucket half full of feed still in his hands.

"Bob, this is Brother Timothy Karr. He is a Baptist preacher,"

"Howdy, preacher. Welcome to our house. We are humble folk as you can see. Excuse me preacher. I didn't intend to bring this bucket of hog feed with me. Don't know why I did."

"Hello, Mr. Matthews. I'm pleased to meet you. Sam told me the way to Spring Hollow Baptist Church last Saturday. I had made the wrong turn and showed up here. He thought I was lost again when he saw me turn into your driveway today."

They all laughed about the incident. Sam spoke up;

"Preacher Timothy, I'm glad you came back today. You've met Mama and Daddy this time. I hope they will promise to visit Spring Hollow Church sometimes."

"Yes, Sam. I hope they will. You will come along with them if they do visit, won't you?"

"You bet. I like the young people over there. All of them treat us well," said Sam.

"I'm glad to hear you say that Sam," responded Timothy.

"Preacher, how about a cool glass of ice tea. Sam, will you go and get Brother Timothy a glass of tea?"

"Glad to Mama,"

"Mr. Matthews, when I first saw your feed bucket, I thought perhaps you had peeped around and had a good look at me and decided I needed some of your hog feed, seeing I am so thin." They all laughed.

"Well I admit you could use something like this. I bet it wouldn't take long before you would be buying new clothes." They laughed. "In fact, the food is not bad. Some of Nancy's laying hens got hold of some of it the other day. Their eggs grew so large the hens had a terrible time laying them. In fact, we had to call in Dr. Brown, the veterinarian, to deliver their eggs." They laughed loud and long about this.

Nancy said, "Bob, you should be ashamed of your self. Don't pay any attention to Bob, Brother Timothy. He likes to joke about everything. But, his heart is as kind as can be."

"I'll be careful not to eat too much of Bobs hog feed, Mrs. Matthews. Bob might get the idea to auction me off as one of his prize pigs at the county fair." They had another good laugh.

"Here's your tea, Brother Timothy. Has Daddy been teasing you? Daddy likes to joke and tease people."

"We've had a couple of good laughs, Sam. Your Daddy is OK. I'd like to stay longer and get better acquainted, but I have another visit to make. Ya'll just plan on coming to church tomorrow. I'd like to see you in church."

"We just might see you at Spring Hollow tomorrow Brother Timothy," said Bob.

"Thanks for the ice tea Sam. You really know how to make a man feel good and welcome. Good bye," said Timothy

"Goodbye Preacher." As Timothy was backing the pickup truck out of the driveway, Bob picked up the bucket of hog feed and walked around the house to continue his chores. Nancy heard him say as he rounded the house corner:

"I sure do like that young man. He appears to me to like people."

Nancy was pleased to hear her husband say such a thing about Timothy. She had never heard Bob carry on a conversation with any preacher before as he did today with Timothy. She hoped this was a good sign for their family, and especially for Bob. Bob had not attended any church for several years. Nancy hoped Bob was turning around from his cold nature. She prayed quietly for her dear husband.

Timothy pulled into the small country store parking place. Two cars were parked along side the store. Another was at the gas pump. As he got out of Josh White's pickup truck, a man came out of the store and headed toward the car at the gas pump. As he did, he looked toward the White's truck and recognized it as that belonging to Josh.

"Howdy mister. That looks like Josh White's truck. Have you bought it?"

"No, I've just borrowed it for a while," said Timothy.

"You're a stranger here aren't you," said the man. "Kin to the Whites?"

"Yes, you can say I'm a stranger. No I'm not kin to the Whites. I'm Timothy Karr, the preacher for tomorrow services at Spring Hollow Baptist Church."

"Oh, yeah, I should have known that by your tall, slim size. Everyone is talking about you in these parts. I live over beyond the school, about twenty-five miles. Names Bill Karn. Well, it's good to meet you, preacher. I've gotta be going."

"Yeah, the pleasures mine, Mr. Karn. Come visit us tomorrow and bring your whole family. Ya'll be welcome."

"Might just surprise you, preacher," Bill answered.

"Do that. I like surprises," said Timothy.

Timothy opened the front door of the store and stepped inside.

"Howdy, are you Mr. Brannon?" Timothy held out his hand to the store owner, the man behind the counter.

"Yep, that's what folks call me around here, except the mister part. Most folk call me Mike," said Mike Brannon.

"I'm Timothy Karr, just a visiting Seminary student preacher for the Spring Hollow Baptist Church. I'm on my way to the Steale home for the weekend. Just thought I'd come by and say hello."

"I'm glad you came by, Brother Timothy. That's what the people are calling you around here, Brother Timothy. Our little girl, Susie, was in church last Sunday. One of our neighbors came by for her. My wife and I didn't get to attend. What I've heard, I wish now we had. Our little Susie fell in love with you. I don't mean that literally, but you know what I mean. She is only ten years old. We have a son who is fifteen. He is not much on church going. I'm afraid I've had too much bad church going influence on him. Other than that, he is a good boy. He's smart in his school-work. He loves sports of all kinds. He plays on the school baseball team. Pretty good if I do say so myself," said Mike.

"What's his name?" Timothy asked.

"Troy," Mike responded with affection. "My oldest son is away at State University. His name is Mike Jr. Can't just tell when he will come home. Most likely when he runs out of funds."

"You've named both well. Troy is a good strong name. It's one a person hardly ever forgets. I like it. Maybe I can meet him tomorrow at church. Do me a favor and bring your family to church. You will feel good afterwards. Well, I have to be going Mr. Brannon. Mr. White might be needing his truck," said Timothy.

"Oh, yeah. I heard about that truck deal. Josh White is a prince of a man, Brother Karr. I've known him for years. The Steale family, they are very reliable people, the cream of the crop."

"Thanks, Mr. Brannon. You're evaluation is just right. Hope to see you tomorrow."

Timothy left and headed for the Steale home. It was 10:30 a.m. when he arrived. Mrs. Steale's cooking caught Timothy's nose as he got out of the truck. "There'll be a feast today," he said to himself. Pat came bounding onto the porch, greeting him as if it had been a year since his last visit.

"Hi, Brother Timothy We've been expecting you since early."

"You have? Why? Am I someone special, Pat? Or is it just you who thinks I am?" Timothy's tease was good for Pat. She realized that she was noticed.

"Everybody hereabouts likes you. We are doing everything we can to keep you for a spell."

"You do want to be our pastor, don't you Brother Timothy?"

"Well, I don't know anywhere else I had rather be their pastor than you folk in Spring Hollow, Pat. You can take that to

Jesus and talk to Him about it. Knowing you, Pat, I bet you will." Timothy laughed to the joy of Pat.

Mrs. Steale heard their talking and came out on the porch to greet Timothy

"Good morning, Brother Timothy. Have you had a good week at school? Pat tells me her week at school has been a busy time for Jesus. According to her, if all the school children and their parents, who they witnessed to this week, would be in church tomorrow, we would have a brand new congregation and no where to put them. Wouldn't that be just grand?"

"I'll say. Let them come. We will just have to move outside, where we will have to sing and preach louder," laughed Timothy.

"Pat, you and your Christian friends are discovering what being a witnessing disciple is all about. You are doing fine. Keep up the good work for Jesus," continued Timothy.

"Sorry you missed Wiley, Timothy. He wanted you to see a part of our community that you haven't seen. Oh well, I expect you will see parts none of us have seen when you become our pastor."

"You sound convincing, Mrs. Steale. The folk here about are wonderful. I'm looking forward to tomorrow."

"Me too," chimed in Pat.

Timothy told of his reason for being late. Pats eyes sparked when he told that Sam Matthews and family planned to be in church tomorrow. Pat knew Sam at school and that she had talked with him about coming to Sunday School.

The clock struck twelve midday, just about the time Wiley turned into the driveway. Josh had already come for his truck. Timothy and Pat were sitting in the swing, waiting for his arrival and eating dinner. All seemed delighted to get into Mrs. Steales cooking. They ate as if no one had eaten anything all day.

Chapter 8

Timothy Karr Called as Pastor

Sunday morning dawned with the rain clouds disappearing. Everyone was thankful for the rain. It had been three weeks since the last rain occurred. Wiley and Timothy left early for the deacons prayer meeting. The deacons were in a high spirit of expectancy. All greeted each other and got down to prayer business. The Lord had blessed them before, and He was blessing again today. Each knew what was coming after the preaching, and they wanted it to be from God. Only Timothy did not know until he was informed at the close of prayer.

"Brother Timothy, the deacons who are responsible for our pulpit supply and search for a pastor have agreed to present you to the church today to become our pastor. We are convinced you are the one whom God sent to us, and we want you as pastor and spiritual leader. Will you become our pastor, if the church votes yes?" asked John Canton.

"I've prayed much about this decision, brother deacons, and I'm convinced that Jesus wants me here in His work. I will accept if the church says yes," said Timothy.

"Let's join the others in Sunday School," Larry Willoby happily said.

Every chair in the Sunday School rooms was occupied. Some children had to sit on the floor. They didn't mind though, because it was a happy time to see so many new faces in Sunday School.

Jim Tilley, the Sunday School Director, was overjoyed to see Spring Hollow Church Sunday Schools growth. He was overheard telling someone that he believed every home in Spring Hollow had been touched with revival.

The bell rang, and people from everywhere began their trek to the auditorium. Several people were already in the auditorium that was not present in Sunday School. The pews quickly filled and added chairs had to be placed in the isle and rear. Several were added to spaces near the choir seats. After all the noise and chatter of adding seats, the worship service began. Brother John Canton stepped to the pulpit and heartily welcomed everyone, especially the visitors.

"Good morning all. Welcome to Spring Hollow Baptist Church. I hope you will join right in and praise the Lord and, above all, let Him have His way with you today. The coming of our visitors among us have made this day more glorious. Brother Dick Reveere, come and lead us to the Lord in singing."

"Good morning all. Let's turn to the hymn "Bringing in the Sheaves." That's what we are doing here at Spring Hollow Baptist. If we sing today, as we did last Sunday, we'll bring in the whole flock. Many of you will need to share your hymnal with a neighbor. You won't mind, I'm sure."

"I believe you were a pure copy of last Sundays singing. Aren't we proud of our good singing?"

Josh White stepped to the pulpit to make all necessary announcements. In closing announcements, he stated there would be a brief business time at the end of the worship service. "Now Brother Dick, lead us again in good singing."

"Please turn to the hymn, "I Know That My Redeemer Liveth." This is a hymn that lifts our hearts in praise."

"Amen, Brother Dick," said Timothy. "You know how to pick hymns to charge us up in the spirit."

"Following the next hymn, "Blessed Assurance," the ushers will receive our tithes and offerings. Let us stand and sing as before. Those of you standing next to the windows, be careful that you don't get hurt from flying glass. If our windows break, they will on this great hymn. Lets sing."

Josh White again came to the pulpit to introduce Brother Timothy.

"We have the same preacher that visited with us last week. I don't think he has changed much in looks, but I believe he is full of Gods Word. We need what God has given you to say Brother Timothy. After this wonderful choir sings, you come preach and we will listen."

"Again, today, the choir will sing an old familiar hymn. It has a great message for us. Please listen as we sing, "Christ For the Whole Wide World."

"Thank you, choir. You have led us well today. And you good people, what a joy to hear your sing. It is evident when you sing like that, that you are happy."

"My sermon for today is God's message for His church at Spring Hollow Baptist. I hope we will listen to Jesus speak to us. Let's pray."

"My Lord and Savior, give Your servant a clean heart, now. Let Thy great Name be glorified. May we all surrender to the Holy Spirit now. In Your Name I ask, amen."

Sermon Title: "My Want List For My Church" Ephesians 1:15-23.

As Timothy preached, he was commended by many amens and praises to the Lord. The Lord blessed the people. Spring Hollow Baptist Church was really in revival.

Timothy prayed a compassionate prayer at the close of the message. It was very evident the congregation listened to the message. The Holy Spirit was dealing with lives and souls of people to respond to an invitation of salvation and service in God's Kingdom. There was a strong spirit of expectancy that Spring Hollow Baptist would be visited again today.

Brother Dick announced the invitational hymn, "Jesus Is Calling." His voice clear and strong, he said, "Please respond to the Lord's will for you as we sing to His glory."

There was no hesitation. Carl and Cynthia Sims moved to the isle from a position in a middle pew. They walked down the isle, she weeping and he bright faced and rejoicing. Brother Timothy greeted them with open arms. Immediately, behind them came Tom Bailey and his wife Juanita. Lloyd and Anna Anderson came next. Sam Matthews came and stood behind the Anderson's, waiting for someone to talk with him. Bart felt strong leadership by the Holy Spirit to move where Sam was and talk with him. He did not hesitate to do so. Sam said to Bart that he wanted to accept Jesus as Savior and needed help to make the decision. Bart took him aside, knelt at the pulpit platform steps, and led Sam to saving faith in Christ. Bart then presented him to John Canton to present Sam to the church.

People, both members and visitors, were openly weeping and praying. Deacon Rufus Dean was on his knees praying and rejoicing in the Lord.

The last to come, but not the least important, was Susie Brannon, the young daughter of Mike Brannon, the country store owner. Susie came trusting Jesus as Savior and Lord. Her decision had touched her Mom and Dad. The invitation closed with Timothy leading in thanksgiving praise to God. It was evident in his voice that God was working in his own life in regards to these spiritual happenings at Spring Hollow Baptist. Brother Canton presented the decisions to the church with great joy. He, too, had never experienced such blessings from God. Carl Sims, Tom Bailey, Sam Matthews, and Susie Brannon came professing Jesus as Savior and Lord. Cynthia Sims and Juanita Bailey came rededicating their lives to Jesus and for transfer of their church letter. Spring Hollow Baptist rejoiced as they greeted them into their church and fellowship. Deacon Rufus Dean had already gotten up from kneeling in prayer. But, he was weeping with joy. He stepped forward and put his arms around Carl Sims and, with a positive, clear voice for all to hear, asked Carl to forgive him for sins of shame he had committed against him.

"Sure I do, Brother Rufus. But, I'm guilty too. Will you forgive me?"

"Yes, I do, Brother Carl." As he said that, he embraced Cynthia and asked her forgiveness. She responded, as did her husband Carl. As they were confessing their sins to each other, there was movement all over the congregation. People were hugging each other and weeping from sheer joy in Christ.

Brother John Canton finally cleared his voice and dried his eyes. He then asked the folk to be seated for a brief time. He then presented the decision of the deacons to extend the call to Brother Timothy Karr to become their pastor. Someone spoke immediately and said, "Yes, get him here quickly." The church responded with a healthy amen.

Brother John turned to Brother Timothy and said, "My brother, you have heard the strongest voice call you will ever hear. Do you accept?"

"How could I ever refuse the leadership of God, Brother John. Yes, all my dear friends of Spring Hollow, I can do nothing else but to follow the Lord Jesus through your call. I believe that I am the most fortunate man alive. What we have witnessed these last two weeks is really a miracle from God." Many amens were sounded.

"Then it's done, church. We have a pastor, leader, and preacher. All wrapped up in one young slim strong man of God. Welcome, Brother Timothy. When can you start?"

"I started last week. The vote was not cast, but God had already done His work."

Before the benediction, Pete and Sandy Carter asked for a moment to speak. Brother John said, "Please do". He did not know what they were planning to do.

Pete and Sandy walked to the front and stood by Brother Timothy He did not know what their intentions were. Pete spoke.

"You folk are aware that Brother Timothy has no transportation of his own. Well, he has now." As Pete said this, he handed Brother Timothy a set of car keys. "These belong to a two-year old Chrysler New Yorker sitting out there in front of the church. It is yours. All you need to do tomorrow is go to the county court house and sign for the title and tag. This was my mothers car. I'm the sole owner. Sandy and I have decided we do not need it, so we are giving it to a man, our pastor, who is worthy of it. Do you accept it, Brother Timothy?"

"What can I say, but yes. Thanks a million miles. I'm rich." Everyone was laughing.

"Now, you can drive it to Brother Frank and Millie Stewarts home for dinner. You will be pleased," said Pete.

"Let's be back this evening for Church Training and Worship," said John as he asked the congregation to rise for the benediction.

"Brother Mike Owens, please dismiss us with prayer."

The departing from the church was joyous time. Several gathered around Timothy's new car and wished him well. As he followed the Stewarts home, he thanked Jesus for all His kindness and future directions for himself and Spring Hollow.

Dinner at the Stewarts was outstanding. Timothy became convinced that the folk in Spring Hollow intended to put a lot of weight on him. Mrs. Millie Stewart was an excellent cook. Timothy enjoyed the meal, but above all, he enjoyed the rich, kind fellowship of the Stewarts.

After dinner, Millie asked Timothy to look at something across the hall. The hall was an open dog trot as it was called in that part of the woods. She opened the door to a very nice clean bedroom. It was completely furnished with a joining bath, which they had added a few years back.

"Brother Timothy, this is your place to stay while in Spring Hollow. That is, if you want it. There is no cost. You will be privileged to go and come as you like."

"What a gift."

"Yes, it is nice," said Frank. We have taken care of it. When we have visitors, this is where they stay. Right now, you are that special visitor."

"You folk are too good to me. I've never enjoyed such love before, outside my family circle."

"Well, you know we have no children. It will be so good for us to have a son, and him a preacher, for a while. Tears came into Millie's eyes. You will make Frank and me very happy. Your meals will be taken with us, if you are here. Many of our folk will be inviting you to their homes also. But, this is your home until we build a pastorium. That subject is already being discussed. So, you can move in this afternoon or wait until next week. Just do as you please."

"Well, perhaps it will be appropriate to wait until next week, since I've got everything spread out at the Steale's."

"That will be just fine. But, you will want to take supper with us before church time, won't you?"

"Yes, I will, but I want to make some visits this afternoon. I'll return in time to not delay our church training at 6:00 p.m."

Henry Nobles had asked Timothy to make a couple visits with him in the afternoon. He was turning into the driveway as Millie was giving Timothy the time supper would be ready. The two walked with Timothy to the porch and greeted Henry and wished them well on their visits.

"We're riding with you Brother Henry?" said Timothy.

"Believe so, Brother Timothy I know the way. But, you take keen notes because you might need to come this way again."

"I suspect that will be the case for awhile. I'll have to learn all directions in these parts. In fact, I want to get acquainted with the area and people. The best way is to ride the roads and stop at every house. Can't learn where they are by telephones, eh, Brother Henry?"

"You are right. And, another thing, I want to encourage you to do, that is, as often as possible, take someone with you and teach them the importance of visiting. Some of our folk need to practice this spiritual duty."

"I'll remember to do just that, Brother Henry."

"Brother Timothy, I'll estimate there are 750 people living within five square miles of Spring Hollow Baptist Church. That figure will double at ten miles. Many, many are just waiting for us to go after them. The Lord Jesus knows who they are, and I believe He is asking us to go witness to them," said Henry.

"Man, I like your spiritual attitude, Brother Henry. That's the spirit to do the job Christ wants us to do. Let's say, if we will win two hundred of these to Jesus within the next two years, where would we put them?"

"That is a big question. However, I believe the Lord will provide. That's what He said he would do. I'm going to trust Him," said Henry.

Henry began slowing down to turn down a small dirt road. For the next mile the road was rough. They were outside the five-mile radius of the church.

"There are three houses down this road with five people in each, children, young people, and parents. They need Christ, and

90

they need us to visit them now. They are not bad folk, but they are shy. Two families are kin, brothers, I believe," said Henry.

"Maybe the Britton woman is a sister to the Wilsons, I'll find out for sure. The first two houses are Wilson's. This one is David and Wendy's." They stopped beside the road. The front yard extended to the road. David was sitting on the edge of the porch with his legs hanging down. As Henry got out of the car, David recognized him.

"Hello Henry. Good to see you. What brings you out this way on Sunday afternoon?"

"Good to see you, my friend. I thought you needed a visit, and I wanted to introduce you and your family to Brother Timothy Karr, our new pastor. He is brand new to us." said Henry.

"Brother Timothy, meet David Wilson. David and his brother work at the same plant I do in town."

"Hello preacher. I'm glad to meet you. You are associating with a fine friend. Henry and I have known each other for a few years."

"I can say the same about you David," said Henry.

"It's good to met you, Mr. Wilson. I hope we will see you often in the time I'm here as Spring Hollow Baptist's pastor," said Timothy.

"Is Wendy home, David?" asked Henry.

"Yeah, I believe so. I just came from the backside of the field five minutes before you folk drove up. I didn't have time to go in and get my cup of coffee. "Wendy," David called. "We have company."

Wendy stepped onto the porch with a tray and three cups of coffee on it.

"Hi, Henry. Good to see you. How's Jean?"."

"Fine, Wendy. She stays busy as a bee, like yourself. Wendy, this is Brother Timothy Karr, our new pastor."

"Good afternoon Brother Karr. I'm glad to meet you," said Wendy.

"The same here, Mrs. Wilson."

"We wanted to make a short visit with you folk and give you a special invitation to our church. We are having a great time down our way. Since we are good friends, we want you to share in this with us. You folks know most of us folks down at Spring Hollow Baptist Church. Your children know all the school children there," said Henry.

They talked about the importance of families involved in church and about other friendly interests. As they did, their coffee was consumed, and it was time to move on.

"I expect we will come down to visit you all, Henry. We've heard a little about the happenings. Sounds good for our community," said David.

"We'll be going, David and Wendy. Hope to see you down there next Sunday," said Henry. By the way, is Mrs. Britton your sister, David?"

"Yes, she is, the best and the youngest."

"Thanks for letting me visit with you also, Mr. and Mrs. Wilson," said Timothy.

"Come by any time, preacher," David said.

Henry and Timothy drove about a half-mile to the home of Norman and Sally Wilson. They were both home and sitting on their porch as if waiting for Henry and Timothy to visit them. Norman was the oldest of the brothers. They were very gentle folk, and invited Henry and Timothy onto the porch. This conversation went about the same as that with David and Sandy. Two of the children, Ben, age 13, and Mendy, age 9, came out to see who was talking with their Dad and Mom. Both were a little shy to meet Brother Timothy, but they knew Henry. As with the other Wilson family, they were encouraged to visit Spring Hollow Baptist soon.

Ted and Angela Britton were standing on the edge of their front yard, near the road. Henry stopped, and they greeted each other as close friends.

"Hi, my good buddy. What brings you out this way?" Ted asked.

"Afternoon, Angela and Ted. We wanted to visit with you, and I wanted you to meet our new young pastor at Spring

Hollow Baptist. Meet Brother Timothy Karr. Brother Karr, this is Ted and Angela Britton. I just found out, a minute ago, Angela, that you are David and Norman's sister" said Henry.

"Hello, Mr. & Mrs. Britton. It's good to meet and know you."

"The same here, preacher," said Ted.

About that time, their energetic children bounded out of the house and ran toward their parents, giggling.

"Brother Henry and Preacher Karr, these are our three children, Cindy, age 8, Will, age 6, and Natalie, age 4. Children, this is Brother Timothy Karr, the new preacher down at the Spring Hollow Baptist Church. You know Mr. Henry Nobles, don't you?"

"Hi, children," greeted Timothy "Did you know that I was about your size and age once upon a time. Now you are looking at me and wondering. Well, he is not too much bigger than we are now. I bet you are saying, somebody needs to feed this preacher a lot." At this they all laughed.

"Ted and Angela, we want you folk to visit us at Spring Hollow Baptist. We are having a wonderful time. The Lord Jesus is blessing more than we deserve. We want your family to be a part of His blessings," said Henry.

"I'll say amen to that," Timothy said.

"We've heard by the grapevine that many good things are happening down there. I'm sure we need what you all are getting," agreed Angela.

"There's enough to go around for us all," said Henry.

"We'll be coming Mr. Henry," Angela promised.

"I've been invited to come to Sunday School by one of my school friends," said Cindy.

"We've enjoyed our visit with you, Angela, Ted, and children. It's been good seeing you again. We should do more visiting for fellowship more often, eh, Ted?" said Henry.

"Preacher Karr, come back to visit us. I can't remember if we have ever had a preacher to visit our home. We will remember this time," said Ted.

"I'll be back." You can count on it," Promised Timothy.

Timothy and Henry left for the Stewart's home. It was 4:30 when they arrived. Henry dropped Timothy off and drove on home. As Timothy entered the hall, he heard Mrs. Stewart in the kitchen.

"I'm back, Mrs. Stewart." I'll be ready for supper when you all are. Right now, I'm going to look over my message a bit."

"O.K., Brother Timothy It will be another thirty minutes. Frank is napping, I think."

Everyone was excited about the morning worship service. Now, there were strong expectations for the evening worship service. By the time Timothy arrived in his new car, several cars were already parked at the church. Timothy thought several of them must be those of the choir. But, Timothy had a surprise coming for the evening service. A duet was to be the special and would be sung by two teenagers, Joe and Callie.

Again, there was a bumper attendance at the Church Training session. Mike Owens was very pleased and expressed it to his new pastor. The bell rang, and people began moving to the auditorium. By this time Timothy and John Canton came in with the choir, the house was full again. The choir led singing was absolutely great. People seemed to have strengthened their voices from the morning service.

After the choir sings, Brother Timothy will preach and lead us to the Lord through the Word. This is the last time I'll introduce him. It is only because we have visitors amongst us tonight. On behalf of our cherished visitors, we are glad you are here. Brother Timothy Karr was called to be our pastor at the morning worship service. Tonight, he is officially our pastor."

Brother Dick Reveere stepped to the pulpit and thanked the choir for the wonderful spirit as they led the singing. He then introduced the duet who would sing the worship special music.

"Joe and Callie Sims will bless our hearts tonight by singing for us. Their mother, Cynthia Sims, will play the piano for her children. Joe has a strong bass voice, and Callie has a strong alto voice. Joe and Callie, we will listen well."

"Thanks, Brother Dick. We are singing for the Lord tonight "It Pays to Serve Jesus." This is a challenge to us all. Pray for Callie and me as we sing." said Joe.

The congregation listened intently as Joe and Callie sang. There were muffled sounds of amen and praise the Lord. Their voices blended so well. Both had studied music in high school and with their mother. It was through their mother that they received this practice. She had worked well with them. At the close of the last verse, the congregation stood and applauded these two brave young people.

Brother Timothy walked to the pulpit and remarked, "Wasn't that great? What dedicated talent. I'm sure there are more who can do things for the Lord that as now we don't know about. Thank you Callie, Joe, and Mrs. Sims."

"My sermon for tonight is titled, "Your Life Makes a Difference When Serving Jesus." The Scripture is found in Mark 5:1-20. Will you pray with me?"

Dick Reveere selected "Have Thine Own Way, Lord," for the invitation.

The first stanza touched the soul of Andy Cline when the words were sung, "Thou art the potter, I am the clay." He turned to his wife, Patricia, and said:

"Honey, I'm giving my heart in rededication to Jesus tonight. It's too obvious to me that He wants me here. I must do it tonight. Would you care to go with me for the same reason? I've already asked Jesus to help me. We can support each other, dear."

"Yes, this burden has been on my heart for several days. I was hoping that we could agree to make our church commitment together. Lets go now."

Andy and Patricia Cline walked down the isle and declared their faith in Christ Jesus as Lord and Savior. They were members of a sister church in another community. They wished to transfer their membership. This young couple would later be influential through Spring Hollow Baptist Church. God always knows what He is doing in the lives of people. What we need to learn is that he wants us to know His work also. When His child commits his all to Jesus, wonders of God's love will overflow.

God blessed His church again on this Sunday night. The Cline's were the only public decisions made. Brother Timothy welcomed them and announced to the congregation their decision for church membership. The church rejoiced again. Many in the church did not know Andy and Patricia. However, before the fellowship service was over, everyone knew each other.

Before the benediction was called, Brother Timothy stated that a baptism service had to be planned within the next two weeks. Since there were no baptistry in the church, he needed to know where, or how, all the candidates for baptism would be baptized.

"Down at the swim hole in Spring Hollow Creek, Brother Timothy" spoke up Mike Owens.

"What we are experiencing here is not our usual time for baptism, Brother Timothy. In years past, baptisms were held in the summer, after the revival. The water was warm then. We will have to work this out this week." said Larry Willoby.

"I'll take Brother Jake down there this week and test the water, him being the candidate." said Wiley Steale. His comments were funny.

"If it pleases the church, I would like to ask the deacon's wives to work with and prepare the women candidates and the deacons can help the men. Will you have some plans in place next Sunday? If so, the ordinance of baptism will be held the following Sunday afternoon." requested Brother Timothy.

"That sounds good. We will do it," aid John Canton.

"Is there anything else that we should know about?" Timothy asked.

"Yes, Brother Timothy I have a solution to our keeping you in a home environment here amongst us for a long time. Frank and I have made provisions for Brother Timothy to home port at our house in our extra bedroom. It is his as long as he needs it, or wants it. You folk know that Frank and I have no children, but it will be strange, but good, to have a son for awhile. And, him being a preacher, he ought to know how to act." The congregation laughed heartily at Mrs. Millie's remarks. They were happy to see her so jolly.

"Well, praise the Lord. This has been an unusual day for me. I've come into the ownership of an automobile and a new home and pastor of my first church all in one day. Thank the Lord. Will you stand and let's be dismissed. Brother Henry Nobles, will you lead us in prayer?"

Mark and Jeremy White, the two small boys of Josh and Sarah White, ran up to Timothy and asked if they could ride to their home with him tonight. The two boys wanted to ride in their pastor's new car.

"Brother Timothy" said Mark. "It won't be too far out of your way to drive Jeremy and me home. We want to see how your new car rides. Will you, Brother Timothy?"

Just then Sarah White came for her boys and heard them request this of Timothy.

"Boys, shame on you for bothering Brother Timothy He would have to go out of his way to our house. No, I'll not allow this. Let's go now, boys."

"Please, Mrs. White, please. I don't know a better thing to do, but to let these boys ride with me. It's not but about two miles difference. That's not far. I think I owe it to their Dad to drive them home, after all you have done for me."

"Brother Josh has loaned me his truck for two weeks. Let me pay him back through your boys; a deal?" said Timothy

"Well, to put it that way, I suppose it is O.K. But, you boys behave, you hear?" warned their mom.

"We'll be good, Mama. We won't cause Brother Timothy any fuss." said Jeremy.

"By the way, Mrs. White. Do you make fresh coffee at your home on Sunday nights after church?"

"Why, yes I do. Josh always drinks a cup and either eats a piece of cake or sandwich before he turns in. You want a cup of my coffee, Brother Timothy?"

"Sure do, if It's not too late and too much trouble."

"We are ready to leave now. You follow us." Sarah said.

On the way home, Mark and Jeremy were all questions about everything in the Timothy's new car. Timothy was in double time trying to answer them all. Finally, he gave up and said;

"Boys, I don't know much about this car. All these gadgets I'll have to learn about. Maybe next month I'll be able to tell you all about them. OK?"

A good fresh cup of coffee and big slice of pound cake was enjoyed by Timothy and the White's. Josh remarked the first thought about letting Timothy use his pickup truck. It made him feel good again and again to have contributed to his pastor's need.

"Brother Timothy, we won't have any need to come by the Seminary to provide your transportation to Spring Hollow anymore. But, while you are on the church field, and if you need my truck, just ask. You are welcome to it." said Josh.

"You are a dear friend, Brother Josh. And, Mrs. Sarah, you are a very good cook. That's the best pound cake I've ever eaten. You know, a few more pieces the size I've eaten tonight might put some fat on these old bones."

Mark and Jeremy laughed a very hearty funny sound.

"We'll get you fatter, Brother Timothy, if you eat with us a lot." roared Jeremy.

"Well, we will talk about that some other time, boys. Right now, I better be on my way to the Steale's home. They'll be out looking for me if I'm too late. And too, your Dad has work to do tomorrow and needs to go to sleep. Remember boys, school is also tomorrow. Before I go, lets have prayer. Mark, do you pray with your family?"

"Yes, Sir. Do you want me to lead in prayer?"

"Please do, Mark." said Timothy.

Mark prayed a very intelligent prayer. It was evident that family worship was part of their family. Timothy hoped it was so for all the church families.

Chapter 9

My Very Own Car

Monday morning found Timothy up early and preparing to leave for the Seminary. Today his trip would be by way of the county seat courthouse. He was looking forward to the act of signing for his first automobile. Actually, all that had happened within the past two weeks seems like a dream. There was nothing in his life to warrant such kindness from the people of Spring Hollow Baptist Church. Only God could receive praise and thanks for so much grace.

Timothy walked to the kitchen and stood in the door enjoying the wonderful smell of fresh cooking pancakes and bacon. Pat and Wiley were sitting at the small breakfast nook.

"Good morning to all." said Timothy.

"Morning, Brother Timothy Did you sleep well?" said Wiley.

"Just great, Brother."

"Hi, pastor." said Pat.

"Well now, that did sound good, Pat. It's the very first time I've ever been called pastor. Congratulations."

"I thought it would sound good too." responded Pat.

"Brother Timothy, be seated and I will fill your plate with hot buttery flapjacks, the best tasting you have ever eaten. A cup of coffee is just about ready. Wiley drank too much this morning." said Katie.

"Pat, will you thank the Lord for our rest and food?" asked her Dad.

"Lord Jesus, thank You for the best rest last night. You have given us a good day. Bless us in school. Bless Daddy and Brother Timothy as they travel. Thank you for this good food Mama has cooked. Bless it to our bodies. All this prayer I ask in Jesus' Name. amen."

After breakfast, Timothy said goodbye and left for the county courthouse. Pat was off to school and Katie stayed home with a thousand chores to do for her family.

The county seat was thirty miles from Spring Hollow. Timothy reasoned it to be very important to observe all the surroundings as he drove along. He knew that this trip would be the beginning of a long pastorate. He wanted to know this community and intended on accepting it as part of his very being. Why? Because the people he had come to love dearly were scattered for miles around him as he drove along. He prayed that Jesus would be first in every home and individual life. His work would be never ending; every moment would be filled with joy. He asked Jesus to endow him with wisdom and love to guide the children of God in Spring Hollow. Timothy prayed that every pastor would have a beginning like his experience here in Spring Hollow. What a day, he thought, to rejoice in the Lord! Timothy parked his car and walked into the courthouse. He asked a young deputy sheriff where the tag registration office was located.

"Down the hall, turn left, and it is on the left." said the young officer.

"Thank you kindly officer. Let me introduce myself. I am Timothy Karr from Willow Bend. I am also the new pastor of Spring Hollow Baptist Church. Come visit us sometimes. You will like us." smiled Timothy.

"Might just take you up on that, preacher. I've heard about a revival going on up there." the officer said.

Timothy walked into the registration office and asked about the information Pete Carter had left.

"Yes, we have it. We've been expecting you. We know Mr. Carter well. He is a good man. You can trust him. You are the preacher out at Spring Hollow Baptist Church? That's what Mr. Carter says."

"Yes, I'm officially their new pastor as of yesterday. I'm looking forward to getting better acquainted with the folk here in the future." said Timothy.

Timothy signed whatever papers were required, received his title and tags and was on his way to the Seminary. What a story of love he would tell to his friends at school! Timothy thanked

God for his friends. They had prayed for him and the church at Spring Hollow.

It was near 11:00 a.m. when Timothy casually drove his new car onto the school campus. He parked at the administration office to register the car and get a campus decal. This task done, he drove on to the dorm and parked in an unmarked space. As he got out of his car and only taken five or six steps toward the walkway, his two friends, Junior and Ralph came out the dorm door.

"There's Timothy, Ralph." yelled Junior.

"Hey, friend. Welcome home. What do you have here?" declared Ralph.

"Timothy, you are not going to tell a big story about earning enough money in two weeks to buy yourself a car, are you?" asked Junior.

"Wow, man! Where did you get this beauty?" chided Ralph.

"It came from Spring Hollow, my friends. No, I've not collected that much money to be able to buy this car. However, I am on salary as of yesterday. Yes, it is a pretty good salary. No, I don't deserve all this. All I can say is that I've come by this pastorate, this car, and a home by the grace of God." said Timothy.

"You mean this car is yours?" stammered Ralph.

"Yes, it was given to me at the morning worship service yesterday by a young couple who inherited it, but didn't need it. I signed the papers this morning for the title and tag. Here they are, friends." said Timothy.

"What a friend we have in Jesus." said Junior.

Timothy moved his car a short distance down the street where there was a water faucet and hose. This was an area where students could wash their cars, and it was provided by the Seminary. It was Tuesday, about 2:30 p.m. Timothy's car had not been washed for a long time, and it was a bit dusty. Timothy also wanted his friends at work to see his shiny car. His work place was about three miles. So to fight traffic, etc., he would leave the campus at 3:30 p.m. to begin work at 4:00 p.m. He only worked five hours each evening. However, tonight He would inform his boss that the Spring Hollow Baptist Church had called him to be their pastor. Therefore, he would terminate his employment on Friday. He began to spray his car when he observed a young woman about 22 or 23 years of age walking toward him on the sidewalk.

"Good afternoon, mam." said Timothy.

"Hello. So you plan to make your car look better, eh?" she said.

"Well, yes, I hope. It's my first time to wash it. It's been sitting in a garage for over a year. I will probably need to wax it, but not today." responded Timothy.

"I'm Timothy Karr. I live in that dorm." Timothy pointed to the dorm of his campus residence.

"I'm Betty Archer, and I live in that dorm." Betty pointed down the street about two blocks.

"What area of study are you pursuing here at the Seminary?" asked Timothy.

"I'm a foreign mission candidate and am attempting all requirements to that end. This is my first year." said Betty.

"What about you.... Timothy, did you say?" asked Betty.

"I'm a preacher. Well, not yet, but I'm preparing to be and to pastor a church. The last part, pastor of a church, has already happened as of last Sunday. You, Miss Archer, are talking with the pastor of Spring Hollow Baptist Church. The church field is about 60 miles from here. Are you a Miss or Mrs. Archer?" asked Timothy.

"Miss." responded Betty.

"This car, Miss Archer..."

"Call me Betty."

"O.K. This car, Betty, was given to me Sunday morning, and ..."

"Really? How wonderful! And you were called as their pastor Sunday morning also? That must be some church." exclaimed Betty.

"You can say that again." beamed Timothy.

"Where are you headed, Betty?" asked Timothy.

"I was on my way to the Library until I was sidetracked by you and hear all these great things about Timothy Karr." responded Betty.

"I'll buy us a coke if you care to ride over to the coffee shop."

"Sounds great. But what about your car wash?" said Betty.

"It'll have to wait until tomorrow." said Timothy.

Timothy bought two cokes and sat down opposite Betty. They began talking about themselves and many things of their homes, school, and plans for the future. Timothy and Betty enjoyed each other's company for about 45 minutes. Betty went on to the Library, and Timothy drove off campus toward his work place. For some strange reason, neither could let go their thoughts of casually meeting as they did, and that meeting turning into a wonderful friendship. Timothy wondered why he had not seen this beautiful young woman before today. She had not been in any of his classes, as far as he knew. Neither had they told where they were from. Perhaps, he hoped, they would meet again.

Betty sought the information for which she came to the Library. As she sat down to review the information, she nodded to two friends who were already seated. Then she broke her silence and whispered. "I met a wonderful fellow this afternoon. I'm telling you, He's tall, skinny, and handsome. I don't know too much about him. He is a preacher and pastor, his first, at the Spring Hollow Baptist Church. I have no earthly idea where that place is. He is also the owner of his new, or used, first car. A young couple in the church gave it to him. Isn't that great!" said Betty.

"Sounds too much to be true. We've never given our pastor a car. Maybe no one has ever thought about such a thing." said her friend.

"Do you plan on seeing him again."

"Don't know. He might not decide his car needs washing while I'm out walking. That's how we met. We started talking, and his car didn't get washed. Do you suppose the Lord has something to do with this? Oh, I'm being silly! It was only a casual meeting and nothing else." said Betty.

"Yeah, I suppose so." agreed the other friend.

"I've got to get this off my mind and get down to business with this report. It's due Friday. If there is further development, I'll let you girls know, OK?" Betty said.

Thursday morning was sunny and warm. "This is a good time to wash my car for the weekend." thought Timothy "I've got all my work completed, even my sermon, so I'll do the job I started Tuesday."

He walked from the dorm whistling an old hymn and feeling up to some good work. He had purchased a can of car wax, but didn't know if he would get that far along.

"Where are you off to, Timothy, my friend?" The voice was that of Junior.

"To wash my car, Junior, care to help?" responded Timothy.

"I might if you will tell me more about what's happening in Spring Hollow. And, I would like to know who that pretty lady is that I saw you with earlier in the week. Man, the news about you is all over the campus." said Junior.

"Well, about all that is left to tell is the plan for baptizing Sunday week. It's going to be in Spring Hollow Creek, that is, if the weather cooperates." said Timothy.

"I'll come along, anyway, and watch you admire your car. Can't say that I blame you at all. If it was mine, I'd polish it every day." said Junior.

Timothy had sudded down his Chrysler New Yorker well. In fact, it was all white and putty against the dark blue paint background. He was rubbing furiously, and Junior was helping, when Betty spoke:

"You fellows seem to be determined to wash the car to last awhile. May I help you?" asked Betty.

"Good morning, Miss Archer...Betty. This is Junior Clark, one of my dorm friends. Junior, this is Miss Betty Archer, a mission volunteer student." introduced Timothy.

"Hello, Miss Archer. I'm glad to meet you, stammered Junior.

"Hi, Mr. Clark. Can I call you Junior?"

"Sure can, I'd be flattered." said Junior.

"Now, Junior, don't go overboard." Timothy chided.

"About you helping us wash, Betty, no need for all of us getting wet. After all, Junior is expecting me to buy him a hamburger or something else for his part." said Timothy.

"I couldn't help anyway. I'm on my way to the Library before class to finish a report. Perhaps you will give me another lift to the coffee shop some other time." said Betty.

"You can count on it, Betty. In fact, Arby's is not too far. How about lunch today? I'm out of class at 11:30 a.m. I'll pick you up whenever you say." said Timothy.

"The time is right, and the place is too. How about picking me up at the front of the Administration Office?" beamed Betty.

"Good." said Timothy.

Betty walked on toward the Library. Timothy and Junior completed the car wash.

"My friend, Timothy, what in this world is going on? I can't believe all this is happening to you. Do you suppose she has a friend anything like her?" Junior asked.

"It's only a casual acquaintance, Junior. I'll ask her if she has a friend. OK?" said Timothy.

Timothy and Betty seemed to enjoy each other's company. They talked about many things while eating their lunch at Arby's. Timothy was convinced that Betty was committed to her decision for a foreign mission appointment. He praised her for her conviction to missions. He assured her that as long as Jesus allowed him, he would support her interest and that of other missionaries. He, too, was a strong mission supporter. However, he knew that Jesus had called him to pastor. Through this great ministry, he would pray for God to call out from his congregation mission volunteers. He also knew that his responsibility would be to develop these toward their future.

Timothy and Betty agreed that this interest in the Lord's Kingdom work was mutual, and that their personal responsibility was very important to God's glory.

Timothy concluded his secular job on Friday night. His boss and his friends congratulated him on his decision to accept the pastorate of the church at Spring Hollow. He felt a burden lifted as he arrived back on the campus.

Chapter 10

At Home With The Stewarts

Saturday morning found Timothy up early, about 5:30 a.m. He went about getting ready to drive out to Spring Hollow. During the week he had prayed for several people. He wanted to visit them, if possible, Saturday afternoon. The excitement of another great worship service was paramount in his plans. The people of Spring Hollow Baptist had been so responsive to the Lord's leadership. He was pleased and rejoiced as he drove his clean, shiny New Yorker toward his earthly heaven.

Millie Stewart had made special preparations for her new Son to take up residence in her home. She knew that his stay would be a joy for her and Frank. Her thoughts in playing the part of mother excited her. Her memory from the experience in her own parent's home helped relieve anxious moments in welcoming Timothy to her house and home. She and Frank would love Timothy as if he were their own son. In fact, they had discussed the possibility that Timothy might be with them for several years. He could live with them permanently, after graduating from Seminary.

Timothy arrived at Mike Brannon's Country Store about 9:00 a.m. Saturday. He needed directions to the Cherry Hill Road. As he entered the store, Mike gave him a hearty welcome.

"Howdy, Preacher. What brings you to Spring Hollow so early? Did you drive in from the city?"

"I left early. How's things with you, Mr. Brannon?"

"Call me Mike, preacher. Everyone else does. I don't hardly know how to answer to Mr."

"I need direction to Cherry Hill Road. Is it North, East, South, or West?"

"Neither, Brother Timothy. It is Northeast, kinda, but you go other directions before you get to Cherry Hill Road. However, it is not too difficult to find. I'll draw you a map."

As Mike was drawing Timothy's map, his daughter Susie came skipping into the store, as happy as a songbird.

"Well now, who is this happy young lady with a cheerful smile?" beamed Timothy.

"I'm Susie. You remember me, Brother Timothy. Remember I accepted Jesus as my Savior last Sunday, and I'm going to be baptized next Sunday. That's why I'm happy. I told a lot of kids at school this week about me being a Christian. Some laughed at me. But there were a lot who asked me what I did and how they could believe on Jesus. I just told them what I did and what Jesus did. I didn't know anything else to say. Did I do the right thing, Brother Timothy?"

"You surely did, Susie. Gee! I'm proud of you. Just think, many of your friends will become believers and trust Jesus as Savior. And, many churches will be very happy when they publicly declare Jesus Christ." said Timothy.

"Well, that might be so, but I told them to come to our church. A lot said they were coming to see me and the others baptized next Sunday. All this is why I'm happy." beamed Susie.

Susie's Daddy, Mike Brannon, was listening to his daughter's happy conversation with her pastor. He realized that he had to change his lifestyle. He did not know if he could match that of Susie's.

"Here's your map, preacher. It won't be hard to follow. It's a few miles up that way. Would you like to telephone that you are coming? I'd hate for you to drive up and not find anyone home."

"That's a good idea. Is it long distance, Mike?"

"Yes, but It's only about fifty cents. I think perhaps I can bear that amount. Here, take the phone and call. Who is it you are calling? I'll look them up." said Mike.

"The Cline's" said Timothy.

"Yeah, I know them. They are good people. I've known them ever since they came into this part of the woods." said Mike.

Timothy dialed the Cline's number and Andy answered. He assured Timothy they would be home and were anxious for his visit. They would be looking for him in about 20 - 25 minutes.

In the meantime, a pot of hot coffee and fresh pound cake would be waiting.

Timothy thanked Mike for the use of the telephone. Susie assured him that she would be in Sunday School tomorrow. He was off to find the Cline's and hoped he would not make the wrong turn. The map Mike drew seemed simple enough to follow. As he drove along, he could not forget the jubilant little Susie and her straightforward witness of her experience with Jesus. It would be wonderful, he mused, if every Christian would be like her. He would pray that she would never lose her zeal for Christ.

Two left turns and one right, and then one mile on, Cherry Hill Road brought Timothy to a light tan house, on the right, which he hoped was the Cline home. He drove into the driveway, and Andy came out to meet him.

"Good morning, Brother Timothy. Welcome to our home. Apparently, you had no problem locating us."

"Hello, Andy. Good to see you. Mike Brannon is a good map maker. It's a beautiful day, Isn't it?"

"Beautiful day." responded Andy. "Come into our home. We are glad you chose to visit us today."

"Hey, Brother Timothy" beamed Patricia. "You've just made our day better. Now, promise Andy and me there will be many more visits, OK?" said Patricia.

"I'll promise. How are you, Patricia? You and Andy look well. The Lord has blessed you two dear people I've prayed for you this week." said Timothy.

"Thank you pastor. My, It's good to call you pastor, Brother Timothy" responded Andy.

"I'm sure your day is going to be a busy one, Brother Timothy. We've seen several people from Spring Hollow this week. They are all anxious and happy about our church's future." said Pat.

"I'm happy about what is happening too, my friends. But, what if this great spiritual revival would last five or more years? How could we handle it? Yes, I know the answer to my own question. The Holy Spirit would work His will and use us as His instruments. Really, there would be no problem, just blessings. I'm dreaming, but they are Godly dreams." said Timothy.

"There is nothing too difficult for God, Brother Timothy. This is His work. We are obligated to let Him use us. Patricia and I have already committed our lives to that end." responded Andy.

"Now, this is the second great statement I've been told this morning. You may be surprised who was the first? It was little Susie Brannon. That child has been a dynamic witness to her school classmates this week. Don't be surprised who you will see at church tomorrow." said Timothy.

"Brother Timothy, we are glad you came to our house this morning. Patricia and I have prayed about starting a new Sunday School class of young married couples. I planned to talk to Brother Jim Tilley and you tomorrow. We can discuss it with you now, over a cup of coffee. If you concur, we can talk with Brother Jim. The way things are going, I hope he will agree."

"Sounds like growth to me." responded Timothy. "We don't have a class of this type and age. I'll agree that we start one. If we wait too long, the church might be hindered." said Timothy.

"Andy and I have had strong Bible teaching in our home church. Our teacher taught God's Word fervently. After we married and moved here, we got away from church activities. We paid a dear price for our sins. Jesus is providing a way for our return and to the work He planned for us to do. We don't want to miss the opportunity again. Young married couples are at a critical age and condition for a strong Christian life, or a destroyed life. We want to give these of our church an opportunity to grow in Christ's grace and honor God with their lives. Do you agree, Brother Timothy?" pleaded Patricia.

"Yes, by all means, Patricia. If this group of people will be provided for to the glory of Jesus, can we imagine what will be the results of such a ministry ten years from now? Oh, God, help us to accomplish this task! Oh, Jesus, use Andy and Patricia that their dream will come to pass! Set all our souls afire with your

Holy Spirit! Give us oil in our lamps, keep them burning! Praise God!" exclaimed Timothy.

"Andy and Patricia, I came to see you this morning to encourage you in your Christian experience. I sensed a burdened spirit when you came forward last Sunday to declare your decision. But, now, everything is O.K. You seem totally different people. Instead of me encouraging you, you have given me the best spiritual lift I've had in a while. Thank you." said Timothy.

"We were in a sad mood for sometime, Brother Timothy But, Jesus has healed all that and we are committed to Him for whatever He wants us to do." said Patricia.

"Have some more coffee and another piece of cake." encouraged Andy.

"No thanks. I've had enough for now. I need to be getting along to my other visit. Let's thank God for this visit. Without Him we can do nothing." said Timothy.

Timothy prayed for Andy and Patricia, his other visits, and for the worship service tomorrow.

"See you good folk tomorrow."

"That you will, pastor."

"By the way, Andy, how far is it to the Carlyle home?" asked Timothy as he opened the door of his car.

"About two miles, Brother Timothy Let Patricia call ahead. They could be out of town or gone for the morning." said Andy.

"Just a moment, Brother Timothy, I'll call." said Patricia.

Patricia's call was answered by Fred Carlyle.

"Hey, Fred. This is Patricia. Are you and Carla planning on being home for a while? Brother Timothy Karr is on his way there and wants a visit with you."

"We are here for the day, Patricia. Tell him to be on his way. We'll expect him soon." said Fred.

"The Carlyle's are home, Brother Timothy. They are expecting you." called Patricia.

"Thanks a million." answered Timothy.

Timothy pulled into the driveway and Fred stepped out on the porch to greet him.

"Hey preacher, what a surprise. You are out and about early in your pastorate. I like that." said Fred.

"Good morning, Mr. Carlyle. It's my pleasure to visit in your home." said Timothy.

"Welcome, my friend." responded Fred.

"Good morning, Brother Timothy. My, it's good to see you way out here, and so early on Saturday." said Carla.

"Howdy, mam. I've been blessed today for being out early." said Timothy.

"Let's sit here on the porch, Brother Timothy This spring weather is just right. How about a cup of coffee? A fresh pot is just now finishing the perk." said Carla.

"I'll be delighted to accept a cup of your coffee. You folk in Spring Hollow Community know how to make coffee. I can't decide whose is the best. Guess I better not say, that is, if I want to continue drinking coffee." laughed Timothy.

"You can come to our home anytime and drink all the coffee you please, assured Fred.

"May I sit here in the swing? I like swings. They keep me moving." laughed Timothy.

"I guess you folk have heard by now that I'm the new pastor of Spring Hollow Baptist Church." said Timothy.

"Yes, the word spread fast. Even though we are not members, yet, we are glad." responded Carla.

"And, you have heard that I have a new car. Well, It's not new as a car goes, but it is new to me."

"That is a great gift, Brother Timothy. You're a blessing to this community. And, the Carters are a blessing to you. All this happened within two weeks." said Fred.

"That's not all. Mr. Frank Stewart and wife Millie have asked me to live with them. They are an elderly couple without children. I believe my decision to stay with them has made Mrs. Millie very happy. They'll have a son for a while." said Timothy.

"We've been doing a lot of talking about getting involved in the Spring Hollow Baptist Church. In fact, we should have before now. Our children need the church activities as well as us. I accepted Christ as my Savior the other week when some folk from there visited us. This week, we decided to join. I for baptism and Carla will move her church membership. I gave up attending church regularly, but never accepted Jesus. That emphasis was not very strong. A person cannot be much of a Christian without Jesus and the church, can they?" said Fred.

"That's right, responded Timothy Jesus first and His church next, and forever. I'm glad to hear of these decisions. You both are doing the right thing. The church plans a baptism service next Sunday afternoon. It will be down at the Spring Hollow Creek. You will be one of several to be baptized. What an experience, three weeks as the church's new pastor and a great baptizing service! If that won't make a preacher happy, nothing will." beamed Timothy.

"We are looking forward to tomorrow, Brother Timothy, and next Sunday as well." said Carla.

"Well, I do hate to leave such good company and conversation, but I better be going on to my new home. Mrs. Millie will be wondering what has happened to her son. They laughed. I don't want to be the cause of her dinner getting cold. She told me dinner would be ready when I arrived. She is a good cook." said Timothy.

"And so is Carla. We will have you dine with us sometime. We'll try to put some fat on those skinny bones." laughed Fred.

"I'll be looking forward to that event. But, for now, let me pray with you before I go," said Timothy.

"Please do." responded Fred.

Timothy prayed with his new found friends. Then he was on his way to the Stewart home. He arrived at his new home at 11:30 a.m. Mrs. Millie was anxiously waiting before she put her fresh homemade biscuits in the oven. Mr. Frank was reading the paper and dozing most of the time.

"Good morning, Brother Timothy, welcome to your new home. I hope you have had a good week at school." said Millie.

"Howdy, Mam. I've had a good week at school. I'm looking forward to final exams next week and whole summer here in Spring Hollow." responded Timothy.

"We will be praying for you to do well on all your subjects." said Frank.

"Get all your stuff in your room, Brother Timothy, and freshen up a bit. By that time the bread will be done and dinner will be served." ordered Millie.

Timothy went about doing the chores necessary in establishing his new home. He was proud of his home away from home. He could not wish for kinder people to live with than the Stewarts. One thing for sure, he did not want to become a burden to these two dear friends.

Timothy had not asked their age. However, somehow he must find out. Nor had he asked about their health. He would find a way about these things. There would be times during the summer that would require him to help Frank with his chores, and with as much as he dared, with Millie's. Timothy knew that it would be laziness and improper for him to receive all the time and never, or hardly ever, give. He was raised to carry his part of the load, whatever it was. The application of this principle would work well with the Stewart's.

Frank and Millie owned several acres of land. Most of it was in Timber of many sorts. But, Frank had kept about ten acres for various crops of their liking. One pet project was their chickens. He had developed about an acre to care for his chickens. It was well fenced as well as crossed fenced for various ages of chickens. It was not a big business, but enough to keep him and Millie busy. He raised and sold fryers, broilers, and baking age chickens. His laying hens were kept in special confinement, with all the necessary nests for laying. People of the community depended upon the Stewart's for poultry products. The community was obliged to call upon them at any daylight hour for their needs. Frank or Millie would make available whatever was asked for. Frank always delivered fresh eggs to Mr. Brannon's Country Store. Town folk would drive many miles for fresh eggs.

Frank and Millie loved their country living. They loved to hear people say good things about their farm produce.

Gardening, but a small one, was a joy also. The garden was for their own use and for two or three other families nearby, whom otherwise did not have time to manage a garden. Five acres were specially fenced for planting green grasses for the older chickens. It was a pretty sight to see various colored chickens against the background of green.

Frank's barn was old, but well kept in good repair. His farm tractor and small repair shop occupied one half. The other half, across the drive through, was for various feeds and whatever. This was his work place, and no one enjoyed it more than Frank.

Timothy moved into this environment of his new country home. He would immediately begin enjoying his surroundings. No one predicted how long Timothy Karr would live in the Spring Hollow community. Only the Lord Jesus Christ knew his future and the Christ-like impact he would have upon future generations of Spring Hollow Baptist Church. Timothy determined to live one day at a time serving Jesus and giving Him all the glory and honor. Timothy proved to be a good son to the Stewart's.

"Dinner is ready." yelled Millie, in a somewhat subdued voice. "Biscuits are never good after they get cold."

Frank and Timothy showed up at the same time and looked over what Millie had prepared. The dinner was far more than they could consume at one sitting. Timothy was assigned a place at the table, across from Millie. Frank's place was at the head of the table. For the rest of his stay with the Stewart's Timothy never changed position.

"Pastor, please asked God's blessings and thanks for our food." said Frank.

"Our gracious Father in heaven, accept our thanks and bless this food and those responsible for it. We are indebted to You, Lord, for all we have and are in this world. Thank you for Your wonderful salvation through Christ our Lord. I ask these blessings in His name. amen."

During the mealtime, many comments were made about the goodness of each food item. Other chatter about many things were also voiced. It was a time of home comfort to Timothy He was pleased that Millie and Frank had asked him to live in their home. He believed their interest in both his physical and spiritual welfare was paramount. He dared not violate their trust.

After dinner, Timothy announced his intended visit to two families, this afternoon, who were not known to be Christian or church members of any other church. He asked the Stewart's to pray for him, Larry Willoby, and Rufus Dean, while they visited Jesse Bagwell and Leon Parmer.

"Yes, we surely will." said Frank. "We know these two families, not too well, but enough to know they are trustworthy people."

"May I use your telephone. I should call these deacons before I drive up to their homes. They may need a little time to prepare for the visit." requested Timothy.

"Sure, Timothy. May we just call you Timothy?"

"I would love for you to call me Timothy.

"You can use the telephone for anything or anytime you wish. Our church should know also, that you can be contacted here for their needs. Perhaps you need to announce to the church about this." said Millie.

"You don't think that would be too much to ask of you?" asked Timothy.

"Not at all." answered Millie.

Timothy made his calls to Larry and Rufus. Both men assured him they would be ready to go upon his arrival. Rufus gave Timothy directions to the Bagwell residence, and they were off to make two very important visits. They prayed for God's guidance for themselves and the families visited.

The Bagwell residence was off the county road and down a lane, about a quarter of a mile. It was a beautiful setting for family and country living. Timothy was impressed with such natural beauty surrounding the Bagwell home. Timothy stopped his Chrysler about ten yards from the home, and off the driveway. The three walked toward the front porch and were greeted by Mrs. Mollie Bagwell.

116

"Good afternoon, Mrs. Bagwell. I'm Larry Willoby. This is Rufus Dean, and the young man is Timothy Karr, our pastor at Spring Hollow Baptist Church." said Larry.

"Good afternoon to you all. I know you, Mr. Willoby. I remember your family a few years back, when we had some sickness. Ya'll helped out a lot. Mr. Dean, I'm glad to meet you. I've heard of you, Preacher Karr. It's nice to meet you. So you are new to Spring Hollow? Welcome gentlemen. But, Jesse is not here at the house. He and our son, who lives a short distance away, are down at the hog pen. If you care to, just drive on down through the pasture to the pens. You'll know you are on the right road by the smell. They all laughed. You folk will see how we make our living. You can also thank the good Lord that our ham and bacon don't smell like that." They laughed again.

"Mrs. Mollie." said Larry, "We are hoping you good folk will visit our church real soon. We are having a great time as our Lord Jesus is blessing. We want your family to enjoy all these good blessings with us."

"I've been hearing about what's been going on up there. Sounds like what's needed everywhere. Our grandchildren have been after us to go to church. They have heard from other children about Spring Hollow Baptist. We're thinking about coming." said Mollie.

"I'm glad to hear about this report from our church children. They are excited." responded Timothy "Tomorrow would be a good time to visit, Mrs. Bagwell."

"Well, Jesse and me will talk about it some more. Ya'll try and convince him."

The three said goodbye and drove toward the hog pens. It was a fact; the smell reached them before they arrived.

Jesse Bagwell was standing beside his pickup truck talking with his son, Ned. They had completed their chores and involved themselves in conversation about where meat prices were going, compared to the cost of feed and care of their hogs. They agreed that profit was going down while costs were rising.

117

Their concern was how to justify expansion, as well as needed repairs, to their industry.

"Wonder who that can be." Ned said. "It's a good looking Chrysler. Suppose they are some kind of inspectors? Why would they be coming around on Saturday afternoon?"

"Don't know." responded Jesse. We'll see in a minute.

Timothy stopped his car, and they got out.

"Well, howdy, Mr. Willoby. What brings you folk down to this neck of the woods? You must of smelled ham cooking." laughed Jesse. "Haven't seen you in a spell. How are you?"

"Hello, Mr. Bagwell. It's good to see you too, Ned. Well, it wasn't the smell of ham. But, to you, I bet it smells like ham and eggs, eh?" responded Larry.

"Who've you got with you." asked Jesse.

"This is Rufus Dean, and this young man is Timothy Karr, our new pastor of Spring Hollow Baptist Church."

"Welcome, gentlemen. This is my son, Ned. He's in business with me. I couldn't take all this scent by myself, so I share it with him. They all laughed. "But, when these animals are processed for consumption, we all like what we taste, eh?" said Jesse.

They all greeted each other with warm handshakes and smiles. Jesse and Ned led the three inside the hog parlor to show off what their prize stock looked like. Pigs and hogs of all sizes were everywhere. The breeder sows were huge as well as the males.

"These big boars are dangerous. They must be handled with special care. You can imagine if one of those giants took a swat at you. He could hurt you very badly, or even kill." said Ned.

"I'll appreciate them from this distance." said Timothy "But, they are beauties. A family could eat on a ham that size for a week."

"Well, perhaps so. But, it's likely when we are finished with his services, he will wind up in ground meat. His hams would be pretty tough to chew on." said Jesse.

"Let's get out of here and go to some more acceptable environment. Ned and I had finished our chores and were about to

118

go to the house. Ya'll drive back there and we'll talk more. That OK?" said Jesse.

Yep, I believe so." said Rufus.

They all sat on the front porch while visiting and drinking ice tea prepared by Mollie.

"Can't nobody rest well without a good cool glass of ice tea. If you men folk want more, just holler." said Mollie.

"Thanks, honey." responded Jesse.

The visit with the Bagwell's was cordial and fruitful. Ned and Jesse agreed with Mollie that some changes need to be done in their families. The talk of what was happening in the Spring Hollow community and at the public schools was obvious that the Bagwell families should not remain neutral. Positive promises were made that they would come to church and began a change in their lives. Larry thanked the Bagwell's for their hospitality. He led in a short prayer, and the three said goodbye. They then headed for the Parmer's home.

Leon Parmer was resting on a patio chair, underneath an old oak tree. His wife, Jean, had just walked down the porch steps, bringing him a glass of ice tea.

"Now, who can that be, Leon?" she asked as Timothy came to a stop in the driveway.

"Good afternoon, Leon and Jean." said Larry. "You look too comfortable to be a working man."

"Hello Larry. Ya'll get out and come sit a spell." welcomed Leon.

"Leon, Jean, this is Rufus Dean and Timothy Karr. Rufus is a deacon in our church at Spring Hollow Baptist Church. And, Brother Karr is our new pastor. We're helping him get acquainted with our community." said Larry.

"Good to make your acquaintance." Mr. Dean, Preacher. Ya'll have a seat."

"It's good to know ya'll." said Jean. How about a fresh glass of ice tea?"

"Well, if it is not too much trouble, Jean." said Larry.

"Not a bit of trouble." responded Jean. "I'll be right back."

"Where are you from, preacher? Did you say your name was Karr?" asked Leon.

"I'm from Willow Bend, a very small town about a hundred miles from here. Have you ever been there, Mr. Parmer?" asked Timothy.

"Shore have. In fact, I was through there two weeks ago. I delivered a truckload of lumber to a man about five miles beyond Willow Bend. He's building a barn." said Leon. "It's a nice community."

"We've been hearing about some happenings at your church, Brother Karr." said Jean as she handed Timothy his glass of ice tea. "Two women from there visited me earlier in the week. They seemed very happy about it all. Can't blame them for feeling like that. The Lord knows this whole area of the State is in need of a good change for the better. Too much bad stuff has been hurting all of us. I'm glad things are turning around."

"Our grandchildren have been hearing about what's happening at your church. They've been begging their Pa and Ma to visit ya'll. They've asked us too. Our son, Will, is their Pa, and lives a mile on down the road. It's about time in our life that we ought to make a change. In fact, it should have been done a long time ago." said Jean.

Timothy, Rufus, and Larry were very glad to hear Jean pour out her heart. It was evident the Holy Spirit was working in this family. They wanted to be sure that their feeble effort would not hinder His work.

They thanked Jean for the tea and both for their welcome and hospitality. Each man urged their visit to Spring Hollow Baptist. The Parmer's were assured they would be warmly welcomed. They agreed to visit and bring their son's family also.

On their way back to their homes, the three were very pleased that God had led them to these families. Each expressed joy and peace in the Holy Spirit's leadership. As they discussed their hopes for tomorrow, there came to them an assurance that Jesus would bless His Word, and His people. How could anyone doubt His power?

120

When they arrived back at Larry's home, and before he got out of the car, Timothy led in prayer of thanks to God. He also thanked God for Larry and Rufus. He expressed in this prayer that positive visitations would become a strong ministry through Spring Hollow Baptist Church. They prayed for the Bagwell and Parmer families. As Timothy was ending his prayer, Rufus broke in and asked Jesus to anoint Timothy in power for tomorrow. With this, Timothy was on his way to Rufus's home, and then back to his new home.

Supper was ready when he arrived. As they ate, Timothy briefly told of his afternoon activities with two needy families. Mollie and Frank assured him that they had been praying for God to do His work. What they heard was evident that He had. Timothy settled in for the evening and began making final preparations for tomorrow. His day had been well spent. He thanked Jesus for the efforts of the day.

Chapter 11

Marie

Earlier in the week, Tuesday to be exact, two members of the Singles Sunday School Class, Ada Jenkins and Becky Skelton, asked Marie Tidwell to have lunch with them. Marie was not a member of their class, nor was she a Christian. The three had grown up together and were members of the same high school graduating class. Marie had been an object of their prayers for several months. Ada and Becky believed this meeting would prove their prayers were being answered, particularly after all the good things happening at Spring Hollow Baptist Church.

Each of these young ladies had an hour for lunch. They would use this time wisely and enjoy the fellowship. After their general comments to each other, and after their lunch order had been given to the waitress, Ada asked that they pray and thank God for the meal. Becky led the prayer. She thanked God for His blessings and for the fellowship opportunity. Ada then made specific comments about their Sunday School Class and the revival spirit in their church.

"Marie, you are a dear friend of ours. We want you to be a part of our joy. I remember when we were little girls growing up together. You were then, and now, a leader. I wanted you to accept Jesus the same time I did, but there seemed to be a problem at home if I remember correctly. As the years passed, you grew up and away from the church. But, It's not too late, yet. What we are experiencing I want you to be a part of. Will you consider this?" said Ada.

"I have Ada. You two girls do not know just how much you mean to me. I've watched you in your Christian life and wished many times that I had a life like yours. Everybody is aware of what is going on at the Spring Hollow Baptist Church. Now, I hear that you folk have called a very young preacher as pastor. If he is strong, his type is what's needed there. My problem is far deeper than you girls may suspect. I can't tell it all now, because we do not have enough time. However, if you will come to my house Thursday night, I'll tell you something no one knows in our community. Will you come?" asked Marie.

Ada looked at Becky and they both agreed to visit Marie in her home. This subject was dropped, and the three spoke about their work. Lunch was served and consumed. Each girl wished the others a good afternoon. Marie was hugged by Ada and Becky and assured they would see her Thursday night.

Meanwhile Mitchell Adair had no scheduled classes for Wednesday. Friday of the following week would end the school year. Tests would consume the whole last week. He looked forward to a rest during the summer months. Mitch had been praying for a friend who was not involved in church nor was he a Christian. He was a very nice, moral, happy young man. He was his friend. His name was David Brown. David farmed with his Dad. He was a hard worker and everyone who knew David respected him.

Mitch called on Tuesday morning to find out if he could come to his home on Wednesday, about 10:00 a.m. David received the call.

"Hey, Mitch. Whatcha know? How's school? Boy, It's good to hear from you." said David.

"I'm doing fine, David. School will be out in another week. It will feel good to be out of books for a change. Maybe I'll come up and do some farm chores with you, ha, ha, ha. Yeah, that would be a laugh." said Mitch.

"Hey, man, That's not too far fetched. There are a lot of things you might be interested in doing here. The pay is terrible, but I love every day of this life." said David.

"David, do you think I'm asking too much of you if I could visit with you tomorrow about 10:00 a.m.? We are having a great time at Spring Hollow Baptist Church, and our Singles Sunday School Class is having a ball. I want to talk with you about this. Could you give me thirty minutes?" asked Mitch.

"I'll take time, Mitch. You are my friend. Come on over. Mama will have some fresh cookies baked and a pot of coffee.

I've heard about what's going on at your church. Sounds good." said David.

Mitch and David met with a warm friendly handshake. It had been more than three months since the last time they had seen each other.

"Good to see you, Mitch. Looks like school is doing you well. How long before I can call you professor?" teased David.

"Never that, David. I don't have that kind of brain power. I'll do well just to shake a professor's hand at graduation." said Mitch.

"Well, good morning Mitch." said Mrs. Brown. She set a plate of cookies and hot coffee before the two young men. "How are your parents? I've not seen hair or hide of them for months. Guess it is about as much my fault as theirs. Anyhow, we ought to get together more often. Tell them I was asking about them."

"I'll tell them, Mrs. Brown. They are doing well. Mama says the same thing about getting out over the community to visit people. She says that years ago, it used to be plum natural for folk to visit each other. Wonder why we stopped a good thing?" said Mitch.

"It oughtn't have stopped, Mitchell. Seeing your friends and neighbors is a healthy thing. We've just got too involved in our personal lives and forgot others. That's too bad." said Mrs. Brown.

"I'll agree Mama. It makes one feel empty to lose friends. said David.

"These cookies are very good, Mrs. Brown. Mama needs this recipe, for me of course." smiled Mitch.

"I'll leave you boys to talk about what you came for. If you want more coffee, there's the pot." said Mrs. Brown as she pointed toward the stove.

"Thanks, Mrs. Brown." responded Mitch.

Mitch was aware David took from his busy time to visit with him a few minutes. He would be prompt to talk about their good Sunday School Class; the happenings at the church, and his desire to see David get involved with him. Mitch and David had

124

known each other all their lifetime. Both had played baseball together, David the catcher and Mitch on second base.

While growing up, they were active in the church. However, David began showing signs of disinterest and, finally, dropped out of attendance. His excuse was that he had too much farm work that took up his time.

David promised Mitch he would come visit their class. But, there would be times of absence he could not help due to chores about the farm. Mitch understood and promised to keep a close relationship.

"David, I must be going so that you can get back to your work. You've been kind to let me visit with you. Thanks for your friendship. Hope to see you Sunday." said Mitch.

"I'll try to work things out so that I can, Mitch. Come out anytime. You are welcome." said David.

With a warm strong handshake, their eyes met with an expression that two friends had exchanged their interests mutually.

Meanwhile Becky and Ada kept their promise to visit in the home of their friend Marie. Neither had questioned the other about what Marie might reveal. Both had prayed for Marie and her family. Marie's Dad was getting along in years, and his health was failing fast. Her youngest brother, Walter, was about sixteen. Marie was twenty-one. Their mother had died five years ago. This left the responsibility of keeping house and home to Marie. Four other children, two girls and two boys, were married and were living out of the community. One boy and girl had a family of their own. It fell to Marie to settle in and keep house and work for her Dad and brother. Ada and Becky knew about Marie's commitment to her family. They did not believe this was Marie's burden.

The girls had been warned to blow the car horn when they arrived, and stay in the car until someone came onto the porch. The reason for this was that their watchdog was very faithful to guard the house. She, Lassie, might attempt to bite. Ada blew the horn, and immediately Lassie appeared from the rear of the house. Marie came out and assured the girls, and Lassie, that everything was O.K. Lassie lay down on the porch, contented.

"Hi, girls. Welcome. Come in and we'll go into the living room where we will be by ourselves. Daddy is reading the newspaper in the den, and brother is in his room doing his homework." said Marie.

"Good to see you." said Ada.

"You look refreshed, Marie." said Becky.

"I've been home all afternoon." said Marie. You know the courthouse is closed on Thursday afternoon. I've had time to clean house a bit, cook some specials, and freshen up." said Marie.

"You are a great housekeeper. I wish mine looked this good." said Becky.

"Before we get too comfortable, let me get you tea or coffee."

"Tea for me." said Ada.

"Me, too." responded Becky.

When they were served, cookies were already on the coffee table, and the three settled down and began the talk about the purpose of the visit.

"We are anxious to hear what you have to tell us, Marie. Again, we assure you that we are your friends, and nothing will be repeated outside of this room. We've both promised the Lord to be true to your request." said Becky.

"Thanks a million. I trust you two as I used to do with my mother. You remember my mother? She was a strong, saintly soul. She demonstrated her love for people wherever she was needed in the community. It's been difficult these past five years to live in this house without her. But, we've managed. I've never hesitated to confide in Mama about anything. She would listen and give me encouragement."

"Now, what I tell you, I told Mama. This event has kept me from joining Spring Hollow Baptist Church because it involved an individual who was a member of the church. He was just a member of the church, not a Christian. Because a Christian would not do to another person what he did to me. Now, I know that I should never blame the church for the actions of one person, but I'm not a professed Christian, and it has been easy for me to hide behind the fault of a bad example."

"I was sixteen years of age at the time. This boy, who was a year older than me, asked for a date. I agreed and thought he was a decent young man. You girls do not know him. His parents moved away soon after, and both are dead. The young man is somewhere in the Armed Services. I don't care where. None of the family members were active in the church. They were just members."

"Well, on the date and after the movie, we were on our way home, when he stopped on a little used road before I could object. He then proceeded to tear at my clothes, drag me out of the car, attempting to rape me. I fought back with all my power, scratching, kicking, and pulling his hair. Finally, he stopped and halfway apologized. I didn't listen to his remarks. I got back into the car and ordered him to bring me home. I suppose my voice sounded so strong that he did what I asked. There was not one word said all the way home. I did not say goodnight, nor did he say anything."

"When I got inside the house, I began sobbing out of control. I was so hurt and felt so ashamed of what I had allowed myself to get into. Mama heard me crying and came to me asking why. Right then and there I poured my heart out to her what I've told you. She was so comforting and understanding. I said, "Mama, he was supposed to be a Christian. I never expected such conduct to come from a Christian." She assured me that it was very improper for that young man to act as he did. Even as a non-Christian, no one should treat another as you have been treated."

"But, that episode, girls, has kept me out of the church. I am a good moral, decent woman. I know that I am. I promised Mama that night I would never allow a man to violate me. It's not right. It's ugly. It's terrible. Someday, I hope to meet a good, caring, decent man whom I can trust. I would very much like to be a good, caring, trusting wife someday, as well, as a good, caring mother of children."

"You girls have heard my life story. I have wished it different. But, I know now, that I've not been fair or honest to myself allowing a mean, immoral person to affect my life. As I trusted Mama with my problem, I should have talked to God about it and trusted Him. However, I didn't, and that is my sin. Even though Mama loved me, she never talked with me about being saved and living a Christian life. No one from your church has ever talked to me about becoming a Christian either, except you girls this week. I thank you for it, and I love you for your interest in me. For the past several months, I've been thinking a lot about my life and the future."

"Let me tell you one more episode; a dream I had about three weeks ago. I told Daddy about it, and he was deeply moved. He told me that he had a similar dream about two months ago. He had not mentioned it to me since he thought it might sound silly. But, now it makes sense that God is saying something to us."

"Well, I dreamed that I was trying to get somewhere that I had never been before. On the way, I came to a deep dark ravine. The road seemed to just stop there. But, on the other side was another road that began and continued into a far distance, into a beautiful place of many colors. I found myself walking back and forth trying to find a way across the ravine. I never did find a place to cross. I remember how frightened I became. Then, I heard Mama call me. She said, "Do you want to walk with me down this beautiful road. If you do, you will have to come another way. There is no way across the way you are going." "I woke up, scared to death. I've tried to make sense of the dream, but cannot. I find myself back at the deep, dark ravine every time the dream comes to mind. What do you think? Can you girls help me?"

"I want us to pray right now." said Ada. "The Lord is saying something we need to hear."

"Dear Jesus, Marie needs an answer for her life. Give us your words to this problem. I ask in Jesus' name."

"What other way is there to heaven?" asked Becky. "Didn't Jesus say, "I am the Way, the Truth, and the Life?" "I'm convinced

Jesus is the answer to Marie's getting across the ravine. Her mother in her dream is telling her the same thing. Marie, your mother is saying to you, If you want to be with me, you must come here the same way as I did."

"Marie, Jesus wants to save you from your sins. Why don't you let Him do that right now? It will end your problem. Will you ask Jesus to save you?" said Becky.

"I don't know how to pray. I'm not good enough to ask Jesus for anything." said Marie.

"Ada and I will help you. We'll pray for you and ask Jesus to guide your thoughts, OK?"

"O.K." agreed Marie.

"My Lord Jesus. Please honor your Great Name and accept my prayers for Marie's benefit. You died for her the same as you died for me. Hear her cry, now, and save her. Forgive her sins and give her Your peace. You, Jesus, are that way she must travel to get across the dark, deep ravine. I ask this prayer in Your Wonderful Name. Amen."

"Marie did you ask Jesus to save you, and do you believe He did?" asked Ada.

"Yes, yes. Oh, how wonderful I feel. I know my sin burden is gone. I'm clean. I have a joy I've never experienced before." exclaimed Marie.

She wept for joy as both girls worshipped with her. Ada and Becky encouraged Marie to read God's Word daily and pray for understanding and guidance.

"Before we leave, we must thank Jesus for saving Marie, and Marie, you personally must thank Him. Let's thank Him for His wonderful presence and fellowship with us tonight. Marie, I believe your dream problem is solved. Your dream will not bother you again. Now, Satan might tempt you from time to time about it, but you have the assurance that you have found the way out of your dark, deep ravine of sin. The devil will leave you alone when you remind him of Jesus' saving grace." encouraged Becky.

"Lord Jesus, we are not deserving of this blessing We've received tonight, but because of Who You are, You love us more than we love You. Thank You for saving Marie. Thank You for loving us. Thank You for eternal life. May Your will be done in all our lives for Your Name sake. amen." said Ada.

Ada and Becky went home rejoicing. Marie went into the den where her Daddy was resting and told him what had happened in her heart. She knew now that his problem was like hers. She could now help him across the road. Mr. Tidwell's dream was like that of Marie's. He could not get across the road to the safe, beautiful land on the other side because of all the massive traffic and mean-spirited people. They all appeared to be his friends, but wouldn't listen to his plea. His wife was waiting for him, but he couldn't reach her. She was pointing upward as if trying to tell him something important. To him it was all frustrating. Now, Marie could tell him that Jesus is the way across. Before they retired for the night, Marie led her Daddy to Jesus, and he accepted Him as his Lord and Savior. There would never be a happier time in their lives than this night. As Marie lay on her bed rejoicing, she thanked God again and again for Ada and Becky. She and Daddy were on the other side of this horrible dream, eternally safe.

Chapter 12

Home From College

Meanwhile, Lisa Boyd was home from Junior College for the weekend. She was an only child, tragically orphaned by an auto accident of her parents when she was 13 years of age. Since then, she had lived with her grandparents, Stanley and Ruth Coon. Stanley and Ruth are active members of Spring Hollow Baptist Church. Stanley had retired three years before the accident as a train engineer. Lisa has been a blessing to them. She had always been an obedient and gracious child. She loved everything about Spring Hollow Church and was actively involved in the choir before going off to college.

Lisa had a deep alto voice. During her teen years, she often sang solos at church, accompanied by her Grandma Ruth. Dick Reveere asked her to sing at the morning worship service. This would be her first time to sing since the coming of Timothy as pastor. She chose to sing "O, That Will be Glory." Lisa knew that this choice hymn offered hope to her and to all who would hear. To her, it meant seeing and living forever with her dear parents. Grandma Ruth would again accompany her at the piano. She also knew that fond memories would swell up in the minds of many friends and bring joy and hope. She promised Brother Dick to do her best. Mitchell (Mitch) Adair would hear her sing. He, too, was home from college. Mitch needed to hear the words sung and the voice of his longtime friend, Lisa.

Mike Brannon was home from college for the weekend. He had chosen State College for his interest toward a Business Major. Prior to college, Mike had been slothful in church activities during his high school years. Nothing seemed to move him. Baseball was his extra curricular interest. Mike was all-star second baseman. However, he did not intend a college career in the sport. He was a good student and was expected to excel in the field of Business. During his first year of college, Mike seemed to drift further away from his early Christian lifestyle. Since his little sister, Susie, had accepted Jesus as her Savior, Mike had shown faint signs of interest. This was mainly because Susie had taken on the task of telling her big brother all that was happening to her and what was happening in Spring Hollow. Susie knew Mike was not living for Jesus, and her crusade was to bring him back.

Today in church, Susie was sitting very close to her brother. In fact, his arm was around her, and she was enjoying the wonderful moment in worship. Now and then, she would sneak a peek at Mike's face and saw what she believed was a very concerned expression on his face. She liked what she saw, and thanked Jesus for it. Perhaps today, she thought her brother would return to Jesus.

When Lisa began to sing, Susie noticed a flush in Mike's facial expression. He tightened his arm around Susie as if he approved of Lisa's choice of hymn. Susie also noticed tears in her big brother's eyes as Lisa finished her solo. Susie took Mike's hand and gave it a gentle, firm squeeze and whispered, "I like her singing." Mike responded with a smile of approval.

Mitch beamed as he listened to his longtime friend sing. He knew Lisa was singing to the glory of God. For several years, he had hoped Lisa would accept him as her fiancee. He had always held her high in character. Someday, he dreamed, she would become his bride. But, Lisa was concerned about a career. She wanted to complete her college career, specifically to make her grandparents happy. Grandpa Coon was investing a lot in her life. It was not right to pursue other matters than college. Perhaps, after graduation, there might be a decision to marry and settle down. Deep down in her heart there was a longing to give all her future to God! Whatever that was, she did not know now. Grandma Coon had often talked to her about missions service. Her years in Girls Auxiliary and Acteens had played a role toward this mission burden. She decided to give everything over to Jesus and wait for His decision.

Mitch sensed the feelings Lisa had toward a Christian vocation. He would not attempt to change her, but decided to wait. They were close friends, and that must sufficed until Lisa decided otherwise. For now, Mitch adored Lisa's beauty and strong alto voice. She sang from her heart as the congregation responded with muffled "Amens" and many tears. She brought joy to everyone. Through her, the Lord prepared the folk for His message through Brother Timothy. Dick Reveere made the proper decision to ask Lisa to sing.

Chapter 13

The Church Grows

The deacons met, as scheduled, before Sunday School for prayer. There were several prayer requests made, specifically for serious needs. They prayed for visible results from all the visits made during the week. Timothy prayed about the over crowded problem that had begun two weeks ago. All the deacons concurred by answering "Amen." When their prayer time was over, each man rose slowly from his kneeling position with conviction of answers from the Lord.

One Adult Women's Sunday School Class, ages 34-40, and the Young Married Class, ages 18-28, had to move to the auditorium due to lack of classroom space. This move offered added spaces for the 8-10 year old class to split and become boys and girls separate classes. The other vacated classroom gave an additional class for High School Seniors, consisting of four boys and two girls.

Three families lived within half a mile of the church. They were involved in the crowded situation, and offered to share their homes until such a time that the church could expand its facilities. These living rooms, dens, and dining rooms would be adequate for a large class, or maybe two in each home. This pleased everyone. To be involved in all that was happening in Spring Hollow Baptist Church was a hallelujah time. Nothing about this spiritual revival was man-engineered. It was indeed a visitation of the Holy Spirit.

Several visitors came into the auditorium before the Sunday School hour was over. Several were not known by the church folk. They had heard the good news through friends or school children. All were made to feel welcome. One man stood out, vividly, from the others. He came alone, and the smell of whisky was very strong. However, his conduct was calm, and he showed no signs of misbehavior. He was welcomed to God's house to hear the good news of Jesus. It was obvious he needed help. He was at the right place to receive the help he needed. Later, it was revealed that one of the church members who worked with this man invited him to church. The member had witnessed to him but did not know if he would visit the church. He knew that the man had a serious drinking problem. It was he, who when he saw his work friend, went to him and greeted him in Jesus Name.

"I'm really glad to see you, Johnny."

"Yes, and I'm glad to be here, Ted. I'm O.K. now, but I had too much last night."

"You are welcome. I pray this will be a good day for you." Ted said.

"I do too, Ted."

With that, the church began to sing and rejoice in the Lord. Dick Reveere announced the first hymn.

"Let's all stand and sing our pastor's favorite hymn "What a Friend We Have In Jesus." Let's sing this hymn as if He is our Best and Only Friend."

The Spring Hollow Baptist Church did sing to the glory of Jesus. The windows rattled, the rafters seemed to bulge upward. All voices blended. Men wept as well as women. Visitors were astonished. And, Brother Timothy wept and responded with several hallelujahs.

"Oh, yes, what a friend we have in Jesus."

Brother Timothy welcomed all, and especially the visitors, to worship Christ. Everyone was asked to feel at home and praise the Lord Jesus. He continued with announcements.

"I'm officially living in my new home at the Stewart's. I like it, and they are treating me like their son. In another week or so, I'll be here on the church field for the summer. I'm looking forward to what will be happening."

"Brother Jake Dawson has an announcement about the baptism plans for next Sunday. Following him, Brother Jim Tilley has an announcement about Vacation Bible School plans."

"About a dozen men will be needed Saturday morning down at the creek to set up for the baptizing. In the meantime, I'll clear the lots where the booths will be set up. Now, don't make me have to call you men." said Jake.

"V.B.S. is scheduled for June 13-24, in two weeks. We need more workers. See me anytime within the next month. We are going to have a lot of children and youth this year. Let's give them our best to the glory of Christ. We all rejoice for our Sunday School growth and attendance of late. We can't stop this good work." said Jim.

"Are there other announcements?" asked Timothy.

"Yes, the Woman Missionary Union will meet at the church Tuesday night at 7:00 p.m.." said Ruth Willoby.

"The Singles Sunday School Class will meet at Becky Skelton's Thursday night at 7:00 p.m.." announced Ada Jenkins.

"The choir will now sing, "When They Ring The Golden Bells." said Brother Dick.

"Will you please turn to the hymn "The Lily of the Valley." Let's sing again to the glory of Christ. The ushers will receive the morning offering at the close of the third stanza." directed Dick.

"And now, we have a pleasant surprise. For our special music, before the message by our pastor, Sandy and Pete Carter will bless our hearts." said Dick.

Pete and Sandy came out of the choir to the pulpit. Sandy announced the hymn to be sung, "All on the Altar."

"Please listen to these precious words of dedication. We hope, if it is God's will for you, that you will give your life in surrender to Him. Please pray for Sandy and me as we sing to His glory."

Pete and Sandy did indeed sing humbly and obediently to Jesus. Many people, including the very young, wept for joy. Brother Timothy was visibly moved as he heard these two dear friends blend their voices and bless God's people. As he listened and saw the reactions of the people, he knew that Jesus had directed the right message for today. His prepared message was "The Urgency of Hearing the Gospel." His Scripture text was John 3: 16-18.

Timothy Karr was a young preacher. By no means was he polished on all aspects of sermon delivery. But, he had the most important element of preaching, a burning in his heart of total commitment to Jesus Christ. There was not now, nor will there ever be, a substitute for the Word of God. Timothy would say what he believed God wanted him to say; and leave the work of the message to the Holy Spirit.

During the invitation, "Have Thine Own Way, Lord." sung by the choir; the Lord convicted people of sins and to repentance. Marie Tidwell, with Ada by her side, walked briskly down the isle. Marie made her public decision to Christ as Savior and desire to join the congregation. Bob Matthew's and wife came forward, he trusting Christ as Savior, and she for transfer of church letter from another state. No one else made public decisions, and the invitation was closed. Brother Timothy presented these to the congregation stating their decision. The church rejoiced with them by giving a hearty approval. Brother Timothy stated that next Sunday afternoon would be a great time to baptize all that had accepted Christ as Savior. Several amens were sounded.

The church greeted these dear souls into its fellowship and loving care. The visitors were warmly welcomed by the church, with the hope they would return and worship with Spring Hollow Baptist folk, again.

The week went well with Timothy and his friends at Seminary. Final tests were over on Thursday afternoon. Friday would be spent packing up, cleaning up the dorm room, and moving to Spring Hollow for the summer. Timothy felt a sign of relief at not having to prepare for daily lessons. The joy in his heart over the wonder of being on the church field every day brought peace to his heart. Many plans were daily forming in his mind about the work of the Lord. It was exciting to just think about the future in Spring Hollow.

As he made the last trip from the dorm to his Chrysler New Yorker, Betty appeared on the scene. He was delighted to see her. It had dawned upon his mind if he should go to her dorm and say goodbye. However, this meeting now would take care of that.

"Good morning, Timothy It seems you are off to Spring Hollow, or to Willow Bend?"

137

"Good morning to you, Betty. I'm off to Spring Hollow. It will be my home for the summer. Do you plan to remain on campus for the summer?"

"No, not all of it. I'll be back in a month for a missions conference. Perhaps you can drive down for a day or so. The conference will last for a week. I'm looking forward to it. The date is July 6-11. Anyone can attend who is interested in missions. I know you are."

"That sounds great. I'll work my schedule for the conference. But, I can tell you now that what's happening in Spring Hollow Baptist Church is going to keep me busy, very busy. Perhaps while you are back here for the missions conference, you can visit our church. If you will, I'll arrange for you to give your testimony on that Sunday morning. Sounds, good, eh?"

"Yeah, it does. I need that kind of experience. Let's plan on it, Timothy"

"O.K. I'll make all the arrangements for the Sunday after the conference. I'll even come back to the Seminary and drive you to Spring Hollow in my Chrysler. I'm sure our people will love to have you speak. Boy, oh boy, I'm glad we met today. You just helped make my whole summer complete, Betty."

"And mine too, Timothy. I'm convinced that God has brought about this meeting today. Isn't is wonderful to know that we are in His will?"

"It surely is, my friend. Well, I need to be on my way to work for a long summer with the best folk in the whole world. See you in July, Betty."

"Have a good summer, Timothy"

Timothy and Betty parted their ways for a short season. But, they did not realize that God was working in them, and for Him, a long, long, life of Christian service.

Meanwhile, during the week, two little girls by the names of Susie Brannon and Beth Sims were hard at work for Jesus. Beth and Susie had become very close friends since each had given their lives to Jesus. As a pair, they are making Jesus known in their school. Before her conversion, Beth was shy and sometimes aloof to attach herself as a friend. But, Jesus made the difference, and now she is actively witnessing for her Savior. Her sweet spirit is contagious. And, because of her friendly attitude, many of her classmates are listening to her testimony.

Susie has always been friendly and forward to make herself involved. However, Jesus was not a part of her getting involved. Now, since He is her Savior, she is unashamed with her testimony. When she and Beth tell of their salvation experience, they get a listening audience. These two girls really do want their friends to hear about Jesus. Both girls will be baptized Sunday afternoon, and they want everyone to know about it. Many of their friends, both Christians and non-Christians, have promised to come witness this life-changing event.

Meanwhile Ted had a few minutes at break time to talk with Johnny on Tuesday morning. Johnny was an auto mechanic, and Ted was an auto body repairman. They both worked for the same dealership in the county seat town.

"Hey, Johnny. How's the day going? I've prayed a lot for you since Sunday."

"I'm doing pretty good, Ted. I've been thinking a lot about my life and that of my family since Sunday."

"Did you feel welcome at our church, Johnny?"

"Oh, yeah. A lot of people said hello to me and shook my hand. All of them asked me to come back again. I came home feeling good, much better than I did going to church."

"Well, I'm glad to hear you say these things, Johnny. I hope you will come Sunday and bring your family. Come in time for Sunday School."

"I told my wife where I had been when I got home from church. She just stood there and looked at me as if I had lied to her. I've told her so many lies over the years; she is hesitant to believe me anymore. But, I convinced her I did go to church. Then I got really brave. I asked her to go with me next Sunday.

She said that she wasn't sure about that, but would think on it this week. Then she said a sweet thing. "Johnny." she said, "I'm glad you went to church. Don't let it be the last time." Her words brought tears to my eyes. I wasn't aware of it then, but my son who is eleven years of age, was listening to us talk. He had come into the kitchen for a drink of water. I went out on the porch and took a rocking chair and was thinking more about the day. Alan, my son, came out and said:

"Daddy, I'll go to church with you. I've been hoping that we could start going to Spring Hollow Baptist. The children at school have been talking a lot about what's going on up there."

"Alan, I'll be back, you can count on it."

Lisa Boyd had been rehearsing the solo hymn that she would be singing Sunday morning. She had selected to sing "It Pays to Serve Jesus." Lisa had a strong soprano voice and had often been called on to sing the special music. Other times she would sing duets with alto voice or tenor voices of choir members. Lisa sang from her heart, not just because she could sing. She could also play both piano and organ. The church appreciated her talents and her willingness to share her Christian gifts.

Dick and wife, Louise, prepared to sing a duet at the Sunday evening worship service. Their talents were often used and both were pleased to share with the church what God had blessed them with. It was well known that Spring Hollow Baptist folk could sing.

When Timothy arrived at the Stewart's, Millie welcomed him and began asking him a lot of questions about the week at Seminary. She was concerned about his involvement at the church, and if they might have hindered his final examinations.

"Everything went well, Mrs. Stewart. I just hope my exam grades are as good as the time I'm having at Spring Hollow. Have you and Mr. Frank been well this week?"

"Yes, very well, only the aging problem which is obvious to all of us. But, I have some sad news, Brother Timothy. You have not met this fine lady, since she was living with her daughter in town. Everybody here abouts call her Grandma Mildred. Mildred Pugh is her name. She died about 3:00 a.m. this morning. Mildred was 94 years old. She had lived a good life and was well liked by all. For the past ten years, she was practically an invalid. She's a member of our church. Word is that the funeral will be Monday at 11:00 a.m. here at Spring Hollow. A former pastor of several years ago, Brother James Barlow, will conduct the funeral services with you assisting. What I've told you is what I was asked to tell you, so that you can prepare the folks as to what to expect."

"Thank you, Mrs. Millie. I'll do as the family has requested. Will the funeral home in town manage the burial services?"

"Yes, but I'm not aware when the wake will be. Perhaps you will need to call this afternoon for that information. Mildred had children living away, so it might be Sunday evening before all the family members can get here."

"I'll check for the information. You have the local phone number, don't you? I'd better get someone to ride into town with me and call on the daughter. Who do you suggest would know the address and the family?"

"Brother Mike Owens. His wife, Bernice, is kin to the Pugh family."

"Thanks, Mrs. Millie. You are a doll!"

Timothy called Mike Owens, and they made the visit into town. The Pugh family was ministered to, as appropriate, in the death of a dear mother and friend. This was Timothy's first funeral, and he knew it was going to be difficult. However, the testimony of a long life and Christian character would make it easier. Their old pastor friend had not arrived. Timothy asked that they call, or have the preacher friend call, sometime in the evening.

Timothy also got all the information about the wake and burial hours. This was important for Spring Hollow Baptist Church. Food would have to be prepared, and the church building made ready for the funeral. The friends of the Pugh family in town took care of all the food there. Spring Hollow would prepare food for Monday, after the funeral. Everyone was aware of the importance of these things, due to such circumstances. These were extra activities for the church and would not interfere with Sunday's services. The afternoon baptism service would go on as planned.

During the week, about twenty men, and a few women, pitched in to prepare the grounds, the creek area where the baptizing would take place, and the dressing area and tents for both women and men. The men of the church had tarpaulins each about 8' x 24'. Posts were secured in the ground, making each dressing area 6' x 6' square. The tarps were secured around the posts and an entrance was provided with an old quilt. Also, an old quilt was hung through the middle to provide privacy between women and girls, and men and boys. Those helping invent the dressing area thought their work was well done. When the church folk saw the dressing area, they too, agreed.

Saturday had been a busy day for Timothy. Mrs. Millie had informed him that he would take supper with she and Frank. This pleased Timothy because he could relax immediately after supper and go to bed early. Millie told him that another family would have him over for dinner on Sunday. Timothy assured her that such unusual care was not necessary, but it did please him to receive such Christian love.

Timothy helped Mr. Frank with some of his chores, those he understood and he would not foul up. Mr. Frank was pleased with his help. It was the beginning of their long acquaintance. About 6:00 p.m., they heard Mrs. Millie call them to supper. Both were ready for a delicious meal. Mrs. Millie did not disappoint them.

The new Sunday School house classes proved successful. Attendance was up considerably. New faces were showing up each Sunday. Some were old members returning to the fold, while others were new people who had moved into Spring Hollow in the past seven to ten years. They were just now finding their way to be involved in Bible study and fellowship with other members of the community. All seemed to rejoice in the fresh, spiritual atmosphere of Spring Hollow.

Again, the worship service was great. People sang with a spirit that had never been voiced with such vigor. There was a great sense of expectancy. When the choir sang, there were no dry eyes in the church. Johnny, the old drunk, was back, and he wept aloud. Ted was very pleased to hear his friend weep, and he believed was under conviction for his sin.

Timothy made all the announcements. Everything was ready for the baptism service at 2:30 p.m. down at the creek. Carl Sims was also asked to assist in baptizing his children. He also announced about Mrs. Mildred Pugh's funeral tomorrow at 11:00 a.m. Lunch would be prepared for the Pugh family and any or all those of the church who wished to fellowship at the meal.

Timothy preached a good sermon. To the best of his ability and knowledge, he explained the Word of God and how the church should respond to it. God did bless the people. If the "amens or other words of praise were any evidence, there would be an unusual number to respond during the invitation. But, Timothy knew that decisions were personal and, he hoped, would be motivated by Jesus. He prayed in closing:

"You alone, my Father, know our hearts. Please, my Lord, be glorified with us in this service which we dedicate to you. amen."

Not one soul moved. All the church seemed to be in solemn prayer. No one seemed surprised. There was a spirit of joy. Timothy breathed a prayer of thanksgiving and was satisfied. The benediction was called for, and the church was again reminded of the 2:30 p.m. baptizing down at the creek.

The visitors were warmly greeted and encouraged to return. The folk were not in a hurry to leave the church. This gave those who were strangers an opportunity to get acquainted. Timothy knew that Jesus was doing the right thing. He would follow His will.

Mike Brannon found Timothy in the crowd and said he was invited to his house for dinner. "We will be going on head to have everything ready. I know you have a busy afternoon schedule." said Mike.

"I'll be right behind you Mike." said Timothy.

"Daddy, I'm going to ride with Brother Timothy. Dana is going home with me also. We'll show Brother Timothy the way." Susie laughed because Timothy knew the way to her house. Timothy was happy to be invited to the Brannon's. He had visited with Mike at the store, but this was an opportunity to discuss vital Christian issues in the home. However, Timothy reasoned time was not on his side for this visit. The baptism service was at 2:30 p.m. He must be there early to make sure everything was in place.

Dinner was served, and it was very delicious. Susie was talkative as usual, but the other two Brannon children were calm. Mike expressed himself as becoming more concerned in church matters. He was cautious with his words as if he did not want to take them back, if events came out different. Mrs. Brannon wondered if what was happening in Spring Hollow would continue. There was a sense of doubt that too much emphasis on church activities might cause people to neglect other responsibilities.

Timothy listened with deep concern. He became aware that much patient work had to be cultivated in this family. He would make it a priority to develop a strong Christian relationship with the Brannon's. They needed spiritual growth, far more than the enthusiastic conduct wrapped up in a little girl named Susie. Timothy concluded it was a field to be developed.

The Spring Hollow Creek bank became crowded by 2:00 p.m. Children were plentiful and running everywhere. Many visitors were there. No one could ever remember a baptizing this early in the spring. The weather was warm, but not hot. The water would be cool, several degrees cooler than it would be in July or August. A slight breeze was blowing, but not enough to make one cold before reaching the dressing areas. There seemed to be no obstacles at all.

Dick Reveere brought his accordion so that they would have music to help keep everyone in tune. There would not be much sound for all to hear, but he would be able to lead in the right tune. Dick announced the hymn "Shall We Gather at the river."

"Sing loud and keep in harmony." Dick pleaded.

The people did sing well. They could have been heard a mile way, as the wind blew. They sang joyously and with praise. Brother John Canton led the congregation in prayer. His voice

was compassionate and tender. After the amens, Dick Reveere announced the second hymn "When We All Get to Heaven." Several strong amens were heard as he announced this old hymn. The people went beyond the call of duty as they sang to the glory of God.

Brother Timothy asked all candidates to join him along the creek bank. He gave them a bit of instructions as to who would be first and that they were to go immediately to the dressing area to change out of their wet clothes. He had asked Carl Sims and his family to be baptized last, and that all stand together. Timothy stepped into the water and waded out to about waist deep. Then he moved back toward the bank for the proper depth for the smaller candidates.

To be baptized:
Sims: Joe, Callie, Beth, Agnes, Cynthia, and Carl
Reveere: Tammy
Brannon: Susie
Matthews: Sam and Bob
Bailey: Tom and Juanita
Anderson: Lloyd and Anna
Tidwell: Marie

This baptizing was very unusual. One complete family was involved. One Dad and son and two husbands and wives. There were fifteen in all. Their ages ranged from twelve years to thirty-eight years.

Timothy was a bit nervous. This was his very first baptism to perform. He wanted to do it right to the glory of God. He assured all that he would be careful not to let anyone slip out of his grip and float away down stream. To his delight, the people gave out a good laugh. Susie Brannon was baptized first. Timothy asked her about the decision she made to Jesus.

"Susie, did you invite Jesus into your heart, and did you promise to serve Him all your life?"

"Yes, I did."

"Then in obedience to the command of our Lord Jesus Christ and upon your profession of faith in Him, I baptize you,

Susie Brannon, into the Name of the Father, the Son, and the Holy Spirit, amen."

Each candidate was asked the same questions, and Timothy baptized them as he did Susie. Each candidate was greeted at the bank of the creek by parents, spouses, or friends. After Bob Matthews was baptized, he stood by to watch his son, Sam, be baptized. The same was so with Tom and Lloyd as their wives were baptized. Marie was met by Ada and Becky and escorted to the dressing area. Timothy had asked Carl Sims to assist in the baptizing of his entire family. Carl placed his left hand behind the right shoulder of his wife, Cynthia, and helped lower her into the water and raise her out of the water. This was an emotional event for Carl. He wept as he continued to help baptize all four children. The people were loudly saying "Amen, praise the Lord, and Glory!

As the Sims family marched out of the water, followed by Timothy, Dick Reveere sounded his accordion to the old hymn "When the Roll is Called Up Yonder." Everyone was greatly rejoicing. The Spring Hollow Baptist Church had never witnessed a service like it was experiencing now.

Brother Timothy asked that no one leave until they all had changed out of their wet clothes. All the new members were to be congratulated and welcomed into the fellowship of the church at this time. It was indeed a joyous time. One most obvious sight was that of Rufus Dean and Carl Sims embracing each other, and both men weeping.

"Carl, what you did with your family today is the most powerful testimony I've every witnessed," Rufus was overhead saying.

"I've never felt so obligated in my whole life as I do now. I am committed to lead my family in Christian growth to the glory of Jesus." said Carl.

Another emotional experience was that of Marie Tidwell's Dad. Mr. Tidwell, though old and in bad health, witnessed the baptism of his daughter. This was the first time in all of his life that he had shown any signs of spiritual concern. After Marie had exchanged clothes, he embraced her as if he cared deeply; and joy seemed to overflow his soul. His actions were very noticeable to all. Several whispered to each other that perhaps the strong testimony of Marie would be a turning point of his life.

All the newly baptized members were now ready to be congratulated and welcomed into the membership of Spring Hollow Baptist Church. Dick Reveere began playing his accordion. Brother Timothy led his church in that meaningful experience. The people were so happy. No one wanted to leave the event. Someone was overheard saying that the church should have prepared a supper meal, and everyone could have remained for the evening. Then an old-time prayer meeting could have concluded the happy event. Perhaps next time this would be planned for. It was evident that a great worship service could be anywhere and at any time.

Mike Owens encouraged all to be present at Church Training. He felt certain that space would be a problem tonight. To the best of his ability, he directed each person to their age groups, with the help of several helpers. The topics in most youth and adult ages were events of the day and how they would make an impact on the Spring Hollow community. The public schools were already affected by the spiritual revival; which, in turn, had an effect on other churches in the county, including other denominations.

Two Negro congregations were experiencing revival. They were not closely associated with any other church, yet revival was being experienced. Most all church leaders of all denominations were being convicted of the need to pray. Business, county, and state employees, openly talked about their Christian experience and witnessed to those who did not know Jesus Christ as Savior. But, as powerful as the revival experience was, and spreading throughout the county, there were some who doubted the authenticity of the work of God. Satan did have his workers attempting to disprove the saving grace of Jesus Christ. During the next three to four years, Satan played his hand heavily upon the county's churches. However, memories of spiritual drought of years past became a clarion call to pray. Spring Hollow Baptist Church committed to Christ their future and, by His power, they would remain vitally involved in evangelistic witness, spiritual growth, and Godly fellowship.

During the summer, and continuing through the first year of Timothy Karr's ministry, many plans were put into action to accommodate the growth of the church. By the time of his seminary graduation, several additional classrooms were added. The preschool and nursery were completely overhauled and refurbished. Plans were made to begin a new auditorium. But, this would come only after adequate educational spaces were completed and paid for. Spring Hollow Baptist Church was reaping Godly benefits for their commitment to their Lord Jesus Christ. Years ahead would record phenomenal growth and missions emphasis that would be felt throughout the convention and world.

Chapter 14

The Community Drunk Converted

Meanwhile, as the Holy Spirit was doing many things to many of the folk in Spring Hollow, Ted Ladnier became convicted to visit and witness to his friend Johnny Jones. He was aware that Johnny had a terrible drinking problem and that it had affected Johnny's family for years. He was not sure what influence his visit would have on Johnny, but he had to try. Perhaps, one thing was in his favor to talk with Johnny. He noticed for several days that Johnny had been fairly quiet and not as talkative. Usually his conduct was coarse and abrasive. Maybe there was a change being made. He hoped so. At the worst, he could fall back on Johnny's three or four visits to Spring Hollow Baptist Church within the past four months.

Ted knew that he had not been a good Christian example toward Johnny for him to want a change in his life. For years, this had been the case. But now, things had changed, and his own life was hungering to grow in God's grace. The revival going on in Spring Hollow had made a tremendous impact on this backslider's spiritual condition. His recommitment to the Lord Jesus, as yet he had not made it public, was a daily joy in Bible reading and prayer. Praying for his family and the family of Johnny Jones had become a very heavy burden. Ted felt that he must talk with Johnny, or lose him forever. He reasoned that no better opportunity would ever be than right now. He walked slowly into the department where Johnny worked. He was asking Jesus to guide in every word spoken. He found Johnny whistling and seemed to be in a good mood.

"Hello, Johnny. How's the work going?"

"Pretty good, Ted. At least I've not hurt my hand or finger, so that I would have to bite my tongue, if you know what I mean."

"Think I do, friend. It doesn't do much good to counter pain with bad words, anyhow. It's kind of an ego satisfaction that seems to get the attention of bystanders."

"Yeah, I know. The hurt is there whatever you say. I bet a prayer would do a lot better, don't you Ted?"

"I'll agree." Ted paused a moment before he spoke again. "Johnny, what are your plans for tomorrow at lunch time? I know you generally bring your lunch as well as I, but I have an offer, if you will take me up on it."

"What's that, Ted?"

"I'll buy you a steak or fish dinner if you will dine with me. Now, That's difficult to turn down by a hard working and hungry man like you. How about an OK?"

"Ted, I'm taking you up on that good deal. However, you need not obligate yourself to pay. I've been wanting to talk with you for some time. I'm glad you asked me to eat with you."

"I'm glad you will join me, Johnny. But, I must pay the bill. It's something I want to do. Let's leave about 11:30 so that we can pick our table. Is that satisfactory with you?"

"Just fine, Ted. I haven't had a good fish dinner in sometime. Think I'll make mine just that."

With the dinner date settled, Ted said so long to Johnny until tomorrow at noon. He walked slowly back to his work place. "Thank you Jesus for making everything ready between Johnny and me. Please provide your presence tomorrow as we fellowship and I witness for you to him. Thanks for blessing me now."

When Ted arrived at home about sundown, he felt so good that he told his wife the good news of plans he had made with Johnny. Before he could say more, she told him that she had felt good for him all day, not knowing why about her feelings. Now she knew. The Lord was helping her to help Ted for Johnny's sake.

"Ted, I believe the Lord is opening the way for Johnny's entire family to get involved in the church. Won't that be just great?"

"Yes, it will. I want you to pray as we meet tomorrow. Johnny has a lot to overcome. But, Jesus can, and will, bring him through to victory."

Johnny and Ted ordered their dinner and began chatting about events of the morning. Both seem at ease.

"Johnny." Ted began. "I've been praying a lot for you lately. I'm deeply concerned about your spiritual relationship with Jesus. I'm your friend, and I want you to accept Jesus as your Lord and Savior. Everything about Jesus Christ is to your advantage. I believe He has been dealing with you lately. Johnny, I want you to trust your life to Him. All Jesus needs to hear from you is that you are sorry for your sins. Ask Him to forgive you, and He will."

"Would Jesus accept me if I just change my ways, like stop drinking and cussing, or fussing with my wife and children? I can't be perfect. It seems there is too much the church expects from a Christian. I don't think I can live up to that."

"No, Johnny. You have it all wrong. The church has nothing to do with your being saved. Only Jesus can do that. You see, all have sinned against God. And only He can and will save us when we repent of our sin. Jesus saves us because He loves us. He died for us. That's wonderful! For God to love you and me so much to die for us is an awesome expression of love. We can't do anything to save ourselves. I'm your friend, and I love you. But I can't die for you, and my dying will not save you. We are all the same. All humans need a Savior if they are to live with God forever. All these other actions or conduct will stop when you give your heart to Jesus. He knows all about you. He knows your thinking right now. He knows that you are afraid you can't hold out to be a good Christian. It is true that you can't, but Jesus can for you. He won't leave you alone. Nor, will He ever leave you."

"Ted, I'm convinced that I need to be saved. But, I don't understand what will come after that. It scares me to think about it. And, it scares me to not let Jesus come into my life. I know that if I don't someday, I'll die and go to hell. The thought of dying and going to hell is frightful. I have been thinking seriously about my life, and I have understood today that I should make the change very soon. Would you come to my house tomorrow evening? In the meantime, I want to tell my wife what I intend to do. Can you come about 7:00 p.m.?"

"You bet I can. I'll bring my Bible, and we will read several Scriptures that will help you make your decision for Jesus."

"Even though it will be Friday, the night I generally do a lot of drinking, I will not drink a drop. You can count on it, Ted."

"I believe you Johnny. I'll see you tomorrow evening. Until then, we better get back on the job. We do need to draw our paycheck, don't we?" They both laughed.

Ted called Brother Timothy to pray for Johnny and his family and for himself as he led Johnny to saving faith in Jesus. He also called Rufus Dean to go with him.

"Brother Rufus, I need your help and presence tomorrow evening. I've promised Johnny Jones that I would come to his home for the purpose of leading him to Jesus. Johnny likes you and puts a great deal of confidence in you as a Christian. Can you go with me?"

"I don't have anything else planned, Ted. Johnny and his family truly need the Lord. I'll be at your house at whatever time you say."

Mrs. Jones had a pot of hot coffee ready, along with some fresh homemade tea cookies, when Ted and Rufus arrived. She was anxious for this visit. She wanted her husband changed, and also was aware that a change must take place in her life as well. Tonight would be an experience the like of such had never happened in her home before. Their two teenage children, Lindy, age 15, and Gene, age 17, needed this family change and their own soul salvation. To have Johnny home tonight, and sober, was a miracle. Surely, the Lord Jesus was wanting to change them. Her heart was burdened and hurting.

"Come on in, Ted and Rufus. It's good to see you, Rufus. You know you are one of my best friends in this community. We are glad to have you and Ted in our home."

"Thanks, Johnny. It's my fault that I have neglected this visit for so long." said Rufus.

"Good evening, Mrs. Jones." said Ted. "Thank you for allowing us to visit."

"You two are always welcome to our house." said Mrs. Jones. "Why not sit at the table. Our coffee and cookies will taste better there."

After a bit of chitchat and a good taste of tea cookies, Ted turned in his Bible to the book of Romans. From there, he and Rufus explained to Johnny and his wife how to be saved. As the Holy Spirit always does, He had prepared Johnny and his wife's hearts to accept Jesus as Lord and Savior. As Rufus prayed, Johnny and his wife began weeping unashamedly. Both audibly confessed their sin to God and asked Jesus into their hearts. What a time of heavenly joy to four friends who loved each other. Johnny and his wife openly shared their joy in Christ for several minutes. They also thanked Ted and Rufus for caring.

Ted confessed that this was his first experience of leading anyone to faith in Christ. But, he promised his friends and Christ that it would not be his last. For several years hence, Ted's promise would find fruition in many souls won to Jesus.

Johnny and his wife came to Spring Hollow Baptist Church on Sunday morning, prepared to make their decision for Christ public, and for baptism. As was the case during these days, the Sunday School and Worship Service were overflowing in attendance. The crowd was so large that it had become a problem getting enough seats for everyone. Dick Reveere had asked Joe and Callie Sims two weeks before to sing at the morning worship service. At that time, no one knew that Mr. and Mrs. Jones would be declaring their faith in Christ, and that their two children, Gene and Lindy, would be present. Most folk in Spring Hollow were aware of Johnny's drinking problem. Up until now, none of the family members were Christians. They had been in the prayers of many for several months. No one, other than Ted and Rufus, was aware that the Jones would bless the church by their public profession of faith.

Joe and Callie Sims were well acquainted with Gene and Lindy Jones. They were school friends, but not close. Gene was a potential ball player, but the problems at home prevented his participation at school. Callie knew Lindy and often comforted her at school due to her home problems. She too had been praying for the Jones's family.

Mrs. Cynthia Sims had heard a beautiful song on the radio. Its title was "I'll Tell The World That I'm a Christian." She wrote for a

154

copy immediately. After receiving the new song, she was playing the music on her piano as Joe and Callie came in from school. They thought it was just what their church needed to hear. For two weeks, after Mr. Reveere had asked them to sing, Joe and Callie learned their new song, both in feeling and words. Joe was aware that the Jones's family was present, but Callie had not seen either of them. When Dick Reveere announced that Joe and Callie Sims would sing the special, the people gave approval with a hardy "Amen." As the brother and sister came to the pulpit to sing, their mother Cynthia sat down at the piano and quietly began to play various notes. After Joe announced their selection, she meshed her playing into the introductions of this beautiful song.

"We're singing "I'll Tell The World That I'm a Christian." said Joe with his strong baritone voice. "Maybe someone will answer God's call. You listen carefully. My family is proud to be Christian."

Callie's voice blended with Joe's so beautifully. Before their singing was half over, the congregation was into the worship with amens, praises, and many tears. Carl Sims was proud of his children. They were singing to his and heart, and he was listening. It was wonderful to observe this congregation accepting his children, and his whole family. They were no more outcasts, or treated differently.

Brother Timothy was deeply moved by what he was witnessing. Surely, he thought to himself, God is working in someone's life, right now. Perhaps Jesus would reveal His purpose to many today. He prayed and thanked God for Joe and Callie. What two dear committed people with talents which are used to praise God.

Timothy thanked Joe, Callie, and their mother, Cynthia, for leading the church in worship and to hear what God was saying. The church responded with a strong "Amen."

Timothy preached with a strong sense of urgency and compassion. He strongly emphasized what God was doing in Spring Hollow. And, with that background, he strongly stressed that God was expecting, yes, demanding, something from all of us in return.

Immediately at the beginning of the invitation, Johnny Jones and his wife came forward declaring Jesus as their Lord and Savior. Ted and Rufus could not hold back their interest in this family. Both men stepped forward and declared to their pastor the experience witnessed in the Jones's home two nights before. They felt very good in support of this family. Then, they took their seats and continued to pray for others.

Joe noticed Gene Jones appeared somewhat uneasy during the time he and Callie was singing. Perhaps, he thought, after the worship service would be a good time to talk with Gene. After congratulating Mr. and Mrs. Jones for their public decision for Christ, Joe made his way through the big crowd of people to where Gene was waiting for his parents, near their automobile. Getting through the crowd was a chore. Many stopped him to compliment his singing. Others asked if he were considering a music ministry. Still others gave him the name of a song they wished he would sing sometimes. He was very courteous to all for their encouragement.

"Hello, Gene, my friend. How are you doing these days?"

"Doing pretty well, Joe. And yourself?"

"I've never been happier in my life, Gene. I don't know what's in my future, but I'll leave that to God. Maybe it will be baseball or religious ministry. Whatever it is, I know Jesus will always be first. What He has done for me in the past few months is worthy of my giving the rest of my life for Him. How about you, Gene. What's your future plans?"

"I haven't aimed at anything in particular, yet. But, for several weeks, I've been doing a lot of thinking about my soul. I need some help. Think you could help me, Joe?"

"I know that I can, and will, Gene. What are you doing this afternoon?"

"I have no plans, just lying around the house."

"I'll be over about 3:00 p.m., my friend. We'll go off to a quiet place and have a good talk with Jesus. Is that OK?"

"Yeah, I think so. Would you consider bringing Callie over? Lindy needs to talk with her. They can go their way, and we will go ours. OK?"

"I'll bring Callie along. In fact, Let's ask her now. There, she and Lindy are coming out the front door."

"Hey, Callie." Joe yelled and motioned for her to make her way to him. At first, for about twenty minutes, the four, Gene, Joe, Lindy, and Callie, talked about things of family interests as they drank their iced tea. No four people in the Spring Hollow community had witnessed exclusion in the past more than they. But, the revival going on had changed everyone. Gene and Lindy were victims of a drinking, unbelieving father and a bitter, unbelieving mother. Joe and Callie were victims of an outcast family of Choctaw Indians. Few social contacts were afforded them. Only at school were they equal, but at times, felt extremely lonely. Christ Jesus was changing all this now in Spring Hollow. Old grudges, bad feelings, and hypocrites were gone. Christians were acting like they ought. Everyone was welcome at church and community functions.

What Gene and Lindy witnessed today at church to Gene's parents was proof what Jesus was doing and wanted to do in their lives.

"Gene, while our sisters talk with each other, why don't you and me take a walk down the road ways."

"OK, Joe."

As the two young men walked along the dirt road, Joe remembered the like experience he had with his Dad a few months ago. He prayed that Gene would be as responsive to the gospel of Jesus as was his Dad.

"Gene, I was overjoyed to witness your parents make their decision to follow Jesus today. I was praying for you and Lindy. But, I knew that no one had ever explained to you how to be saved from your sin."

"I almost did go forward, Joe. But, I didn't know what to do or say."

With this opportunity of interest from Gene, Joe explained to him that Jesus Christ loved him very much. He led Gene to repent of his sin and, in simple faith in Jesus, asked forgiveness. Not under-standing all that was happening, Gene asked Jesus to come live in his heart and life forever. Gene began to sob softly, but was not ashamed to let Joe witness his emotions. The joy Joe had told him about was now overwhelming him. He felt changed as if he were a new person. Standing in the middle of the road, these two young friends embraced each other and wept aloud. Joe remembered a Scripture that said; "Angels in heaven rejoice over one sinner saved."

"Gene, did you know that you caused the angels in heaven to rejoice at this very moment?. It is why we all should rejoice when sinners repent and are saved."

"Well, Joe, if they are as happy as I am, they have something to rejoice about. Let's go back to the house and tell Dad, Mom, and the girls what I've done."

When the two arrived at Gene's home, Callie and Lindy were on the front porch, laughing and weeping. About that time, the parents came onto the porch and asked what was going on. Lindy replied that she had just been saved, as they had been earlier, and she was happy. Gene spoke up:

"Dad and Mom, I, too, have given my heart to Jesus. Joe and I had walked down the road a ways to talk about my salvation. We left the girls here and the same thing happened with Lindy."

Both parents embraced their children in such a tender love that they had never experienced before. Joe and Callie looked on as they praised the Lord for the peace and God's salvation that had come to this home.

"Mom, Dad." said Lindy. "We are a Christian family now. We won't have to witness the harsh things of the past again."

"That's right, child." said her Dad." Never again will Satan rule this home. We belong to Jesus now, forever."

"Oh, how true that is John." responded his wife. "Jesus has cleansed this family. Oh, thank you Jesus." They all said "Amen."

During the evening worship service, Callie and Joe sat with their friends Lindy and Gene. At the invitation time, Joe and Callie walked down the church isle with their new Christian friends and told Brother Timothy about the experience of the afternoon. Spring Hollow Baptist Church rejoiced because Jesus had transformed another family in the Spring Hollow Community.

Chapter 15

Class Testimony

Timothy had seated himself and was talking with two students across the isle before the professor entered the classroom. No tests were scheduled for today, and that was cause enough for all to relax. Timothy had been very reluctant over the past several months to talk about happenings on the church field in Spring Hollow. He felt strongly about not taking any credit for what the Holy Spirit was doing. He was fully aware that no man, nor a group of people, could cause revival of the spirit in man. Only God could change people's hearts. However, some four or five students had asked their professor to let Timothy talk to the class about his experience in the Spring Hollow community. Today was that day. But, Timothy did not know that he was to lead the class in such an event.

When the professor entered the room and the class was in order, he asked Timothy to volunteer his time for the benefit of his classmates. It was a surprise, but he accepted.

"Thanks, fellows. I'll remember to try this on you sometime. I know all of you, but it makes me nervous to be standing before such a mass of intelligent minds. Don't hit me too hard with your questions. The class had a good laugh.

"Well, I'll begin by saying that I am only a tiny speck in God's work in Spring Hollow. It's not me nor them, but Him, the Lord Jesus Christ. What we, and I emphasize "we", have experienced within the past year, I wish would continue for my lifetime. It is profound, yet so simple. Really, it is the Lord's people letting Him do His work, His way, through them. His people are listening, accepting, and obeying. There is nothing strange about what's happening when it is compared to the Scriptures command. The key is; God is in control and His people are obeying His voice. I didn't cause this revival to happen. It was going on before I arrived in Spring Hollow. Spring Hollow is a place one must plan to visit. You don't get there, nor pass by it, on a major highway. The people are plain honest, dependable, and trustworthy. They love God, their families, land, and neighbors. Above all, they love, and they know how to worship Jesus at His house of prayer."

Timothy explained the best he could how the Lord Jesus was working in Spring Hollow. The class was spellbound for the entire period. He never once claimed credit for anything. "Why, he said, would a human being attempt to claim credit for something as glorious as what was happening in Spring Hollow?"

His class friends really did have a good laugh when he told of his first week's experience. No one could every forget how a young preacher was called to his first pastorate, given his first automobile, and a new home, all in one package.

"Again, he said, Only God could do a thing like that."

At the close of the class period, the class roared their approval for what they had heard. The professor was amazed. All he said was; "What a testimony. Praise God for what He is doing in Spring Hollow."

Chapter 16

Mary's Death

George Nichols and wife Mary were pecan farmers. George estimated he had between 75 and 80 acres in rich, healthy, bearing trees. Their work consisted of disking, fertilizing, pruning, and harvesting. Climate conditions determined the outcome of the harvest. This work was indeed a condition of faith.

George and Mary are 51 and 49 years of age. They have been members of Spring Hollow Baptist Church for 30 years. During the last six years, they have become very active in attendance and supportive of the church's programs and finance. The revival emphasis going on now has also been a great boon to their spiritual growth. They have no children living. Mary gave birth to a son who lived five years and a daughter who died just after her 12th birthday. She was advised by her doctor not to have any more children due to her health conditions. At the time of her children's deaths, the community of Spring Hollow grieved deeply with Mary and George through their loss. Spring Hollow is known for its response to the needs of anyone. It is a community that cares.

Timothy was awakened at about 1:00 a.m. on Tuesday morning by Frank Stewart. George had called for his pastor to come immediately to the hospital. Mary had a massive heart attach about 12:00 midnight, and George rushed her to the hospital. Her condition was poor. No one was with George at this time but the hospital staff. He was lonely and afraid.

Timothy dressed quickly and was off to the hospital about 25 miles away. He asked Frank to call John Canton and inform him about Mary's condition. John would notify other deacons and church folk. They were all asked to pray for Mary and George.

As Timothy drove to the hospital, he asked God for his safety. Mary was constantly on his mind, praying that Jesus would see fit to spare her life. It was not to be. When Timothy walked into the hospital a nurse led him to where George and the doctor were waiting. George rose from his chair and embraced Timothy, weeping uncontrollably.

"Mary is gone, pastor. Oh, I feel so alone. I wish it had been me instead of her. The doctor told me I was fortunate to get her to the hospital. She was so sick and hurting terribly."

"I feel for you deeply, my friend. We will have to turn this loss and grief over to Jesus. He will know how to deal with it. Let's trust Him to heal your heart and hurts. There is one dear and strong consolation. Mary is joined with your children, forever. Let me lead us in prayer. Doctor, will you join us?"

Timothy prayed a comforting prayer. He wanted to be sure that God received the praise and glory for Mary's life and her death. She was His child and knew what was best for His children. After the prayer, George introduced Timothy to the doctor who had helped him so much.

"Brother Timothy, this is Dr. Stanley Windham. Dr. Windham, this is Timothy Karr, my pastor." said George.

Each man greeted the other with a warm handshake. Each thanked the other for the help and comfort given to George.

"Brother George, with your permission, I should call John Canton. I know it is late, but he needs to know, and others of the church family." said Timothy.

"Yes, please do. They need to know." said George.

Dr. Windham had excused himself to attend to other business before going home.

Timothy and George walked to the waiting room and made the phone call to John Canton.

"Hello, John, this is Timothy I have sad news about Mary. She died before I arrived at the hospital. George is here. I will be following him home as soon as we finish things here. Please pray for him. I haven't asked him, but it would be good that I spend the rest of the night with him. Call Frank, and tell them my plans. I'll see them sometime this morning. Try to rest, if you can. The Lord knows our needs."

"Thanks for calling, Timothy Be careful and stay with George." said John.

As Timothy and George were passing the nurse's station on their way out and leaving the hospital, Dr. Windham asked Timothy to give him a minute to talk.

"Brother Karr, would you be my guest for lunch a week from Monday? I've heard a lot about Spring Hollow Baptist Church in the past four or five months." said Dr. Windham.

"Yes, I believe that would be possible, unless I have an emergency. Where will I meet you?" asked Timothy.

"Drop by my office about 11:30 a.m. We will go from there." said Dr. Windham.

"Doctor, you have heard right about our church." said George. We not only have a thriving church, but also have a great pastor in Brother Timothy"

"I believe that, too." responded the doctor. "Mr. Nichols, if I can ever be of help to you, please call me. I'll be in prayer for you during these next several days. You have a lot of adjustments to make. But, you can do it. Right now, you may feel that you are the only one suffering. But, many are going through your experience, tonight."

"Thanks, doctor. You are a friend." responded George.

Timothy and George left the hospital and went home for a few hours. It was a comfort to George that his pastor would spend these hard difficult hours with him. This was the third time for George to experience grief and loneliness. His two children had died, and now his beloved Mary. This was different. Mary's presence helped to comfort in their children's death. Now, he had no wife to weep with and share his agony.

Timothy returned with George to the funeral home, around 11:00 a.m. to make plans for Mary's funeral. Two couples from the church were waiting in the front lobby. The women were a great help to George in suggesting correct clothing suitable for Mary. George was deeply appreciative to them. They also informed George that everything at his home was being cared for. All he had to do is accept it and rest the best he could.

George had called his only sister and two brothers before leaving home for the funeral preparation. Mary's brother and aunt had also been called. All George's kin, as well as those of Mary's, lived in other counties. They agreed to call other kin for George. He thanked them for their help and prayed for their safety in travel.

Mary's funeral was scheduled for 2:00 p.m. on Wednesday at Spring Hollow Baptist Church. The wake would be from 6:00 B 9:00 p.m. today, Tuesday. This was possible because the funeral director had no other commitment. George agreed that it would be best.

Spring Hollow community responded in love and kindness. George was deeply moved by the Christian response. His family members and those of Mary's were likewise happy from such outpouring of love.

Mary was laid to rest in the church's cemetery, next to the graves of her children. George was assured by all his many friends that they would lift him up to the Lord Jesus in prayer daily. The whole funeral service was a worship experience. Spring Hollow Baptist and other neighbors know how to make one feel loved through an experience like this. George was strengthened for the weeks ahead. His friends would not forget him.

The Wednesday night prayer service was an experience of a great worship service. People of all ages expressed love for each other and to the Lord Jesus for what was happening in their lives. The newborn Christians were eager to participate in prayer and sharing of their faith. The older membership rejoiced to witness prayer meetings to be what they were designed to be. The singing was lively, worshipful, and with meaning. Christ Jesus was being allowed to live in His people as His salvation was designed to do.

Along with the membership of Spring Hollow Baptist Church, Timothy Karr was bathing in God's grace and growing in the experience of being a pastor. Week after week, after week, Jesus was pouring out His Spirit. People were being saved during the week and on Sundays. A great time of refreshing had come to the Spring Hollow community. No one could take credit for it. Only God held the answer.

Timothy walked into Dr. Windham's office at 11:30 a.m. on Monday. He told the young lady at the reception window why he was there. She immediately buzzed Dr. Windham, and she was instructed to show Timothy Karr to his office. The two greeted each other with a warm handshake. They talked briefly and left the office for lunch.

"Let's use my car, Brother Karr. Now that didn't sound just right, did it? said the doctor.

"It's O.K. I like my name, Karr, better than truck or vehicle." said Timothy with a laugh.

"By the way, we are both young and professional. Why don't we drop the professionalism and call each other by our first names?" said Dr. Windham.

"Great idea." responded Timothy "I won't feel so uptight."

"Timothy, my wife, Hannah, and I have been here for one and half years. We like the people. They have been very good to us. My practice has grown rapidly. However, we are not happy in our church. God is saying something to us, but our church is not giving the answer. I want to talk about that. We are both concerned. Mind you, we are not critical toward our church's many activities, nor the preaching. It's the mission emphasis That's lacking." said Stanley, as he parked in front of the restaurant.

The two entered the restaurant and were greeted by one of three waitresses. She led them to a window table and away from several other customers already eating. Stanley and Timothy ordered their meal, and the waitress was gone for a few minutes.

"Timothy, I believe missions is the heartbeat of the church. If that focus is lacking — the church may survive, but not with power — all else it may do, is for naught." said Stanley.

"You are right, my friend." Responded Timothy "And, it means more than giving of money."

"We have purchased a small acreage out toward Spring Hollow Community. It's about fifteen miles out. The house is old, but repairable. Sometime in the near future, we plan to build. We are thinking about coming to Spring Hollow Baptist, not because your church is nearer, but more spiritually alive and missions minded. My wife is a nurse and works with me. We are a team. We've talked with several folk from Spring Hollow Baptist who are my patients. They have impressed us, and we are considering the move. I'm glad I met you before we visited, but I didn't know it would be under stressful circumstances. I hope, Timothy, you don't think we are church jumpers. We are not. We both grew up in the same church. This is our second church to ever be a member. What I am saying, but beating around the bush to say it, we need a strong spiritual push to send us onto the mission field. Can you understand that, Timothy?" asked Stanley.

"I've been listening to your heart's interest, Stanley. You and Hannah will be welcome at our church. Yes, we are missions oriented. Spring Hollow Baptist has not always demonstrated such a missions spirit. The revival we are now experiencing is of God. I believe, yeah, I'll prophecy to that fact, that God is preparing a work through Spring Hollow Baptist Church, which, within the next ten years, will yield a great harvest in His kingdom. Perhaps he wants you there to work toward this harvest. Our church membership is made up of many kinds of occupations. Yours and Hannah's will just add to the many gifted people." said Timothy.

"Thanks, Timothy You have been a decision-maker for me. Now Let's change the subject. How is George Nichols? He is a strong Christian, but adjustment is going to be difficult for him."

"He was at church yesterday. He is not lacking for friends. Some of his relatives were with him. They, too, were appreciative of the church's care."

"Well, It's about time I got back to the office, Timothy I'm sure you have plenty to do at Spring Hollow. We will see you out there pretty soon."

After a warm farewell at Stanley's office, Timothy headed back to his church field. He stopped by to visit with George for a few minutes. His relatives were leaving as Timothy drove up. They assured him that George was in good hands at Spring Hollow Baptist. George seemed happy to have had his kin with him for a few days.

"George, you know where I am if you need me. Either call or come over. As much as I can, by the Lord's good grace, I'll help you through your grief." said Timothy as he was leaving.

"Thanks, pastor. You are a dear friend. I'll call." said George.

Timothy turned down the lane between George's pecan orchard and a stretch of timberland. It was three miles to Leon and Jean Parmer's house. He did not want to lose the opportunity, while in the area, to visit the Parmer's. Both were home. Leon was not operating his sawmill today, because a few repairs needed to be taken care of. So, they sat on the front porch and talked for about an hour. Timothy was satisfied that his visit was profitable and would bring results. After a prayer, he left the Parmer's to their chores.

Chapter 17

The Confrontation

Gene and Lindy Jones were not among the "In" group of students at school. Gene, in particular, was not popular. He was brash, ill tempered, and seemed ready to fight over little things. He was not a bully. That title belonged to a town boy. He would not be so unless the small group of boys, five or six, were always in his company. However, Gene avoided confrontation with the Bully group as best he could. He knew the cause of his non-acceptance, that being the son of a drunkard father. It was often thrown up to him that he had no more brains than a bottle of whiskey. Such language and accusations hardened his heart toward any change. He would observe his father's drunken stupor on weekends and wish he was not a member of his family. Gene was truly a young man hurting from the stark facts of bad home environment. About a month after Gene's marvelous conversion experience in Christ, he was confronted with the Bully group, and particularly by the leader. It was during the lunch hour. Many high school students observed the confrontation, particularly chosen time by the bully, to embarrass Gene. Joe Sims was present, but made no attempt to intervene. He prayed for Gene to reveal Jesus to this haughty, vulgar, sinful group of young men who needed Christ as their Savior and Lord.

Gene took the abuse about himself and his family with no outward display of hostility. His countenance did not change. Gene did not respond to their sinful filth so long as their talk continued. He felt very sorry for his enemies. Gene knew that some of the things said about him had been true. But, no more were they true. Jesus Christ had made him a new person, cleansed of all his past sin and prepared him for a bright and different future. He was proud that Jesus was in control of his conduct at this moment.

Casually, Gene rose from his seat at the table. He was a fair sized young man of 5' 10" and weighing about 165 pounds. He grew up in the country, on a small farm, and knew what hard work could do for the body. He was not afraid of his accusers. He spoke without fear.

"Jack, I'm sorry for you. If you had confronted me and said these things about me a month ago, I would have taken you on, with your friends, and beat the tar out of you. And, you know I could have. I want you and your friends to hear what happened to me four weeks ago, this past Sunday afternoon."

Gene vividly described his conversion experience. The entire group of students gathered in the lunchroom heard him clearly. His voice was firm, compassionate, and convincing. Those who had stood and moved near the exits for fear of a fight began taking their seats or moving nearer to Gene to hear what he was saying. Many began weeping and sniffles were heard from most of the students. There was no anger in Gene's voice, only love. He told about his parents being saved, of Lindy's experience of Christ's salvation, of Joe and Callie's influence upon them. As Gene expressed his concern for the whole student body, the small group of his enemies began to take a seat and most became teary-eyed. Even Jack sat down and hung his head in shame. Joe, Callie, Lindy, and many more Christians present were beaming with joy.

Gene spoke. "Jack, and you who are his friends, I forgive you for what you have said and done. I hold nothing against you. Only, I hope that you will come to know my wonderful Savior Jesus Christ. You will never have peace until you do."

When Gene finished his testimony and pleas, he stepped forward, extending his hand to Jack.

"I love you, my friend. Please accept my forgiveness."

Jack stood, tears streaming from his eyes. He didn't take Gene's hand, but instead, embraced him.

"I'm sorry, Gene, very, very sorry. I do want this peace you spoke about. Can we meet after school and talk about it? I'll drive you home afterwards."

"Sure we can. But, I'll ride home with Joe. You will need to hear what has happened to Joe, too."

"That's O.K. with me." said Jack.

The bell rang for classes to begin. The afternoon passed with great anticipation about the after school meeting. Two teachers were present in the lunchroom and heard what had occurred. One, a deacon in his church, was very pleased about the outcome of the confrontation between Jack and Gene.

The teacher went to the Principal and asked permission to use the lunchroom for the after school meeting. He reasoned that students attending would be more comfortable seated than just standing around outside. The Principal agreed, and the word was passed down through the classes. Instead of Jack and his friends, Gene and Joe, the deacon, and another teacher, about fifty students showed up.

Joe Sims asked for calm during this time, since it involved spiritual matters about their lives. He told of his own salvation experience and that of Gene. After Joe spoke, Lindy gave her testimony. Her words were effective. Then Gene related the earlier comments made that initiated this meeting. With calm and convincing words, he appealed to all present to do what he did, repent and receive Jesus as Savior and Lord of their lives.

Jack raised his hand for a question. "Gene, how may I know, for sure, that Jesus will save me? Is there anything in particular that I should say?"

"You will have to trust Jesus to do what you want done in your heart, Jack." With that he took from his shirt pocket a New Testament and turned to John 3:16. "Listen to what God said, "For God so loved the world that He gave His only Begotten Son, that whosoever believes in Him would have eternal life." "You see, Jack, God has already done everything for us. All we have to do is accept what He has done. That's what everybody who has ever become a believer did, and must do now to become a Christian. God cannot do more than what He has already done. I believed Him and trusted Him to save me from my sin. He did just what He said He would do. You know by the change in your heart about things good and evil. I changed from hating you to loving you. Only Jesus could cause me to do that."

"Gene, can I do what you have talked about, right now?"

"Sure thing. Just confess to Jesus your sin. Be honest about it. Ask Him to forgive you. He will. Thank Him for saving you. Then begin living for Him. Let's all bow our heads, and all who will, do what I've instructed Jack to do."

Gene prayed: "Lord Jesus, none of us are worthy of Your love. But, You gave Yourself to us anyhow. I once did not know You, but I do now. I was once lost in sin, but now I am saved from my sin. I once hated You and Your people, but now I love You and all people. We are all praying and confessing our sin to You. Accept our repentance and save us all for Your Name's sake, amen."

Students wept and became emotional as they asked Jesus to forgive their sin. Many embraced and asked forgiveness for sins done to each other.

Joe stepped beside Gene and laid his hand on his shoulder and said, "Thank you, brother. Jesus has won the battle." At the same time, Jack got up off his knees and embraced Gene and Joe, weeping like a little child. When he became calmer, he said, "Thank you Gene and Joe for not hating me and for leading me to Jesus."

Many other students who were not Christians made public their faith in Christ at this meeting. None were ashamed to say so. It was an emotional time for all present. Joe encouraged them to join a church of their choice and get involved in Christian living to change their communities. He then asked the deacon teacher to lead in a closing prayer.

News of the after school meeting traveled fast. It was the type news which made families whole and persons strong. What happened at the High School corrected many problems prevalent among the students. Classroom attitudes changed because people changed. Where there had been tension and suspicion, now a spirit of happiness and trust prevailed. The school Principal and teachers were pleased that their school was released of harsh conflict.

Among those affected by the meeting, from the Spring Hollow Community, were five young people of the Wilson families. They were Altha and Ben, daughter and son of David and Wendy Wilson. There were Earl, Nathan, and Lynn, sons and daughter of Norman and Sally Wilson. When they arrived home that afternoon, immediately they told their parents of their decision to accept Jesus as Savior and Lord.

"Dad and Mom, I wish you could have been present. No one could have doubted what has happened to Gene Jones. I've known Gene for several years as you have. He has always been defensive and would fight. He disliked what Mr. Jones was doing. As a drunkard, the family was deprived of many things. Deep down, Gene was a good guy. But, he resented his family environment."

"Today, Gene was confronted with a bully, and he won. Not with fists or foul language, but with a testimony of what Jesus Christ had done in his life. What we witnessed today was convincing. Jesus Christ can change lives. That's why, when we were given an opportunity to accept Jesus as our Savior, we did and made it public to all the students and two teachers present. Now I, and I know Nathan and Lynn, feel the same. Gene didn't preach. He just told us what Jesus had done for him about a month ago."

Nathan spoke; "Mom, Dad, We children know that things are not alright in our family. Since now, Earl, Lynn, and I have become Christians, why can't you also? Really, It's a happy feeling I can't explain but I know I'm saved. Right now, Altha and Ben are telling Uncle David and Aunt Wendy what we are telling you. Why can't we invite Gene and Lindy Jones and Joe and Callie Sims to our house on Friday night and have Uncle David and Uncle Ted's family to come over and hear what Jesus will do for us? Will you ask our kin to do this?"

"It's a great idea, Dad." said Lynn.

Norman looked at Sally. Her eyes were wet with tears. "Sally, dear, we do need what our children have experienced. I'll call David and Ted. If they have any misgivings, Earl can go over and explain to them what has happened."

"David, this is Norman. How's the day been?"

"Just fine. I've been exceptionally busy. Nothing unusual happened until our children came in from school. They've been chatting every since."

"So you've heard of the goings on at school. Well, to be honestly frank, Sally and I are proud for what our children did. How do you and Wendy feel about what has happened at school and what is taking place in Spring Hollow?"

"Well, Norman, there is no question about the change in people's lives I know. It really can't be nothing else but good."

"Look, David, our children want us to invite the two Sims young people and the two Jones young people to our house Friday night, around 7:00, to tell their story about what has happened to our children. Can you and Wendy come and bring the children?"

"Hold just a minute while I ask Wendy. Hey, Wendy, would you agree to meet at Norman's Friday night and hear more about what's happening in Spring Hollow?"

"Sure, David. I think we need what our children have experienced."

"It's O.K. Norman. We'll be there if no emergency happens."

"Good. Thanks, David. Have a good evening."

Norman called Ted and Angela. "Howdy, Angela. Been busy today?"

"Not too much, Norman. Just trying to keep tabs on the children and Ted. It's kinda the way Wendy has to do with her old man and children."

"Watch it, Angela. I'm not that old, yet. Say, Angela, we're having two young couples, brothers and sisters, coming to our house Friday night and talk with us about what happened at school today and the goings on in the Spring Hollow Community. Can you and Ted come over and bring your children?"

"Sure we can, Norman. Our oldest, Andy, heard about the large number that were saved at school. He is all excited and asked us to help him and Will to understand it. Frankly, we can't because neither Ted nor I are Christians. But, I know we ought to be because of the responsibility of rearing children."

173

We'll see you Friday night, then. Have a good evening and say hello to Ted."

Earl called Joe and Gene and asked about them coming to his home on Friday night. Both agreed to come, but were surprised that they had been singled out for the occasion. Earl assured them there would not be harsh questions or bad attitudes of doubt toward them. They were to simply tell what Jesus had done in their lives and those students at school. Also, Earl assured, the Wilson and Britton parents were deeply concerned and had agreed to the meeting. Everything was settled for the Friday night meeting at Norman and Sally Wilson's home.

After the telephone call from Earl Wilson, Joe called Gene.

"Hey, Lindy. This is Joe. Is Gene home?"

"Yes, just a minute and I'll get him. He's out back feeding the cats. As you may not know, Gene is crazy about animals, especially cats and chickens. He pets them as if they were breakable."

"Gene." called Lindy. "Joe is on the phone. Can you break away from feeding for a minute?"

Joe heard Gene answer in a seemly far away voice, "Coming, be there in a second." Joe waited.

"Hey, Joe. What's up."

"Hello, Gene. It's about the call from Earl and Friday night. I believe you and me need some praying together."

"I'll agree, Joe. We've got a couple of days."

"Let's meet, first, at school tomorrow. Are you willing to fast at our lunch period and pray?"

"That's a good idea. Why not meet in the homeroom. No one is in there at that hour. I'll call Brother Timothy."

"Great! See you tomorrow morning at school, Gene. Good night."

"Good night, Joe."

Joe and Gene met for prayer for two days. They were facing a witness opportunity that would challenge their ability and faith. It was in this vein of thought that prayer for direction and words were asked for. These young men wished above everything to honor Jesus; and these three families would see Him as God's gift of life and become their Savior. It would become their lot to tell with simplicity, what Jesus had done in their lives and in their families.

Joe called Brother Timothy and informed him about their invitation. He asked his pastor to hold them up before God on Friday night. Timothy had already heard about the spiritual event at school. He rejoiced that so many had witnessed the saving power of Jesus. Timothy was most pleased that Joe and Gene were leading participants. But, he was also aware that they were obedient servants, just as many others were, in the Spring Hollow community.

Friday evening at 6:30, Joe and Callie picked up Gene and Lindy, and they headed up County Road 10 toward the Norman Wilson's home. It was about 12 miles to the turn off onto a gravel dirt road. Another 3 miles would bring them to the middle house on the road. The road had no name. However, the three families living on the road were kin. David and Norman were brothers and were married to sisters. Ted Britton was married to the third and youngest sister. All these families were farmers, cattlemen, and timberland owners. Their property ownership had come to them through inheritance by the wives.

Norman, David, and Ted were well known for their good farm management principles. They were honest and trusted by businessmen throughout the region. Their children were well mannered and obedient. Work ethics were taught from very young childhood age. This conduct was displayed in public, as well as at home. Public school was their institution for learning; not a place or time to frolic. Earl, the oldest son of Norman and Sally, and the oldest of the three families' children, was in his High School Junior year. He would graduate from County High School at eighteen, if all goes well, and would be the first of many family kin to do so. Altha and Nathan would follow Earl in about two years. Then they would set a precedent to continue for many years.

Even though good work ethics, moral principles, and obedience were taught, somehow religion and church attendance were neglected. Historically, the families were not atheists, but church activities were never a part of their lives. This was about to change.

175

Earl, Nathan, and Altha met Gene, Lindy, Joe, and Callie as they arrived.

"This is a happy time for us." said Nathan.

"It is for us, too." Callie responded.

"We've been praying as much as we know how." said Altha.

"We've been doing the same." responded Gene.

"All this is new to us." said Joe, "But we will trust the Lord."

"Ya'll come on in the house, and I'll introduce you to the rest of our family." said Earl.

"Uncle Ted and Aunt Angela, Andy, Will, and Natalie, Uncle David and Aunt Wendy, Altha, Ben, and Mindy, Mom and Dad, me, Nathan, and Lynn, these good friends of ours are; Joe and Callie Sims and Gene and Lindy Jones. Ya'll say welcome to them and to our house."

With handshakes, hugs, and yes, a few tears, the welcome was warm and cordial.

"Earl, before we settle down to the purpose of our gathering, Let's all enjoy a refreshment time. I have baked cookies. We have coffee, ice tea, or milk, whichever you choose. Just help yourselves and make yourselves at home." said Sally.

After a few minutes of fellowship, Joe was asked to relate his Christian experience. Joe was precise, but cautious for fear that someone might not understand. Gene told of his salvation experience. He told of how his Dad and Mom were gloriously saved and how their changed lifestyle affected him. Lindy was crying as Gene told how proud he was of his father, how he had won the battle over drinking. From his own experience, he led the conversation into the confrontation at school. As he retold the story of the situation, Nathan began sobbing. What young Nathan had witnessed, both in actions and words, brought him face to face with Jesus. At this time, Gene spoke to the parents with such conviction and simple faith in Christ, that Ted began crying.

"You see, friends, we have nothing to do, nor can we do anything to be saved. It is a simple matter of telling Jesus we are sorry for our sin we've committed against Him. If we mean it, then ask Jesus to forgive us. Believe me, He will, just as He said

176

He would. It's not a matter of learning a lot about religion, or church, or how you might change to be good, or even changing your habits. Jesus Christ has done everything for us. He wants all of us to trust Him as our Savior and Lord. Joe, turn to John 3:16-17. Read it slowly so that we will not misunderstand. Now, turn to Romans 10: 9-10."

Joe read these Scriptures as if they were the most important words spoken tonight. Callie bowed her head and was praying that everyone present would hear these glorious truths.

"Let me emphasize Jesus saves all alike. Dad or Mom, you cannot be saved differently than your children. Do you have questions about what I've said? I am a new Christian. It was about five weeks ago that I said yes to Jesus. Joe was with me and led me in prayer of confession of sin and, by faith, trusting Jesus as my Savior. I know what happened to me. I also believe you can have this salvation tonight."

"May I know for sure that Jesus will save me when I ask Him to?" asked Wendy.

Lindy spoke. "Mrs. Wendy, let me give you an example. Did you know when you gave birth to your children?"

"Why yes, I even remember the hour of the day each were born."

"Well, the assurance of you being reborn by Jesus will be the same. The Holy Spirit works in ways too great for our understanding. He wants us to trust and believe Him."

"I see. It is simple, Isn't it?" responded Wendy.

"Do we have to be in church or a worship service to become a believer.? asked David.

"Not at all." responded Joe. "Right now is the best time you will ever have. There is no better place than in the home. Our parents were saved at home."

"And, ours were also saved at home." said Lindy. Later, Gene and I were saved. I was on our front porch. Gene was off down the road somewhere. Any place and time is the right time and place."

"I witnessed five of your children being saved at school this week." said Callie.

Joe spoke. "We ought to talk to the Lord Jesus now; and we all can say to Him what we want and need to do. After all, it is His gift of salvation, and we heard His promise that He wishes to give it to us. I can pray for you, but I can't ask Him into your heart. Each person must do that. "My Lord and Savior, You have heard our hearts. Please extend Your mercy to these parents and children, and, by Your grace, save each and their families. Accept each repenting soul and give us Your eternal life. amen."

There were quiet whispers and sobbing. Each was expressing his own spiritual needs to God. The time belonged to Jesus and a few of His created. The work of God was being done, recreating His children to His glorious nature. Angels began rejoicing with exceeding gladness. Heaven's floodgates of joy swung open, and God's children entered through praising the Great Name of Jesus Christ!

Andy got up from his kneeling position and walked across the room to his mother, hugging her and said:

"Mommy, I gave my heart to Jesus, and I said that He could use it in any way He chooses. I feel so good. Daddy, I'm going to be the best son for you. I want our whole family to be the best for Jesus. Will you and Mommy be the best parents for Jesus?"

"Yes, Andy, my son. We will be the best Mom and Dad for you and for Jesus. I have accepted Jesus into my heart as you did. Mommy did too, because she is agreeing with me."

"The same goes here with us," spoke up Wendy and David.

"Me too, Dad." responded Mindy.

"And us." said Norman and Sally.

Nathan leaped to his feet and ran to his Dad and Mom, embracing them in affectionate love.

Gene sat quietly, beaming with joy that three families had been saved and entered into the Kingdom of God. He thought heaven must be like this. Here with these families were joy, praise, and gladness. Yes, heaven must be like this moment.

Suddenly, with a deep strong voice, Joe began singing: "Amazing grace, how sweet the sound, that saved a wretch like me. I once was lost, but now I'm found, was blind, but now I see." Callie joined in as the two sang: "When We've been there ten thousand years, bright, shinning as the sun. We've no less days to sing God's praise, than when we first begun."

Many comments were made, by parents and children, about their immediate future. All agreed, and planned, to be in Spring Hollow Baptist Church on Sunday morning. This would be the first time in their family history to be in church together.

Gene, Lindy, Callie, and Joe left the three families to themselves until Sunday morning. They had witnessed the work of God tonight as they had witnessed in their own families. Each reflected on the whole week; the school experience of many students being saved, and three sister families accepting God's salvation tonight. For them it was spiritual growth and commitment to Jesus. What would become of their lives, no one knew? Only God held that secret, and He would reveal it in His own time. When Joe stopped his car at Gene's house, Lindy asked if she could lead them in prayer.

"Sure thing, Sis." responded Gene.

"Lord, what our eyes has seen and our ears have heard tonight is of Your love and is most holy. Thank you for allowing four young people to witness Your power and saving grace. We are undeserving of such blessings. Yet, You chose to let us be your servants for tonight and boldly say what You did for us and our families. Thank You for the Wilson and Britton families. Please, wrap Your arms around us and guide us into a surrendered life for Your kingdom. I pray in Jesus Name."

"Amen. Thanks, Lindy." said Callie, as she gave her a hug. "We'll see you Sunday at church."

180

Chapter 18

Mrs. Wilma

Sunday was glorious day at the Spring Hollow Baptist Church. No time in the church's history had it experienced such revival and particularly on this day. The congregation singing was revealing. The choir special was not too outstanding, but well done. The pastor's preaching was strong, informative, and compassionate. Most importance, the congregation was expecting the Holy Spirit to reveal His power. This worship attitude had become paramount in every service, even the Wednesday night service. The Sunday evening service had long ceased being a time to conclude the day. Also, this was true with the Wednesday night prayer meeting. The midweek service had truly become a time of great expectation and closeness with Jesus.

When the invitation time came for anyone, or whosoever would surrender their lives to Jesus; David and Wendy Wilson and their three children, Altha, Ben, and Mindy; Norman and Sally Wilson and their three children, Earl, Nathan, and Lynn; and Ted and Angela Britton and their two children, Andy and Will, fourteen in all, and all kin, came confessing Jesus Christ as their Savior and Lord.

Stanley and Hannah Jean Windham came on transfer of church letter. Stanley is a physician, and Hannah is a nurse. They are mission volunteers waiting for the Foreign Mission Board's appointment.

Wilma Lucky, a longtime member of the church and old in years and very feeble, asked to be helped to her feet. She then proceeded to walk very slowly down the isle. She had to hold to the pews as she walked along to keep from falling. The church became silent. Folks were wondering why Wilma was going forward. Gene Jones stepped alongside her and asked permission to help her along. She took hold of his arm and said:

"Thank you, young man. You are a blessing."

"My pleasure, Mrs. Wilma."

Wilma held out her hand to Brother Timothy as she said aloud so all could hear:

"Brother Timothy, I'm publicly trusting Jesus Christ as my Savior today. I want to be baptized and become a member of Spring Hollow Baptist Church. When I was a little girl, about twelve years of age, I joined this church. But, I wasn't saved, nor have I been all these years. Last month, I was convicted by the Holy Spirit about this matter. I asked the Lord Jesus to forgive my sin and trusted Him as Savior and Lord of my life. I know now, for sure, that I'm saved, willing to follow and serve my Lord and go to Heaven when He calls me."

Wilma Lucky turned and slowly walked to the front pew and sat down. Brother Timothy did not have an opportunity to respond to her decision. He accepted her decision as from the Lord. All the church heard her profession of faith. As they listened, tears flowed freely. There did not seem to be a dry eye in the house.

A little girl was overheard asking her mother about Mrs. Wilma. Everyone believed her to be such a good person. "Mother, why did Mrs. Wilma need to be saved? She has always been real good and kind."

"Everyone needs Jesus, child, the good as well as the bad."

Dick Reveere signaled the choir to stop singing and to be seated. The congregation followed their action.

"Praise the Lord!" said Timothy. "You have witnessed His presence and work today. His power is a marvelous display to our eyes. I don't deserve what I've witnessed for the past year and a half, neither do you. But, Aren't we all wonderfully blessed for having seen this? Let's welcome these families into the family of God. Mrs. Wilma, you may sit in this chair for your comfort."

"Thank you, Brother Timothy. By the time all these people come by, I might get a little tired if I had to stand. I know most, but I'll enjoy all the hugs I'll get."

The congregation responded lovingly to Mrs. Wilma. She was that good person everyone knew and loved. But, the church folk witnessed one of their members being saved. Her act caused serious searching of the soul by many. To many, the Scripture came to mind in their search: "Man looks on the outward appearance, but God looks on the heart." Mrs. Wilma made the decision of trust to be saved, and to Whom she knew, would get her to heaven. To her, it was Jesus only, and no one else.

Brother Timothy asked the congregation at the evening worship service to prepare for baptism soon as possible. The weather was warming a bit, for the winter chill was beginning to be replaced by early morning warmth and sunshine. It was the middle of May. The last Sunday afternoon was selected.

The number to be baptized was, by far, the largest ever recorded by the church. What was happening in Spring Hollow Baptist Church was proof that preparations be made in the new building for indoor baptizing or a baptistry. In earlier time in the church history, summer revivals produced nearly all candidates for baptism. The creek, known as Spring Hollow Creek, was sufficient. And, it was always an unusually joyous time for the church to gather at the creek for their summer baptismal service.

If all continued to go well, and there were no setbacks by the weather, this summer outdoors baptizing would be the last for Spring Hollow Baptist Church. The new church was already being prepared. This building program was the only one since the present structure was built many years ago. Spring Hollow Baptist was not building for the sake of a new church building, but out of necessity. The new church building was designed for several years in the future. Everyone was excited about what was happening in Spring Hollow.

Another fascinating thing about the church was its financial growth. There had been no emphasis made toward giving by anyone. Giving to the Lord in response to His saving grace and happiness was accepted to be right and just. The Bible said it was so and the people obeyed. To disobey God in the matter of personal finance was as sinful as denying Him personal talents to His glory, or to be a witness at anytime an opportunity afforded itself. Bible study in the home, church, at school, or some workplaces were daily events. No one portrayed a fanatical attitude. Rather, it was an inner urge of hunger and thirst to know what God was saying and wanted each to know. The simplicity of working out, what God was putting in, became common practice. Spring Hollow Baptist Church members were doers of God's Word and not hearers only. It was the New Testament belief being empowered and led by the Holy Spirit in bodies of clay, which have been regenerated. The old self was gone. The verse from the old hymn, "Since Jesus Came Into My Heart" says it right; "What a wonderful change in my life has been wrought, since Jesus came into my heart."

Chapter 19

The Second Summer Baptizing

The new church building was not ready for use. The winter weather had hindered building progress. However, it was no concern to the folk at spring Hollow Baptist Church. They would just have another great rejoicing at the creek, in an old-time baptizing worship service.

It was decided that the third Sunday afternoon in May would be the time for the first baptizing. April had been warm, and if the weather didn't change too much, Spring Hollow Creek should be fairly warm for the baptizing. Prayers were being offered to the Lord for beautiful weather. And, as Spring Hollow folk believed, God did give warm and pleasant weather.

Preparations were made at the creek, as were done last summer, for a large number to be baptized. The candidates were asked to bring blankets or large heavy towels to wrap around them when coming out of the water for the short walk to the tents. This was a good precaution for not getting too chilled. It was also a time that the church prayed for the health of its new members. Baptizing in Spring Hollow was a joyous occasion, a real worship experience.

Following the example of last year, at baptizing times, no night worship service was held at the church. The people made the decision, and it proved a good practice. Here to fore, it had been a rush to return home, do all the chores, and return to church on time. Since the baptizing service was a singing and praise time, and above all, a mighty demonstration of personal testimonies; all were assured the time with family was well spent on Sunday evening. Many visited each other's families, because time allowed it. Most family visits during the week were denied due to work schedules.

The third Sunday in May arrived. It was again announced at the morning services that everything was ready for the afternoon baptizing in Spring Hollow Creek, at 2:30. Among the numbers to be baptized, were four families; two Wilson's, one Britton, all kin, and the Jones's.

Dick led the people in singing "Shall We Gather at the River." It was a refreshing hymn. On the last stanza. Timothy waded into the water to a proper depth for the candidates. Josh White and Jake Willoby followed Timothy into the water for the purpose of safety and assurance of their help if needed. The water was a bit chilly, but not too uncomfortable.

The Jones family was first to be baptized. Jeanette was first. Then the two children, Gene and Lindy. Johnny was last and showed deep emotions for his family. David Wilson's family was next. Mendy, and last David. Next, Norman Wilson's family. Sally first, and then the three children, Carl, Nathan, and Lynn. Last was Norman. Next was Ted Britton's family. Angela was first and the two children, Andy and Will, and last Ted. As each family came out of the water, the congregation applauded and with many "Amens."

Dick led the people in singing "I'll Go Where You Want Me to Go," as Timothy and the two deacons walked out of the water. While the folk changed out of the wet clothes, the people had a good fellowship time. Then, all the baptized formed a line for the church welcome as all sang "What a Friend We Have in Jesus." Timothy spoke a few words of encouragement and led in the closing prayer, thanking Jesus for a wonderful experience in worship.

Chapter 20

Marriage Proposal

The summer church activities went very well. Everything was far above average. The Vacation Bible School attendance and missions offering exceeded all expectations.

Betty Archer proved her worth. The testimony she gave about the assurance of her call to the mission field fit the demeanor of her conduct. Spring Hollow Baptist was very pleased with her. In fact, they assured her that a return visit was absolute. What they didn't know, nor could have known, was that Betty Archer would return to Spring Hollow for a long time.

Two more very unusual baptism services were held during the summer. They were the results of Spring Hollow Baptist membership doing what they ought. No revival was scheduled this summer. No special revival services were needed. Spring Hollow Baptist Church had been in revival for several months. It was God's way of doing things as He had planned. At several worship services and Wednesday night prayer services, personal testimonies would be given. People felt fine to speak about what Jesus Christ was doing in their lives. These times were wholly given their place.

Timothy had no need to preach. It didn't bother him at all. He rejoiced with the good folk as Jesus was working His will among His people. Several people had been saved because of the strong spiritual testimonies of young and old alike. During one baptism service, two families were baptized. What a change Jesus was working in the Spring Hollow Community!

Timothy had made all preparations for his third and final year at Seminary. Instead of plans to stay in his old room at the dorm, he decided to commute from Spring Hollow. His decision to commute was good news for all the church folk. If needed for any emergency situation, he would be nearby. Frank and Millie were very pleased. Millie had thoroughly enjoyed having her son through the summer. Now, Timothy would be there all year. She thanked God daily for him.

The third year of Seminary seemed to fly by. It was a challenge and blessing to commute to school. Two evenings each week would be spent in library research. This, too, was no chore. God was blessing so wonderfully at Spring Hollow. That time spent in school gave Timothy opportunity to pray, prepare for his people and share with other students his many experiences.

Timothy and Betty saw a great deal of each other. Betty seemed to grow on Timothy, and he liked what he was feeling. Betty acknowledged that she was very fond of Timothy. This relationship grew beyond fondness to that of falling in love. They finally agreed that they were brought together by the Lord and for His purpose. Neither knew what God's purpose was. Betty thought God was preparing them, as husband and wife, for the mission field. Timothy believed Jesus was conditioning them for a rich pastorate. They both agreed that whatever the outcome, God's will must be done. Neither would question His wisdom.

During one library study period, Timothy and Betty became frustrated about their inability to grasp the truth of their dilemma. They both needed an answer from God for their future, her for foreign missions, and he for the pastorate. Timothy reached across the table, took Betty's hand, and invited Betty to pray with him. When Timothy said "Amen." he looked into Betty eyes and said:

"Betty, my dear friend and the girl I love, will you become my wife? I want to become your husband."

"Timothy, I love you and believe God sent you to me to be my husband, and I your wife. Yes, I will become your wife. I believe we both received our answer during the prayer. I'll marry you and believe God will work out all His plans for our life."

Marriage could not be until after the end of the school year. It was left up to Betty to set the date, time, and place. She promised Timothy to give him an answer within two months. In the meantime, their secret would remain between them. Their choice of each other for marriage released a stressful burden;

and in its place, brought joy and peace. For the next several weeks, Timothy felt as if he had passed a great milestone in his life. The people at Spring Hollow knew something had happened, but did not know what. They were reluctant to ask Timothy. His preaching was strong, positive, and purposeful. His energy was remarkable. He visited in homes of people, within a twelve-mile area, that never had a preacher to show any interest. On the other hand, people from these homes were visiting regularly, or becoming members of Spring Hollow Baptist Church by profession of faith or transfer of church membership. Each Sunday the worship services were packed to standing room only.

Six weeks had passed, and Betty had not mentioned their wedding plans.

"Timothy, I'm going home after classes on Friday. I'll have our answer when I return Monday. Let's have lunch together on Tuesday and talk about it. Is that OK?"

"Sounds good to me, Betty. I'm anxious to announce the wedding to my family and to my church. Hey, I've got a good idea. Since my family has not met you, Let's go to Willow Bend on the following Saturday and give them a big surprise. And then, on Sunday, I'll break the news to my church."

"Let's do just that. Can I have your permission to tell my family who I'm planning to marry, when I go home? They don't know anything about this part of my life. I've kept it from them, as you have, until now."

"By my leave, tell them." said Timothy.

Timothy asked John Canton for a brief time to make an announcement to the deacons, after their prayer time on Sunday morning.

"Gentlemen." Timothy began, "I have a deep secret to share with you. I want your word not to reveal it to anyone, not even to your wives. I must go to Willow Bend next Sunday. That's not the secret, but part of it. You see; I'm getting married. I ..."

"Wow! Brother Timothy. We thought this was something very strange, as you put it, a secret. We knew something has

189

been happening, but none of us knew what. Boy, oh boy! We are glad." said Josh.

"Maybe I went about this in a wrong way. At least it sounds odd now, to think about it. Well, I wanted to break the news to my parents and church at Willow Bend first. Then I wanted to announce it here so that it would not come as second hand information. Ya'll do understand? However, you will keep it a secret, won't you?"

"Sure thing, Timothy We are delighted to hear this good news." said Jake.

"This will be a first for Spring Hollow, Timothy All our past pastors have been middle aged or more and married with families. I'll betcha you and your bride will be treated special here. By the way, who is she?" Wiley asked.

"I was coming to that, but I got sidetracked." laughed Timothy, and the deacons laughed with him. "She is Betty Archer, the young mission volunteer who visited us last July. I am convinced that God has made this choice for us both. We both have prayed much about our decision. We are happy. Betty is breaking the news to her parents today."

"Now, getting back to next Sunday. Do I need to ask someone to preach in my place only for Sunday morning? I'll be back Sunday night." said Timothy.

John Canton spoke up: "If you men don't mind, I would like to speak at the morning service next Sunday. I've been wanting to encourage our people about a couple of things. Is this O.K. with you men?" asked John.

"Sounds good." responded Rufus.

"Brother Timothy, we will keep your secret."

With this assurance, the deacons went to their Sunday School classes.

Timothy met Betty at a coffee break on Tuesday morning. They talked briefly about their coming event and the trip to Willow Bend on the weekend. Since it would require extended mileage for Timothy to return to the Seminary on Saturday to pick Betty up, they decided to make arrangements for her to spend Friday night in Spring Hollow. It would also be arranged for her to spend Sunday and Monday nights, since they would be returning from Willow Bend on Sunday afternoon.

Timothy announced to the church on Wednesday evening that Brother John Canton would speak at the Sunday morning worship service. The church was encouraged to be present and hear what he would say about the future of their church, preparing for its growth. These times were exciting in Spring Hollow. Everyone seemed pleased. The Holy Spirit was doing a work that no one could take credit for. It was truly a time of rejoicing.

Timothy asked Ada Jenkins if she would consider letting Betty spend the night with her, since she was single and a very active member of the Singles Sunday School class.

"Brother Timothy, I'm thrilled that you asked me to do this. Becky and I had talked about doing something for Betty the next time she visited us. This is great! You don't mind Becky's involvement, I hope?"

"Not at all, Ada. You women do what seems best for you. While we are discussing Betty, she will be here on Sunday and Monday nights. I'm taking her to Willow Bend on Saturday to meet my family. We'll be back around 4:00 p.m. on Sunday afternoon. On Monday, I plan to give her a good tour of Spring Hollow and our town. We'll probably eat lunch in town."

"I'll prepare for her, and we'll enjoy her company. Becky will surely want her to stay at her house on Sunday night. But, you just don't worry about a thing. Brother Timothy, you just don't know how much the folk here appreciate you, and now you are bringing Betty, and we all suspect, to be with us permanently, if you are listening to what I'm saying? Are you listening?"

"I think I am. Is it that obvious? I've tried hard to keep it a secret. But, you won't tell until we return from Willow Bend?"

"I promise, not even to Becky. And now, about Monday at lunch, would you allow three of your single women members to honor you and Betty at lunch in town? We often lunch together and would be overly pleased to have you two join us."

"I'll agree for both of us, now. But you might mention it to Betty on Saturday evening."

"We'll be listening for you to reveal the secret and all the plans Sunday night. Have a good trip, Brother Timothy"

Timothy and Betty arrived in Willow Bend about 1:00 p.m. on Saturday. Timothy's two sisters, Eunice and Bernice, were having a ball washing their car and getting each other wet. Both were in college, Eunice in her senior year and Bernice in her freshman year. There were four years differences in their ages. As Timothy drove into the driveway and came to a stop, both girls called out:

"Hi, Timothy, big brother. Welcome home."

"Hello, girls. It appears you two are full of mischief. Is it safe to get out?"

"Not if you are unwilling to get wet." said Bernice.

"I have a friend I want you to meet. She's special."

Eunice and Bernice threw down the water hose and wet wash cloths and ran to meet Betty.

"Girls, meet Betty Archer. Betty, these are my mischievous sisters, Eunice and Bernice."

"Hi, Betty. Welcome to our home. We have heard so much about you."

"Hello, Bernice and Eunice. I'm glad to meet you. I've heard a lot about you two, also." The girls hugged Betty and Timothy, even though they were wet.

"If all Timothy has said about you is true, you two sisters will be very special to me. But, men do not know all the good makeup of us women. So, I'll be privileged to add my values about you. Just give me a little time." said Betty.

"Timothy may have exaggerated, Betty. We have given him a hard time down through the years." said Eunice.

"We are proud of Timothy, Betty. And, we are very happy that you two met." said Bernice.

Just then Karen Karr came onto the porch, with a big smile. With a jubilant voice, she called out: "Welcome home son. Bring your beautiful friend to me that I might meet her. Oh, you are so beautiful. Welcome to our home. Karen gave Betty a long, motherly hug. You are more than what Timothy had described."

"Hey there." roared Rance Karr. "Who do we have here?"

"This is Betty, Daddy." said Eunice.

"Welcome, Betty, to our home. My, my, Timothy didn't tell the half about you. We'll forgive him though, or thank him for letting us make up our own mind about you. You are just lovely," said Rance.

"Hi, Dad, Mom. It's good to be home. I'm glad you approve of Betty. She is special to me, and I believe will be a great addition to our family. said Timothy.

"I'll say, amen to that, son." said Karen.

Dinner was served with all the good hospitality the Karr family could muster. It was 3:00 p.m. before anyone suggested clearing the table. Both family histories were thoroughly discussed. It was decided that God had brought these two families together for some great future purpose. They would wait for His will to be done and would not ever question His judgment.

Willow Bend Baptist Church was very pleased to welcome their young preacher home for the day. They were as pleased to welcome Betty to their church and God's plan for her life in association with that of Timothy's life calling.

During their return to Spring Hollow on Sunday afternoon, Timothy and Betty made plans for Timothy to visit her family. Until then, Betty's family had not met her future husband. They only knew him as Timothy Karr, and a student in Seminary. It would be another month before this visit would take place.

Upon arrival in the Spring Hollow community, about 4:30 p.m., Timothy drove directly to Becky Skelton's home. Becky was expecting Betty and had everything arranged for her comfort. It was a joy to have Betty stay in her home. The two women exchanged hugs and kisses and told Timothy to go on about his business. They would see him at church later that evening.

As Timothy drove to his church home at Frank and Millie Stewart's, he thanked God for such good, dependable people.

193

Surely, it was a great joy to serve the Lord among such a great community of people.

Millie had supper ready and within a few minutes, Timothy was enjoying the warm fellowship of Frank and Millie. It never ceased to be a wonderful joy to the Stewart's to have their son home and enjoying Millie's cooking. They both knew that one day Timothy would be gone. But, for now, Timothy was a great comfort to two aging people. Many a time since Timothy's coming to them, Millie reflected on the experience of Hannah of the Old Testament and Elizabeth in the New Testament.

John Canton met Timothy as his car came to a stop.

"Good evening, Brother John. How has the day gone? I bet your sermon was right on target." chided Timothy.

"Howdy, Timothy. Yes, everything went well here. There was such a good response to what I said that the entire congregation stood in approval. Along with two committees, the deacons will inform you about our church plans. You'll be happy. Now, about your secret, will our church hear about it tonight? They are expecting something, but no one knows what. Someone asked if you were away preaching somewhere in view of a call. I told them, no, that you needed to go home for a day."

"I'm pleased to hear all this, John. Yes, I'm telling my secret. But, It's not so much a secret anymore. Ada, Becky, and Marie had already figured out what was about to happen. However, neither have said anything."

"Brother Timothy, our folk in Spring Hollow are family wise and discrete. Perhaps after tonight, you will have several to say to you, "I thought so." about your secret. But, you and Betty can be sure they all have your interest at heart. We all love you, and we will love Betty too." said John.

"I am very fortunate to be the pastor of Spring Hollow Baptist Church." responded Timothy.

"About today and all that was said and planned, the folk asked that we spend Wednesday evening prayer time to further discuss the needs of our church. You, Brother Timothy, will be pleased with what we are thinking and planning. I'm overjoyed

194

with the positive spirit our church has committed itself to do the Lord's work. Another great thing happened today. Gordon Lamb, an auto mechanic, and David Brown accepted Jesus as Savior and Lord of their lives. We handled everything just fine. We were the Lord's church doing its work." said John.

"I'll say amen to that." Timothy said.

Church Training was over, and the people were hastily making their way to the auditorium. As usual, the church was packed. The people were jubilant. Brother Dick Reveere asked the congregation to sing, "Blessed Assurance, Jesus is Mine." This great hymn, sung as only the people of Spring Hollow Baptist could, set the worship tone for the evening worship service. After a warm welcome by Brother Timothy, prayer and announcements, Dick Reveere challenged the choir to out-sing the congregation in singing "We're Marching to Zion." The singing by the congregation sounded as if any voice could be a legitimate choir member. The children rejoiced because they had been a part of this great singing. People wept unashamedly, and joy filled their hearts.

Finally, Brother Timothy came to the pulpit. He announced, with hesitation but clearly, the plans for his marriage to Betty Archer.

"Amen. Praise the Lord." someone said.

There was laughter and clapping of hands for a minute or so. Someone else said,

"You are full of surprises, pastor. We like what we are hearing."

"This will be a first at our church, Brother Timothy" chimed in another.

Timothy stood speechless for a moment. Then he said:

"For the benefit of some who have not seen, nor met, Betty Archer, I need to introduce her to you. Betty, will you stand so that all may see what a beautiful girl you are? Betty is a mission volunteer and presently in her second year seminary preparation. We will let you know, soon, about the wedding date. Until then, we should get on with our worship services."

Chapter 21

First Wedding Plans

Timothy and Betty met at the Seminary Library after the last morning class. Since neither had another class schedule until 2:00, they decided to go off campus to a fairly small restaurant, but with very good food, near the edge of the city. They wanted to be as private as possible. Today, they would decide the date of their marriage. Both had mentioned the latter part of July as the marriage date for some time. The details would be worked out today during this meal. Betty seemed relaxed, but anxious for her marriage to Timothy be finalized.

"Timothy, I'm suggesting the third Sunday in July for our wedding. Is that O.K. with you?"

"That is the best date we could choose, Betty. I've thought about any later date would be too close to you starting your last year at Seminary. Let's make it final."

"I hoped you would agree, Timothy I believe our families would be in agreement, with their time and plans, to share with us in this great moment of our lives." Betty smiled broadly, and Timothy answered with a hearty chuckle.

"Your words are great wisdom to me, dear."

"Now, now, Let's don't go too far with that kind of talk. I might change so much that you would need to retract your words."

"I'm surrendered! I'll bear the burden and hope for the best." responded Timothy.

"Now, hear me out on some thoughts I've had about our marriage. I have not been able to dismiss from my mind. Will you help me, my dear Timothy?"

"Sure, I'll listen. It must be pretty good that it does not allow your peace of mind." laughed Timothy.

"I think it is a good and practical plan. Here it is. Timothy, my family is not wealthy. They fall far short of that goal. A large church wedding is out of the question. My parents struggle to keep me in Seminary. I want you to know this now, and also that you are not marrying a middle income society girl. The expense for the wedding ceremony would be prohibitive."

"Your own family, Timothy, is not able to share their part for you. Your sisters are in college, and I believe your parents are strapped with a heavy financial burden. Many more factors enter our immediate future that we do not realize now. They are just waiting to happen."

"Now, the big question to you. You have been all ears, I've noticed. What do you think about our getting married at the Spring Hollow Baptist Church?"

"Wow! How about that! Wow! What a brilliant thought. Betty, my love, you are a wonderful girl."

"Well, you surprise me, Timothy I didn't know, nor had I any way of expecting, how you would react to my idea as you have. But, I'm proud of your acceptance."

"Allow me to further interest you about some plans. Our families could come to Spring Hollow. They have never seen our new home place. It would do them well to visit on this occasion. I believe both families will like the idea. I'm sure the folk at Spring Hollow Baptist Church will thrill over such plans; don't you, my future husband?"

"Why, Betty, I'm convinced our church will go all out to make it a great event. They love us, my dear girl. Our wedding would be another first for the church."

"But, Timothy, Let's not permit our wedding to become a big affair. That's what I'm trying to prevent. Let's make it a church-wide worship wedding. And, Let's have it at the morning worship service. Your home church pastor can preach that morning and marry us at the close of the service. Doesn't that sound great? My pastor will not be able to attend."

"Yes, it does, Betty. You know, Betty, I am convinced that I'm getting a very intelligent girl for my wife. Don't you agree?"

"No, Timothy, I'm only a plain down-to-earth girl who believes God's economy is worth more than ours. A wedding of two of His children in this type setting will honor His institution of marriage and greatly honor our Heavenly Father."

"We have talked about all these plans, but we do not know if Spring Hollow Church will accept it. You better ask this week, Timothy. If they accept, we will plan. If not, we will have to go another direction."

"I'll do just that, Betty. However, I'm a believer in these folk. If my feelings are correct, they will rejoice to have their young pastor and his beloved fiancee wed in their church. It would be nice were it to take place in the new sanctuary. But, that is not possible. For now, my dear, we had better get back on campus and to class. It's been an enjoyable lunch, don't you agree?"

"Yes, it has, and very important. Do you sense the Lord Jesus is preparing us for some special work in His Kingdom, Timothy?"

"Anything Jesus wants to do with us is acceptable to me, Betty. Will it be the same for you?"

"I'm a believer, Timothy Whatever are the plans of God, are acceptable to me also."

Timothy was nervous and somewhat reluctant to ask the folk of Spring Hollow Baptist Church for permission to be wed in their church. He stammered through a couple of announcements hesitating to present his case. He had believed all details had been worked out in his mind. But, now he was not sure. Finally, he said:

"I have one final announcement and request to make. Please don't judge me too harshly. Betty and I have set the third Sunday in July for our wedding date."

The congregation applauded heartily. There were even some low-key whistles.

Timothy continued, "With your permission, we would like for the wedding to be here, with you folk."

Again, he was interrupted by applause. Someone said, "It couldn't have a better setting, Brother Timothy." Everyone was jubilant.

Timothy continued, "The reason for such a request is that Betty and I thought it would be proper and right to have your young pastor and his wife wed in the church he was serving. We discussed it thoroughly and came to believe it a good idea.

"My pastor will preach the morning message, and at the close, we will bravely stand before you very good, kind, and loving people and be wed by him. Betty's pastor will not be able to attend, but her family will. My family will drive down for the special occasion. Her family will travel too far for a one-day trip. The wedding will not be elaborate, no frills, just a worship service with you dear folk."

Brother John Canton walked to the pulpit. Timothy stepped aside so that John could face the congregation.

"Do I hear a motion from the church that we grant our Pastor's request to be wed at Spring Hollow Baptist Church?"

Alice Dubose stood immediately. "Brother moderator, I move that we allow our pastor and his dear beautiful bride to be wed here with all our blessings."

Seconds to the motion came from everyone. Even the children chimed in.

"All in favor, say amen."

"Amen, amen." roared the congregation.

"Then, it shall be so ordered." said John.

John turned to Timothy, "Brother Timothy, my dear friend and pastor, you are a miracle to us. Since you came, we have not stopped having first things happening to us. What a time to be in fellowship with Jesus!"

"Thank you my dear lovable people. It's a joy to be serving the Lord here in Spring Hollow. You are a wonderful family. I've never heard before, a congregation willing to be led by the Holy Spirit as you are. It really seems that I do nothing, but you are doing everything right. No one, no committee has to beg you to serve the Lord. All of us are growing so fast in the knowledge of Jesus Christ. We are all so happy. People from all sections of the State, and some out of State, have heard of your commitment to the Lord Jesus. Let's keep our lives pliable to the Lord's use. Jesus is doing a great kingdom work here in Spring Hollow. We are all pleased that He is using us to the glory of His Great Name. amen."

"My sermon thoughts are based on Matthew 5:6: "Blessed are those who hunger and thirst for righteousness, for they shall

199

be satisfied." Timothy continued emphasis upon the nature of being devoid of life's necessities; the danger and consequences of neglect. He made comparison to the spiritual needs of people. When the right decisions are made for the benefit of life, healthy bodies, minds, and attitudes are the result. It is also true when He, who is the source of our spiritual needs, is asked for help, we are filled up to complete fullness, forever and satisfied.

Timothy stated the purpose of the invitation. The burden was left to each person to make his or her decision; what will you do with Jesus?

Dick Reveere announced the invitation hymn, "Jesus Is Tenderly Calling." The sound of many voices were echoing the call as if to each other. It was a strong pleading call.

Susie was not singing, but praying for her brother Mike. She still held onto his hand believing her touch would affect Mike to surrender to Jesus. Suddenly, Mike released her grief and moved from the pew into the church isle and walked toward Brother Timothy Susie wanted to go with her brother, but held back. It was his decision. She could tell him later of her joy. Mike spoke to Timothy about rededication of his life to Jesus. Many changes would be radical, but very necessary. His promise to Jesus was that he would not forsake his Savior again. He knew that his life had been miserable and without purpose. Now, it would have meaning.

Chapter 22

The Treasured Gifts

Timothy arrived at his new home, feeling very good about his day the Lord Jesus had blessed him with.

"Good afternoon, Mrs. Millie. Have you had a good day?"

"Yes, both of us have." said Millie. "Frank has been quiet, but busy. That's a good sign he is happy. We've missed you, though. Will you be here for supper? Frank has something on his mind to discuss with you."

"I'll be around. Right now I want a glass of ice tea, which I'll get, and then sit on the porch for a spell. I have some meditating to do."

Timothy sprawled himself onto the swing with his feet hoisted high on one arm of the swing, while his head rested on a pillow on the other. He was comfortable, contended, and above every thing else, happy.

He was awakened by a gentle touch on the shoulder. With a show of a little embarrassment, he sat upright and attempted to explain what happened to his meditation.

"You have been asleep for an hour, son." said Frank.

"I must have been tired." responded Timothy.

"You probably are from what you have been through for the past several days. Don't apologize for a good nap. I came out earlier to talk with you about a matter of importance, but you were resting, and I would not disturb your rest. We'll talk about it at supper, which is now ready, that is if you are awake." laughed Frank.

"I'm ready, and I'm also hungry." said Timothy.

Millie was pleased with her new responsibility of preparing additional food for her expanded family, her pastor, Timothy. Frank was pleased also, that he had another man to share his interests during his aging years. After Frank thanked God for their food and care of the family, the three filled their plates with delicious food of Millie's special cooking. Minor chit-chat of the day's activities was said, and then Frank asked to be heard about a proposal he had in mind, and had prayed about a great deal.

"Timothy, our church building is in dire need of expansion, as you well know. Millie and I have no heir to leave our fortune, however much that might be. We have discussed selling most all our land and giving the proceeds to Spring Hollow Baptist Church. That would be a considerable sum. We also have accumulated a sizeable amount of money in the stocks and bonds over the many years. Right now, they are not doing anyone any good. They are worth a little fortune. We are planning on liquidating them into cash. After all taxes are paid, we are giving the remainder to our church for building purposes. Again, I say, we have prayed about this gift for some time. This is not something we are doing for publicity, but for the glory of God. Whatever we have is a gift from Him. He has allowed us to manage what is His; now we are returning it to Him in our old age, I hope with interest."

"Our church building has been adequate for us folk, middle-aged and up, but it is not so for the future generations. Our community and church are growing rapidly. Spring Hollow children and youth need new and larger facilities to accommodate their spiritual growth. Millie and I are proud to be a part of this preparation. I'm convinced we should begin within the year."

"I'm not a deacon, nor a member of any committee. I'm too old to function in these responsibilities. I trust the good membership of our church to do the best and right thing. I have mentioned this to John Canton, not in detail, but casually. He agrees, as well as several others, that we must do something soon."

"Timothy, what I say to you now is personal about you and is the thoughts of all the church. You are humble, not pushy. What you told us the first Sunday you visited spread through this community like wildfire. We liked what we heard and do believe Jesus sent you to lead us in His great blessings. It's time of the young to dream and the old to see visions. The two must mesh and become reality. Many others, besides Millie and myself, will be partners in this venture."

"At the next business meeting I want our proposal to be presented, if the deacons concur. There will be no strings attached. It is a stewardship adventure, and we want Jesus to be praised. What do you think about this, Timothy?"

"If I would do what I feel like doing, I'd jump up and shout for the next hour. But, I am shouting! It's glorious! You are doing what Jesus blessed you to do. Frank, you and Millie are responding to a need God designed for you, and you are doing it to His glory. That's what He wants from his children. I say amen to your decision."

All the time Frank was speaking, Millie was crying quietly; and her face was radiating the love of Jesus. Even though she had never given birth to a child, her children would continue to be born in Spring Hollow and beyond because she helped plan God's kingdom, here, for their spiritual welfare. She, too, was shouting.

Timothy prayed at the end of supper time:

"Lord Jesus, You have heard far more than I because You interpreted the hearts of Frank and Millie. I heard a response to Your love. You, Lord, put Your love in their hearts. Thank You, Lord Jesus. We await the leadership of Your Holy Spirit in this matter for the community and to Your glory. Give us wisdom to do Your will. May Your peace abound in every thing Spring Hollow Baptist Church does. I ask these petitions in Jesus' name. amen."

Pete and Sandy Carter owned 25 acres of timberland joining the Spring Hollow Baptist Church property. For some time, since the death of the two widows, they had discussed selling this tract of land to homeowners. No one had approached them about buying any acreage of this particular property. It had never occurred to them that the church might need a new site for future building until the quarterly business meeting of the church.

When Frank presented the proposal he and Millie had agreed upon, Pete whispered to Sandy and said, "Honey, we can be a great help in this matter of future building. Since we have not offered our land for sale, Let's consider offering our church some acreage for expansion."

"Sounds good. It's O.K. with me. We don't need it anyway. Do you want to make the offer tonight?" asked Sandy.

"Why not? Since the interest is running so high about building, this seems to be the right time." said Pete.

"Brother John, I mean Brother Moderator." Pete's voice was clear as he stood up.

"Sandy and I have an offer to make to the church. It has to do with our land that joins the church property. If the church will accept it, we want to make available enough land to satisfy future building needs. We offer this in good faith and with no strings attached." said Pete.

Laird Dubose rose slowly to his feet. He cleared his throat as if he was very nervous.

"Ah, Brother John, I've been a member of some other churches in my life. Neither of them showed interest in community needs and mission causes as Spring Hollow Baptist. This church wants to prepare for a long time. Our great grandchildren will benefit from our plans today. I believe this is the right spirit, and we are heading in the right direction. This has not always been the spirit of Spring Hollow Baptist. But, the revival God is blessing us with now, is the real purpose of His will for us. I'm glad to be alive and witness what's happening here. There were several loud amens. I also believe we all should commit ourselves in applying our talents to the use of these gifts real soon." Several praises and amens followed his comments.

The Treasurer, Brother Jake Dawson, gave the financial status of the church.

"Brethren." said Jake, "Spring Hollow Baptist Church is financially sound. We have never had so much money at our disposal before, as we do now. All I can see is a very bright future for whatever we wish to do. I thank God for what our membership is doing."

The quarterly business meeting ended with the church singing, "Praise God from Whom all blessings flow."

Chapter 23

Timothy Karr's Ordination

At the regular monthly deacon's meeting, Timothy reminded the deacons that Spring Hollow Baptist Church should request his home church, Willow Bend Baptist, to take proper steps toward plans for his ordination. It was not that he wanted to be ordained for prestigious reasons, but for purposes dealing with legal matters; such as performing marriages, certain taxes, and legal paper signatures.

This matter was understood by the deacons to be proper and in order. The request was approved by the church in business meeting. The clerk wrote the request letter for ordination to their sister Baptist church in Willow Bend. Their action was approved, and the ordination date set for the second Sunday morning in June.

Several people from Spring Hollow Baptist made plans to attend. Since Timothy must be away and present for his own ordination, someone would have to speak in his absence. A number of persons were very capable to speak. There was never a shortage of talents. The continued revival was producing talented people who before never realized they had a talent of any kind. Even the youth were aware of their importance in God's kingdom, and offered themselves to whatever God wanted for them.

Dr. Stanley and Hannah Jean Windham were newcomers to Spring Hollow. They were Foreign Mission Volunteers awaiting their appointment. He had a strong testimony as to why he and his wife gave their lives for missions. It had been nearly a year since Betty Archer, also a Foreign Mission Volunteer, and soon to become Timothy's wife, had spoken at Spring Hollow. Stanley Windham was asked to speak at the morning worship service while Timothy was away. Everything went as it should at Spring Hollow. Stanley Windham was effective in his presentation and appeal to commitment of lives to Christ Jesus for whatever area He might choose.

Joe Sims went forward surrendering his life to Jesus call to the gospel ministry. For some time now, he knew this was what the Lord wanted of him. Joe's decision did not surprise the congregation. He asked for their prayers that his life would count big for Jesus.

Bart Dean walked calmly down the isle and stood by Joe. He said with strong conviction that he was giving his talents to the Lord in music. Bart was still in High School. He was liked by so many at school. Neither he nor Joe was ashamed to witness for Jesus. The church also had heard Bart's strong tenor voice on several occasions.

As these two young men stood before the church, Carl Sims, Joe's father, came to stand with his son. About the same time, Rufus Dean, Bart's father, did the same. The two boys were deeply moved to have their Dads stand by them and give their approval to the Lord's call.

The church wept, many aloud, as Callie began singing "I'll Tell The World That I'm a Christian." Everyone present greatly rejoiced in the Lord. Dick Reveere began singing "Leaning on the Everlasting Arms." At the end of the worship service, the benediction prayer was led by Jim Tilley, the Sunday School Director. The church gave their warmest congratulations to Joe and Bart. Carl and Rufus were very pleased. Stanley Windham was very happy to be a part of this great worship service. The church was very pleased and happy to have such a wonderful, committed man in their midst.

Betty was at her home on this day. She wanted to attend Timothy's ordination, but commitments at home prevented her from being present. Timothy would write her and give details of the ordination during the following week.

The ordination service was an unusual experience for Timothy and to most folk in Willow Bend Baptist Church. It had been twenty -five years since anyone had been ordained to the ministry or sent out as a missionary. Timothy gave his testimony again, about his call of the Lord. He mentioned the great revival going on in the Spring Hollow Community. He claimed no credit for anything happening, only that he was there and receiving many blessings from the Lord Jesus. Timothy reaffirmed his wedding date and asked all who would to come for the grand occasion. Willow Bend Baptist Church laid their hands on Timothy Karr as they asked God's blessings upon him. All the membership and Christian visitors prayed over him that God would empower His servant to His glory. Timothy was greatly impressed and deeply thankful to the Lord Jesus. Only God knew how effective Timothy would be in the future. Only God knew where he and Betty would be serving. All God required of Timothy was to be faithful and obedient.

When Timothy arrived back in Spring Hollow and to Frank and Millie's home, he got a big surprise from them as they related the wonderful worship experience.

"Timothy, my boy, I'm grateful to you for your choice to have Dr. Windham to speak. He said the right things and with deep conviction. Surely, the Lord will do great things with that young couple." said Frank.

"And, another wonderful thing happened, Timothy. Joe Sims surrendered to preach the gospel, and Bart Dean surrendered to the music ministry. Their Dads came forward and stood by them. It was a moving experience. Timothy, I just don't believe our Lord Jesus could ever blessed any other community more than He has us. I know we don't deserve it, but, I'm glad He is so forgiving. There are times I'm so happy that I almost lose my breath. I hope, Timothy, that many more of our youth and young adults will surrender their lives to the Lord. What we need to do is set up financial support for this very special cause. Don't you think it will work?" asked Millie.

"Well, I'm elated to hear this report. It is no secret that at the same time in Willow Bend we were experiencing a wonderful worship time. Yes, Millie, it would be wonderful for our church to assist our students financially in the Lord's work. Let's pray about this and later announce the Lord's leadership in the matter."

"Praise God for Joe and Bart. What two fine young men! I've watched their spiritual growth since I've been here. It's no surprise that the Lord has called them. He will call others later as He chooses. I believe every church should prepare young people for the Lord's Kingdom here on earth. If His church is not concerned about sending mission volunteers, preachers, music ministers, and many more, then it is failing the Lord Jesus. Surely, our Lord has a great mission for Spring Hollow Baptist Church. I wish, yea, I pray, that every church would experience what we are experiencing. I believe the key to all of it is obedience to the will of the Holy Spirit of God. This great revival is not what we are doing, but what He is doing. We are only the recipients of many blessings of grace." said Timothy

"Oh, I believe what you said is true. No one can change lives but God." responded Millie.

"Well, I better get out of this comfortable swing and get busy for tonight. Who knows what great blessings God has in store and ready to give it to us tonight. Let's go to His house of prayer believing He will."

"I'll say, amen to that son." said Frank.

Timothy called Dick Reveere and asked him to select "A Child of the King" as one of the hymns for the evening worship service. He also asked Dick to sing a solo, "Near To the Heart of God." It had been sometime since Dick had blessed them with his great voice. He could sing any hymn and make it sound fresh and new. Dick was indeed a blessing to the church.

Timothy assured the church tonight that he felt no different toward them and his Lord after the ordination. He was the same person committed to his dear Lord Jesus. The ordination of laying on of hands by the church was simply the completion of setting aside, for God's service, by the church and the church's support in his ministry. Timothy's obligation was to uphold every responsibility to the glory of God. If he ever dishonored his church, he would have already dishonored his Lord and Savior. His ordination was a covenant made through Willow Bend Baptist Church by Almighty God; and for the purpose of preaching the good news of His Son, Jesus Christ, wherever he would be sent.

Chapter 24

Horace

In the meantime, Gene was sitting in the front porch swing when his friend, Horace Dixon, drove up. The two young men were of the same age, and both were entering their senior year of high school. It had been more than three years since Horace had visited. Neither parents liked the other for various reasons. Two in particular, Johnny Jones was a whiskey drinker and mistreated his family. Jim Dixon was an atheist and bigot. This influence by parents affected the children's relationships. Several times, Horace and Gene had hard words but did not come to blows.

Since Gene's Christian conversion, their friendship had changed for the better. Horace was still reluctant to talk about God, Jesus Christ, church, or Christian faith. His Daddy had made his atheistic lifestyle to strongly mar the life of his son. Gene had been praying for him that some evidence of change might occur. Other Christian youth of their school and Spring Hollow Community were praying for Horace. What many had witnessed in others because of prayer, they believed could happen to Horace.

"Hey, Horace, my friend. Get out and come in."

"Hello, Gene. How's things going?"

"Fine. It has not been ten minutes ago that I was thinking about you. Now, here you are. What do you think about that, eh, Horace?"

"I don't rightly know, but it must be good. I've been wanting to come over and talk with you, privately, for some time. There are so many questions that I have no answers for. I trust you, Gene. Since you became a Christian, you have changed a lot."

"Horace, my friend, I'm delighted you came over. I may not have an answer to all your questions, but I'll help if I can. Gee, It's good to see you."

"Gene, all this Christian stuff that is happening around Spring Hollow Baptist Church has come way out where we live. All the talk about it at school has got me worried and all upset. To make things worse, I've tried to tell my parents what's going on, but I can't explain it as it should be said. To make things worse, they curse and fuss at me and even warn me of bad consequences. I've never been inside a church of any kind. Many times, as a small boy, I've wanted to and often wondered what all those people did when they were at a church house. Right now, I feel all alone. It seems everyone else is experiencing something good, and I'm left out. Am I all that bad, Gene? If there is a God, do you think He does not consider me as worthy as He does others, say like you? I really would like to be a part of whatever is going on. Really, I feel like I've been squeezed out like a sponge. Maybe it is all my fault. Anyhow, That's why I've come over to talk to you."

"Horace, you have told me more about yourself within these few minutes than I've ever known or suspected. Yes, I will help you. Are you willing to listen and believe what I say, even though you do not understand?"

"Yes, I'll try hard. But, Gene, I don't want to be tricked."

"I promise you that there are no tricks in being a Christian. First off, God has sent you here today. Now, I realize that is difficult for you to accept, but it is so. God loves you as much as He loves me, Horace. He has no favorites. Second, a person has to accept God as He is. No one sees God. He is Spirit. We are flesh and cannot see God. But, we can, and do, experience Him in many ways. He is the Creator of everything. Even those who don't believe there is a God experience all His good gifts of daily life. Third, and most important, is how God revealed Himself through Jesus Christ, His Only Son. It is a fact of pure record, recorded in the Bible, that His Son, Jesus Christ, came into our world to tell us, and show us, He loves us sinners enough to save our souls from damnation. When we believe this truth about God, it becomes so simple and clear that God, the Creator, would want all His human creation to believe and trust Him as Savior."

"Horace, all that I'm saying is true. But, not all can be grasped within a few minutes. It is by faith that anyone believes God and what He did for the sinful human race. Even the faith we use to believe is a gift from God. Since you have never been privileged to hear about the wonders of God in your home, it is more difficult for you to understand. But, understanding comes after acceptance of God's love in Christ Jesus. It was somewhat difficult for me too. However, my parents were not declared atheist as your parents are. They were just sinners, knowing there is a God, but doing nothing about their lives. Finally, they did, and Lindy and I followed. It might just be that God will use you to bring your parents to God's salvation. I hope this will be the case, Horace."

"Well, I've listened, Gene. I also believe you are truthful with me. You believe what you've told me, but it sounds strange to me. It is the very opposite of what I have heard all my life. However, I feel much better and have heard things that changed you. I hope I will be changed also. I promise to think about what you have told me. I also believe that I can come to accept that there really is a God who loves me. I don't know anything about praying. I've never prayed in all my life. But, I will try to talk to God somehow. If He is Who You say He is, do you think He will listen to me, Gene?"

"Horace, I am absolutely sure that God will listen to you. In fact, He is listening now." As you talk with Him, don't try to impress Him with your own intelligence. Just be open, honest, and willing to believe. Also, Horace, spend a lot of time listening to God. He will talk with you in many ways. At first, ask God to defend you against evil and the devil. He will. Horace, my friend, you can be sure that I will be praying for you, as well as several others you know, who are very interested in your life."

"Thanks, Gene. You have been a real good friend, and a lot of help. I must be going. As you know, I must help Daddy with the many chores. Sometimes I wonder how much longer he can hold out to do so much. He is a hard worker. I love my Dad and Mom. For what little I know, I wish they would have been believers so that I could have been. So long, Gene. I'll see you in a few days."

"Goodbye, Horace. I've enjoyed your company. Come anytime. You are welcome at my house anytime."

Chapter 25

Second Wedding Plans

Timothy graduated from Seminary during the third week of May. Betty completed her second year. Both became busy preparing for their wedding. Betty went home for six weeks. She was making all plans for her family and a few other close friends to attend the wedding. In all, there were fourteen, or possibly sixteen, who would need a place to stay for two nights. She had written Timothy for help in preparing for her family and friends.

Millie and Frank prepared for the parents of Betty in her extra bedroom. Laird and Alice Dubose prepared for Betty's brother and his wife. Ada Jenkins prepared for two of Betty's sisters. Becky Skelton prepared for three family girl friends. Stanley and Ruth Cory prepared for four girls, other family friends. Larry and Ruth Willoby prepared for two young men, family friends.

Timothy wrote Betty about a week later to say that all accommodations had been met. The church was excited about their hosting the wedding. Betty would stay at the home of Sandy and Pete. Marie Tidwell, Jean Nobles, and Marsha Wimple were responsible for rehearsal, decorations, and reception. They were encouraged to ask for help from anyone else for any needs that might arise which they did not foresee.

There had been many wedding at Spring Hollow Baptist Church back through the years. But, none for its pastor. This wedding was for all the church family. Everyone would have a part. In fact it was our wedding.

The local county seat newspaper had been alerted of its importance. The editor assured them would print the story. The Seminary agreed to send representatives for pictures and write-ups. Neither Timothy nor Betty initiated the Seminary's decision. It was a first, and the school wanted it recorded. Certain members of Spring Hollow Baptist requested the Seminary's action. Upon their investigation, the story seemed reasonable and proper since both bride and groom were students. Several of their close friends would be attending the wedding.

Marsha, Jean, and Marie decided they better look further into Betty's needs than just having the wedding at Spring Hollow Baptist Church. Since so much was to be done by the women of the church, someone suggested it would be a wonderful gift to have Betty's wedding dress made right here in Spring Hollow. All they needed was her dress size, her choice of materials, color, and a few other incidentals, along with shoe size.

Jean called Timothy to get Betty's home address and telephone number. She would take care of all Betty's needs. Marsha called two women of the church who were good seamstresses, Sally Canton and Katie Steale, both deacon's wives. But, being deacon's wives had nothing to do with asking them to help with sewing. They were known far and wide for their sewing ability.

When Marsha stated her request to the two women, they were overjoyed about the plans to make Betty's wedding dress.

"Marsha, my dear, you are so thoughtful to suggest this for Betty. I'm sure she will be pleased. I'll need two week's time for what I'll be doing. If we can sew to her exact size, no problem should be expected when Betty arrives before the wedding." said Sally.

"Wonderful, marvelous idea!" said Katie. "Sally and I will dress Betty so pretty that she might not want to get out of her dress after the wedding laughed Katie. We will do whatever is best for our new bride. What a wonderful and exciting time we have coming. Isn't it just great to have the wedding at our church? Pat is just about besides herself." said Katie.

"As soon as we hear from Betty, we will give ya'll the information. I'm so pleased with everything and with you two dear women." said Marsha.

Marie called Ada and Becky. She asked Ada to talk with Patsy and Alice for their help. Becky was asked to call Louise, Cynthia, and Ruth for their help in the early planning. Others including some teenagers were also asked to help.

When Jean asked Timothy for Betty's telephone number, he asked; "What's cooking between you women, Jean?"

"I'll let you know after I talk with Betty, Timothy. You will have to wait and guess. But, I'll bet you will be surprised and happy." said Jean.

"O.K. I'll wait." said Timothy, and gave Betty's telephone number and address to Jean.

The next evening Jean called Betty and talked for about forty-five minutes.

"Betty, this is Jean Nobles of Spring Hollow Baptist Church. Hi."

"Hi. Why, yes, I remember you. It's good to hear from you. Is everything alright there?"

"Oh, yes. It couldn't be better. We are going all out for you and Timothy. You two deserve everything, and more, than we are planning."

"Well, I might question that, Jean. By the way, what are you planning?"

"Well, I hope you concur, Betty, but we are planning your whole wedding just as you will want it. Does that sound O.K., Betty?"

"Anything you good people will do will be alright with me, Jean. You are so kind and thoughtful. I've wondered a lot about how I should go about the wedding. It has bothered me somewhat."

"Don't you worry one bit more, Betty. We women folk have everything going your way. I believe you will like what we are doing. We'll keep you posted as progress is made, and the wedding date approaches. But, right now, I need to ask you personal questions about yourself. Please don't say no. Because what we are planning for you and Timothy is marvelous. Our church is so happy about it all. I need your dress size, shoe size, colors, etc."

"Oh, my goodness! This is a dream. Why is the Lord so good to me?"

Betty gave Jean all she asked for and preparations were underway within two days. It was discovered that Ada was almost the same size as Betty. She became the model for Betty's dress.

Betty wrote Timothy a few days later and asked what plans he had made toward their wedding. Since she had decided on pale pink for her color, she thought perhaps a white suit would be appropriate for him.

"Betty, I don't know too much about selecting colors for weddings. You see, I've never been the principal subject before. If you think white for me and pink for you is appropriate, it suits me fine. Perhaps I could wear the white suit during future summer events. It's O.K. with me. Your choices are just fine." wrote Timothy.

Betty wrote Jean that the colors suited Timothy, and that he would wear a white suit and white shoes. No one else would need special colors. She would let her sister, who would be her maid of honor, pick her own color. The same would be for Timothy's best man, who by the way, would be his Dad.

As promised, Jean kept Betty appraised of the progress toward the wedding date. Her dress was gorgeous and fit Ada as perfectly as it would fit Betty. They teased Ada for not wanting to take the dress off after modeling. Ada liked herself dressed up for a wedding. "If, she said, "I could just find me a good man to match my wants."

Larry and Dick had been selected by the men of the church to take Timothy into the city and fit him up with a white suit and shoes. Timothy was reluctant to go along with their plans, but after friendly persuasion, went along graciously. It was a gift from the church, and they wanted him to represent his people properly, as Dick and Larry suggested.

Timothy was pleased. Never before in all his life had he been the object of such love and concern. He thanked God for these many blessings and asked Him to continue His blessings upon the people of Spring Hollow. Betty's family arrived Friday afternoon before the wedding date set for Sunday morning. The various hosts were at the church to receive their guests for the weekend. It was a joyous time to meet Betty's family. Timothy was there to meet them also. He had not met any of them and was very anxious to do so. What he witnessed was indeed a great pleasure. They were so cordial and receptive of him, and he of them. Betty beamed with joy as she witnessed Timothy hug her mother, father, and sisters. It was a definite sign of good

215

taste. Timothy told them they would meet his family the next day, Saturday afternoon.

Betty was whisked away by Marsha to the home of Sally, and later Katie, for the final dress modeling. Both women were very pleased to see Betty. When they showed her the wedding dress, she gasped for breath.

"What a beautiful dress. How did you do such work?" asked Betty.

"Wait until you see the veil and train together with your dress. Katie is on her way over with them. I hope you like them too." said Sally.

"Oh, I know that I will." beamed Betty.

In the meantime Betty tried on her dress. It was a perfect fit. Ada was indeed a good model. Betty twisted and turned about in front of the long length mirror, admiring her beautiful dress. Just then, Katie came in with her veil and train.

"Hi, Betty. Gee, you look beautiful. Just wait till we finish you out with the veil and train. Will you promise to take them off?" laughed Katie.

"I promise, Mrs. Katie."

"O.K., here goes. Marsha, help with the train. I hope it is not too short. Do you like it?"

Betty was again twisting and turning before the mirror.

"Oh, my, my. It's the most beautiful wedding dress I have ever seen. It's a miracle. I could not have ever dreamed this would happen to me. Why, may I ask, are you doing this?"

"Because we love you very much, Betty. You are to be part of Brother Timothy's life among us. It's the lease we can do."

"Mother and Daddy are going to like this gift very much. They could never have afforded this dress."

"Actually, Betty dear, it is not the material that makes the beauty, but what we did with it. We prayed about it, and our Lord gave us the talent and ability to make it beautiful for you. We are glad you are satisfied with our work." said Katie.

"Oh, I am." With that, Betty gave all three women a big hug and kiss.

Chapter 26

A House for the Pastor/Bride

Once again, Pete and Sandy Carter would come to the need of an event eagerly awaited in the Spring Hollow Community. The event is the wedding of their pastor, Timothy Karr and Betty Archer. This wedding was the most talked about coming event, second only to the great revival going on in Spring Hollow.

Pete and Sandy were the only heirs to the estates of two widows who had died a few years before. Both widows, neither kin, left either her son or daughter considerable land acreage and each a house. Both houses were fairly old, but in good livable condition.

Pete and Sandy had allowed a couple in their early fifties to live in Sandy's house, free for taking care of both properties. They were trusted people and the deal had proven very valuable for Pete and Sandy. Jim and Pearlie Barker were faithful members of Spring Hollow Church. He was a carpenter and painter and very good at his profession. Most of the community depended upon Jim for their repairs. Pearlie was mostly a house-keeper, but many times, she would help her husband in work too difficult for him to accomplish alone.

On Saturday morning, a week after Timothy made the wedding announcement, Pete and Sandy drove over to talk with Jim and Pearlie about the livable condition of the other house. During the week they had discussed, and came to the conclusion, that Pete's house would be offered to Timothy and Betty to live in as long as it was needed. They felt very good about this decision to help their pastor and wife off to a good start.

"Good morning, Jim, Pearlie." said Pete as he got out of his car.

"Hi folks." beamed Sandy with a big smile.

"Hi to ya'll. It's good to see you." said Jim.

"Yes it is, and just in time for a hot cup of coffee. And, Pete, if you have been good to Sandy this week, I might just sweeten you up with a fresh cut of lemon pound cake." said Pearlie.

"Wow! I knew there was a good reason for us to come over this morning, Pearlie. No one in two hundred miles can bake a pound cake like you. Let's get to it now." beamed Pete with his big smile.

"Come on in and have a seat at the table." responded Pearlie.

"Pearlie, don't pay too much attention to hungry Pete. He is always eating. I don't know why he doesn't get as big as a barrel." smiled Sandy.

"He works hard." Jim chimed in.

"Let's enjoy it all as we talk about a project that needs attention." said Pete.

"Pearlie, I admire the way you keep this old house. It's so neat. You and Jim are a great blessing to us." said Sandy.

"Jim, how long would you say it will take to put my old house in shape for living in again?"

"Can't just say, Pete, but would not be too long. Why? You ain't figuring on selling are you?"

"Oh, no. Now what we talk about here today must not be uttered again outside this room. Ya'll promise?"

"Why, shore Pete. Pearlie, you heard what Pete said. I don't want another woman to hear this news. "Ain't you women the gossipers of the community anyhow?" laughed Jim.

"Now, look here, Jim, Pearlie and I are special. Aren't we, Pearlie?" smiled Sandy.

"We shore are, and if I hear much more of this, I'm a good mind to take back this pound cake." laughed Pearlie.

"Can ya'll break away for a while to ride over and look the house and place over. It shouldn't take more than an hour or so. Pearlie and Sandy can look over the inside, while we look about the outside, etc. Does that sound fair, ladies?" Pete said.

"We'll do whatever is necessary, Pete. Don't look for too much that is needed to be done. The house is in good shape. It might need a little paint here or there and dusted out. We keep it up pretty well. After all, that's the deal you made with us." said Pearlie.

"We'll make sure the water pump is working properly. Sometimes when a pump is not used much, it will dry out. But, that should not be too big a problem. I've not noticed any roof leaks. To tell the truth, Pete, she is in pretty good condition. Let's go over and look her over." said Jim.

"What's the occasion, Sandy?" asked Pearlie.

"We are thinking of offering it to Brother Timothy and Betty to live in after they are wed. Would you and Jim like to have them as neighbors? They will need a place to live until their own house can be built."

"What an act of love, Sandy. You and Pete are the best folks. I wish the whole world were full of people like you two. You are always willing to share. Jim and I often talk about how blessed we are to know you and Pete. You have been so good to us. That's why It's a pleasure to take care of your property. It really is a good home for us." said Pearlie with tears in her eyes.

"Well, Pearlie, thanksgiving works both ways. You and Jim are a great blessing to us. We are fortunate to have good trusting friends to help us. We both love and serve the same wonderful Lord and Savior. He is the reason we love and trust each other."

"I'll say amen to that, Sandy. There's not a day goes by that Pearlie and me don't pray for ya'll." said Jim.

The house, outbuildings, and immediate grounds were looked over thoroughly. A few things were agreed upon to change. The yard fence needed replacing, as well as the fence around the garden and small barn. Some painting was needed inside, but all thought it best to wait and let Timothy and Betty make their recommendations of colors, if they chose to live in the house.

Sunday morning was a bright, sunny, and fairly warm day. Sunday School was again registered above enrollment. This had become the usual for more than a year. Joyous times reigned at Spring Hollow Baptist Church during Bible study and wonderful fellowship. No one wanted to be absent. Every Sunday there was a fresh, vibrant spirit among each class. This same spirit carried over into each worship service. It was a great time to be alive and experiencing the work of the Holy Spirit.

Pete looked for Timothy among all the many people pouring out of their classes and into the auditorium. He got his attention and drew him aside for a moment.

"Timothy, has anyone invited you to lunch with them today?"

"Not yet, Pete, but if things go as usual, someone will. Why?"

"You've got your invitation. Sandy and I have a thing to discuss with you. Preach up a good appetite, and we will see you at our house around 12:30 p.m."

"I'll need to get away soon after dinner. The hospital called me earlier about an old man who is a patient. He gave them information that he was a member here. He does not live in this community. The hospital said his name was Lon Ables, very old, perhaps in his early nineties. Do you know him?"

"Yes, many years ago. I thought he was dead. None of his people live here anymore. I might ride into town with you, if that is O.K."

"Sure, company is always appreciated. See you later."

Timothy pushed his plate away after eating and listened to Pete and Sandy tell of plans for his and Betty's future. Deeply concerned, he silently asked God why he was receiving all these special favors from the folk of Spring Hollow, and especially from the Carters. In answer, he felt a warm, calm feeling come over him that gave assurance that all was well.

Timothy promised to check out Betty's plans for next weekend, without revealing any secrets to her. The three agreed it would be a joy to see her surprised. Timothy wondered how could she not like living in such a good community. He would not see the house until next Saturday. Actually, there were surprises for him, also.

When Timothy and Pete arrived at the hospital and inquired about Mr. Ables, the receptionist directed them to a couple seated in the waiting room. The receptionist told them that Mr. Ables had died about twenty minutes before they arrived. The couple was waiting for a telephone call from another relative.

Timothy and Pete introduced themselves, and Timothy asked what he could do to help in their need. The woman was a niece and in her mid-sixties. There were no Able children living, only a few nephews and nieces. It would be up to them to make plans for the funeral. Mr. Able's wife, who had preceded him in death, was buried in a Methodist Church cemetery about one hundred miles to the north, and in another county. This niece assumed they would bury her uncle there, alongside his wife. Her pastor, who was a Methodist minister, had been in contact and willing to assist with funeral plans. She thanked Timothy and Pete for coming and showed deep appreciation for their effort. After prayer, led by Timothy, they left; feeling their visit was accepted.

Lunch with Betty had become a regular event. Generally, they met at the school cafeteria. Today, Tuesday, was a full day for both. Only thirty-five minutes were allowed for them to eat and get to their class. But, it was always a joy to see and talk with each other after a long weekend.

"Betty, I have a bit of news for you and a proposition for you to consider. We will not have time today to discuss all details. They can come later and with more clarity. The church is flabbergasted over our choice to have our wedding there. I wish you could have heard their response when I suggested the idea. We have no worry at all, none. Would you like to live in the country, in an old house, but very sturdy and comfortable?"

"Timothy, dear, what are you trying to tell me?" Are the folk at Spring Hollow providing us a house too?"

"I'll say. It's not all the folk, but two dear friends of ours. Remember Pete and Sandy Carter? Well, they own land and two houses left them by each of their mothers. Neither the widows were kin. They left everything to Pete and Sandy. Sandy's part and house is occupied by a couple who cares for both properties. Pete's house is the one we are offered. Give it your best thoughts and tomorrow we'll say more about it. Right now, we had better be on our way to class. I'll see you tomorrow. By the way, plan on going to Spring Hollow with me on Friday afternoon."

221

At lunch on Wednesday, Betty was all smiles. All this goodness promised from the folk in Spring Hollow seemed like a dream, but she knew it was so. She also knew that it was an act of love. How she wished that all of God's churches were of a like spirit.

"Timothy, I'm free to go with you Friday. But, where will I stay? Am I becoming a burden? Are you sure that this is not just your idea that you want me to get used to your preaching?" she smiled.

"You will be Sandy's guest for the weekend. Bring your necessary classwork. You will have time to do it all. We'll drive to school on Tuesday morning. She probably has some plans for your spare time. I'll bet you all will discuss wedding plans. My suggestion would be, let loose and let them go, go, go." beamed Timothy.

"I'm happy about all this, Timothy But, I hope it doesn't spoil us. God must have something very special in His plans for us in Spring Hollow. Shall we wait and see?"

On the way out of the city, Betty asked Timothy to stop by a novelty store. She wanted to buy Sandy something in token of appreciation for her hospitality. What she bought was appropriate for Sandy. She knew Sandy would accept any gift of a worthy item. It was indeed an act of love from Betty.

They arrived at the Carter home around 6:30 p.m. They were already on the front porch before Pete heard their steps. Sandy rushed to the door to greet her dear friend.

"Hello, Betty. Welcome again to our home. This is a visit we have been anxiously waiting for."

"Hi, Sandy, Pete. It's good to see you again, and so soon."

"Evening, folks. I bring you the heart of my heart. Ya'll make her behave, now you hear." Timothy smiled jokingly.

"You leave her be, Timothy. We will give her the best. Betty, you look tired. Has school been hard on you this week?"

"Pretty much so, Sandy. I'm looking for a little peace in about four weeks. I'm planning on enjoying this summer a lot, including all that is to happen here in Spring Hollow. I really don't know how to respond to all the love you folk are giving. To tell the truth, I hope it never stops."

"Oh, it won't, Betty. Spring Hollow people know how to treat friends. I'm glad to be one of them, especially at this time. All we want you and Timothy to do is relax and let us show our appreciation."

"Timothy, please stay long enough to have supper with us. Everything is ready to be served. Why don't you call Millie and let her know. Then, she won't be worried about her son." said Sandy.

"Are you sure that you have enough cooked? I'm starved."

"In that case, none will be left over. Pete doesn't like leftovers."

"I'll call Millie."

At supper their conversation was about many things. Betty thought it such a joy to be a guest in this dear Christian home of Pete and Sandy. However, their conversation began, it would finally get around to the wedding plans of Timothy and Betty.

Plans for tomorrow morning were discussed, and time set for the inspection of their new home. Timothy left the Carter home delighted to be a friend of these two dear people. As usual, Frank and Millie were glad to see him. They knew he would not be with them in their home much longer. Their son was a blessing in their old age. Timothy gave his heart to them, knowing how precious the meaning of family was to his dear friends. He slept well during the night. Frank had to call him for breakfast, because he had overslept. As usual, he was hungry, and past his usual coffee time before he ate.

"Eat your fill, son. I know you will have a busy day. Before night falls, you will have gone over this whole community, maybe even without dinner. It's not good for you to do without eating."

"Mrs. Millie, thanks for being concerned about me. But, I'll be O.K. I'll promise not to starve."

Timothy told Frank and Millie about the plans to live in the Carter house after the wedding. He asked that they not give out the word about it. Neither he nor Betty had seen the house. But, this morning they planned to see it all. Millie was excited. For Pete and Sandy to offer their house for their pastor was just wonderful.

Timothy drank another cup of coffee with Pete, Sandy, and Betty before they departed to view their new home. Timothy loved Pete's coffee. He brewed it strong, just right for him.

"Betty, I want you to be fair with yourself about the house. If you do not like it, or its location, your decision to not accept it will be O.K. with Pete and me. We are not trying to push something off on you and Timothy, just to have you as our neighbors. We mean to be of help. It's an old house, but sturdy. It's where Pete's mother lived for many years. She took care of it, as you will see. Its design may not meet with your liking."

"Sandy, I believe being a neighbor near you could be the best thing to ever happen to us. I was born and raised poor. Our house was, and is, old too. Living in the country is a pleasure. There is no better environment to bring up children. Even unseen as yet, we will like your house."

The four arrived at Pete's aunt's house. The yard fence had been repaired and weeds cut. Jim and Pearlie had washed the windows and painted the porch furniture, including the swing. From the outside, Betty liked what she saw. Her heart pounded with excitement. If the outside looked this good and all the surrounding area, including barn and garden, surely the inside must be beautiful.

"Betty, I like what I see." whispered Timothy.

"Me, too, dear."

They went inside. What a surprise they had! It was beautiful, so clean and neat. All the widow's furniture was still in place. It was like walking into an occupied house. Timothy and Betty felt the old house saying, "Welcome home, children."

Betty overheard Timothy say, "Lord, why are you doing this for us? We don't deserve such courtesy."

They toured the house carefully. Every room was in order, every chair in place. The kitchen was actually ready to begin cooking. Betty put her arm around Timothy and began crying.

"Timothy, this is unbelievable. It's like a dream. Although I've never had a dream like this. It's a miracle, That's what it is. Do you think our friends will believe us when we tell them about it?"

"They won't. But, we know It's true. Do you like it? Think you will be happy here? Do you think Pete and Sandy are doing too much? We can have our own garden, and raise chickens. You know preachers love chicken. We might even have a cow or two, and pigs. Boy, I love country-cured ham. We will have to have all that to feed our family." laughed Timothy.

"Silly boy, But I like your dreams. Sounds practical." responded Betty.

"It's a place, and we will make it a home. Many people will come to visit us. I like it. Do you?"

"Yes, very much. Shall we tell Pete and Sandy we will accept their gift?"

"Let's do. They are still on the porch. I think they wanted us to see it all and make up our minds without their presence, don't you?"

"Yes." said Betty.

Timothy and Betty walked slowly through the house and out onto the porch. It was obvious to Pete and Sandy that they liked the house. Betty had a radiance on her face that made Sandy very happy. Pete caught a bright gleam in Timothy's eyes, about the same time Timothy gave him a wink of approval. After all, how could anyone turn away from a love gift like Pete and Sandy was offering?

"Sandy, Pete, you are dear, dear friends. Timothy and I are not deserving of such generosity. But, if we refused this gift of love, you would not be blessed. It is a blessing to us, and our accepting is a blessing to you. Timothy and I will take extra care of your property. We love you for this also, and we accept. However, there is one question. Does the furniture go with the house? If it does, how much more will be added to the rent?"

"Rent?" Sandy responded with a hearty laugh. "Honey, there will be no rent. Yes, the furniture goes with it. We have no need for it. We have discussed several times about selling the house and furniture and perhaps an acre of land. As you see, we never did get around to doing it. I'm glad. Our Lord saw further into our future than we could. So, He preserved this gift for you.

Now, all this was a long time before we ever heard of Timothy Karr and Betty Archer. God does work in marvelous mysterious ways, doesn't He?"

"Oh my, yes. That's why we love Jesus so much. I don't know how anyone could doubt His love and awesome power."

Pete and Timothy just listened and were beaming in smiles.

"What two wonderful women, Brother Timothy Aren't we blessed a whole bunch?"

"Yeah, boy, and there will be more and better times in the future."

"Betty, the only expense you will have is the power and propane gas. Think you can manage that? There is a good dependable fireplace, and plenty of wood to burn, as much as you can put Timothy to gather up. Best of all, you will be neighbors to Jim and Pearlie and us. There will be no strings attached. Whenever you please, you can move. Everything is left to you. I'm speaking for both of us. I hope you two are around a long time." said Pete.

"I've been admiring that swing. You just can't imagine how much time I plan to occupy it for my naps. Betty will be in the kitchen laboring over my hot meals, and I'll be resting, waiting to eat. That sounds great."

"Not too fast, my dear. We will have to learn to cook country style before I turn you loose on your own. You might get too rested to enjoy my cooking." laughed Betty. Sandy agreed.

Pete stood by listening to Timothy tease Betty. He was enjoying the conversation. However, he knew Timothy had much to learn and experience about marriage. His smiles were approval of how Betty and Sandy responded to Timothy. Pete also knew that he felt good about the prospect of Timothy and Betty living in his old house. They would be comfortable and to them, good neighbors. He thanked God for all His great and good blessings. None of this had cost him anything. The very least he could do would be to help someone, in this case Timothy and Betty, with God's gift. He was pleased to do so.

The church folk were surprised to see Betty visiting again on Sunday morning. However, they were pleased as always. Some few teased her about spying them out to determine if she really did want to live among them. The children loved her and asked that she visit them every Sunday. Betty's big smile assured them that her love was mutual and for them to wait patiently a few more weeks for her permanent residence. She also assured them that parties would be at her house, just for them. Betty did not realize just how long God, in His providence, would allow her promise to the community children to last. In later years, her own children were the reason community children were always at her house, and hers at theirs. It is always best that we do not know what God has in store for us. We need only to trust Him and thank Him for whatever plans and blessings He wants to give us. Whatever the gift, it is divine love from our Heavenly Father.

Chapter 27

The Wedding Day In Spring Hollow Baptist Church

Sunday morning was a bustling time at Spring Hollow Baptist Church. The Sunday School broke all records in attendance, as well as the Worship Service. This was the day in church history to forever be remembered. Many visitors were present. The membership was asked to stand in the rear and down the outside isles of the auditorium, if necessary, to make room for visitors.

Several Seminary students were there on behalf of Timothy and Betty. They were awe struck to see so many people honoring their friends. Among the students were Junior Clark and Ralph Gates. They had wanted to come to Spring Hollow for a long time, but their work and school would not allow it. However, for the wedding of Betty and Timothy, they would not be denied.

The visitors heard singing of the like they never heard before. Dick Reveere led the choir in singing "The Banner of the Cross." The choir was absolutely wonderful. Christ's message in song was strong and effective. The congregation erupted into applause at the conclusion. Everyone knew where Timothy was. But, he was not on the pulpit platform. John Canton was in charge of all the worship activities for which he had been assigned. He announced the wedding at the end of the worship service. He also asked that all remain seated while the bride walked down the isle. Everyone would be able to see her if all would remain seated. The children would be disadvantaged otherwise.

John introduced the preacher for today. "Our preacher for today is Brother Thomas Green, pastor of Willow Bend Baptist Church, the home church of our Brother Timothy. Several of his congregation are with us today, including the family of Timothy. Also, we are deeply honored to have with us the family and friends of Betty. Brother Green, we are indeed pleased to have you to lead us in preaching God's Word today. You will also conduct the wedding as planned. We will pray for you and for each other. After the special music, please lead us as Jesus leads you. Now, a word from Brother Dick Reveere."

Dick announced, "Joe and Callie Sims will sing "I'll Tell the World That I Am a Christian." They will be accompanied by their mother at the piano. Please listen. These two young people will bless our hearts."

Jack, the ex-bully at school was present as well as two other ex-bad boys of the same group. Their lives had been dramatically changed by Jesus to serve Him. They listened to Joe and Callie sing, and praised the Lord for the privilege of being in this special worship service. Joe and Callie got a standing ovation at the conclusion of their special song. They did, indeed, bless the congregation.

Brother Thomas Green stated his deep appreciation to the church for this special privilege of leading in worship and the wedding of Timothy Karr and Betty Archer. His message emphasized the continuance of encouragement to each other for spiritual growth and mission support. Several times, the congregation responded with hearty amens and praises. He was a blessing. In his concluding remarks, Brother Green praised God for Timothy and Betty. He showed deep emotion as he thanked Spring Hollow Baptist Church for calling Timothy as pastor and also for their unusual tender love to allow their wedding here. His comments brought many to tears.

Brother Green emphasized the purpose of the invitation. His plea was salvation for the lost and surrender to Christ's service to His children. Dick announced the invitation hymn "I Surrender All." On the very first stanza, Jack stepped to the isle and came forward. He had already joined his home church, but wanted his many friends to know the change that had occurred in his life. He thanked the church for Gene and Joe. Then he took his seat.

"Now my friends, we all are honored to witness the wedding of your pastor and his bride."

The pianist started the wedding march "Here Comes the Bride." Timothy and his father had quietly entered the auditorium from a side door and moved to the front of the pulpit. Betty and her father were standing in the front door and began their slow walk to the front. There were a lot of oohs and aahs as she came down the isle. She was beautiful in her pale pink wedding dress. Timothy waited in his white suit. They were indeed a gorgeous pair, and very special to the church.

Brother Green performed the ceremony without a flaw. After, he announced the reception in the fellowship hall. He stated that the situation would be very crowded. He encouraged all to meet and greet Timothy and Betty and to move on so that others could do the same. There would be food for all. He told them to please enjoy themselves. The Bride and Groom departed to the reception area to meet their friends. Today was a time in the history of Spring Hollow Baptist Church never to be repeated again.

Chapter 28

The Honeymoon

Timothy and Betty left for their wedding honeymoon shortly after the reception. Timothy had made reservations for a cabin in the beautiful mountains about fifty miles beyond the home of Betty's parents. Betty promised her mother they would spend a day or so with them on their way back to Spring Hollow. At that time, she would be picking up all her belongings, including all the gifts her neighbors and friends had given since the news of her wedding. It was hoped that their car would hold all the various stuff.

Her mother laughed with Betty while they discussed items almost as old as her daughter. Perhaps, some of these things need another home, for instance the trash heap.

"Betty, you do not want your new home to become cluttered with your old and discarded antiques. I know they remind you of precious memories of events and people. But, some things need to be forgotten. Not people, of course."

"I'll decide Mom, what to do when we stop by. I won't have much time to figure out what is most important, will I? Whatever I leave, you can keep or throw away. Would that be too much to ask, Mom?"

"No. I'll do whatever you desire. Please be careful on your travel. We will be praying for you and Timothy. Timothy is such a fine young man. I'm so glad you chose him for your husband. Our Lord has blessed both of you. He must have great plans for His Kingdom in His choice of you two dear people. Timothy's family is just adorable. They are so loving and caring. Betty, you also have roots in a strong loving family. Keep that bond going through your family now. We all will be expecting great things from Spring Hollow in the future. Remember, God's work is just as important in Spring Hollow as it is anywhere else. So long, Betty. We will see you in a few days. Be careful."

"Bye, Mom. We will be praying all this time for us and our families."

The old Chrysler was loaded and ready to go. Someone had written with white chalk "Just Married, Be Careful, God loves you," on the rear trunk lid. Most of the people were out front and waving goodbye as Timothy and Betty drove away. No one followed them. Before, while everyone who could get inside the fellowship hall, Brother Green led in prayer for their safety and well being.

Betty suggested they stop for the night after Timothy had driven one hundred and fifty miles. Just outside of the town, Betty spotted a restaurant advertisement, and they decided to check it out. It turned out to be a good clean family type restaurant. Each ordered a light dinner and enjoyed themselves for about an hour.

"Betty, It's been a good, long day, and we need the rest. Will you agree that we stay the night here, that is, if there is a hotel available?"

"I like the idea. We can't reach our cabin tonight anyhow. Let's ask the restaurant manager about a hotel."

Timothy was given directions to a hotel owned and operated by a deacon of the First Baptist Church. He was assured they would be taken care of.

"By the way; asked the manager, where are you folks from? You look like newlyweds."

"We are from Spring Hollow, and we are newlyweds. I'm Timothy Karr, the pastor of Spring Hollow Baptist Church, and this is my beautiful wife, Betty."

"Well, now. I can't accept your money for your visit with us because it would not be appropriate. This is indeed an honor for ya'll to have dinner with us. We here have heard about the revival going on in Spring Hollow. I don't know where that community is, but it must be a good place to live. Please excuse me for just a minute. Now, don't leave before I return."

"Well, OK, if you say so." responded Timothy, as he and Betty stood aside to let another couple pay their bill.

The manager phoned the hotel and informed his friend about Timothy and Betty. He was assured the wedding suite was available.

"Thank you young folks for waiting. I've been told it paid you to wait." he laughed. "My friend at the hotel has reserved for you the wedding suite. It's very nice. And, I told him who you are. So, my friends, you have chosen the right time, town, and place to spend the night."

"We could not have known all this, Betty." said Timothy.

"Sir." said Betty, "Do you believe in miracles?"

"Why, sure, why do you ask?"

"Well, it seems everywhere we go the things happening to us is beyond our power or anyone else." said Betty.

"All I can say is that the Lord takes care of His children. I love to help Him do it." responded the manager.

When Timothy and Betty arrived at the hotel, the deacon and his wife were waiting to greet them.

"Welcome, Brother and Mrs. Karr. You will be our guest for tonight and breakfast tomorrow morning."

"Thank you, my friend." responded Timothy "But, you should not go to all this trouble for us."

"No trouble at all. To have you two people spend the night with us is a blessing from God. We have heard about God's great work in Spring Hollow. I wish you could stay a week and tell us all about it." said the Mrs.

"It is not what we are doing my friend, but what Jesus is doing. The people are allowing Him to do His work and will through their lives. They are greatly blessed, and God does His work." said Timothy.

They were taken to the bridal suite and left for the night. Timothy and Betty embraced each other with all the tenderness and compassion they knew how to give. Timothy prayed for Jesus to consecrate their marriage to His glory as they became one in consummation.

At breakfast, Timothy was asked to pray for God's blessing upon the fellowship, food, and travel safety. The hotel manager and his wife had asked Timothy and Betty to dine with them during breakfast. Timothy talked about what the Holy Spirit was doing in Spring Hollow. It was a refreshing time for the deacon and his wife. He asked permission to discuss with the local newspaper about writing an article concerning their visit there and about the revival in Spring Hollow. It was O.K. to do so, said Timothy But, not to glorify them or anyone else other than God. This was agreed to.

Timothy and Betty continued on their journey and arrived at their secluded cabin about noon. It was a beautiful place and so quiet and peaceful. Several couples occupied other cabins in the area. On Tuesday evening, four couples enjoyed a cookout together. It became a sharing time with newfound friends and what their plans were in the future. Wednesday, about 2:00 p.m., Timothy and Betty left for her parent's home, which was about fifty miles away. Betty got busy separating old stuff to take home or throw away. Before nightfall, the old Chrysler was packed full. They laughed a lot as armload, after armload was somehow pushed into the car. Some items were important and valuable. Others only had sentimental memories so touching, she could not dispose of them. Mrs. Archer was pleased to see her daughter so happy. Timothy was accepted into the family as one of their loving children. He was pleased to hear kind words of acceptance. He promised the Archers he would love Betty very much and take the best care of their daughter. The family was given the address of their new home and was urged to write often. Timothy assured them Betty would complete her Seminary work. He thanked them for sending her to the Seminary. Otherwise, he would never have met her, married her, and be in this home today. He gave Jesus all the credit for their being together.

They took another route home, one that neither had traveled. It afforded beautiful scenery and places both needed at this time in their lives. Some places where people have ruined God's beauty for selfish reasons, is stressful to see. They wanted to avoid those kinds of scenes on their way home. What Timothy and Betty experienced was God's marvelous beauty, and it gave them rest in mind and body.

234

Timothy and Betty arrived back in Spring Hollow, and to their new home, late Saturday afternoon. As they passed through the county seat town, Betty suggested they stop at a grocery store for necessary food items to hold them over until Monday. Several people in the store recognized Timothy and congratulated them on their marriage.

When they drove into the yard of their beautiful, clean new home, there was an appearance that much activity had been going on. Four or five green flower baskets were hanging on the porch. What they saw inside was unbelievable. The entire house had been appropriately decorated. On the dining table was a note telling them to check out the refrigerator and cabinets before going off to grocery shop. There was fresh cooked food in the refrigerator, along with milk, tea, colas, juices, and other items of food. Candles and place mats were on the dining room table. The small kitchen table was set and a wish in each place.

Betty went into the bathroom and found good smelling soaps, bath towels, and face cloths ready. She began to cry. Timothy ran to her asking what was wrong.

"Timothy, my love, I just can't understand why these good people are doing all this for us. What have we done to deserve such kindness? I feel so unworthy."

"Honey, I believe it's Christ working through them to accomplish His kingdom's work. I see no other answer. People, in general, are not this responsive to sincere commitments. Only Jesus can prompt folk to do righteous acts. There is no telling what will be the future outcome for what is happening in Spring Hollow. Oh, I enjoy what I'm experiencing. If it lasts into my old age, I'll still be young when the end comes."

"What a truth! It's a happiness with eternal dimensions. We really should not question what's happening to us. I believe Jesus wants all His children to be blessed in ways that cannot be explained by human lips. His ways are never our ways, nor His thoughts our thoughts."

"Yes, I'll agree. Now, shall we indulge in a portion of this good food? I'll put on a pot of coffee. If I know Millie Stewart as having anything to do with what's in the kitchen cabinets, there is some of her coffee just waiting to be brewed. She taught me how to brew coffee. Yep, here is her gift. In a few minutes, you will be smelling an aroma that will make your nose twitch with glee." Timothy laughed.

Supper by candlelight was a pleasure. Tonight set the stage for many more like evenings in this lovely home of the pastor and his beautiful wife of the Spring Hollow Baptist Church. After supper, Timothy turned in his Bible, lying on the table, to Psalm 8 and slowly read aloud its magnificent message. Betty began praying as they bowed their heads to God in reverence. After their devotion, Timothy reached to take Betty's hand.

"My dear sweet wife, I love you so much. Only Jesus knows how much."

"My dear loving and honorable husband, I love you deeply, with all my heart. Surely our marriage is God's gift to us. Let's cherish it to His honor, forever."

"Amen, amen. May I now ask your permission to finish preparing the message for tomorrow? Or, do you wish me to help with the dishes, etc?"

"I'll handle the kitchen affairs while you finish your sermon thoughts. You haven't had a lot of time to prepare your message this week. Take you another cup of coffee and get along."

Betty spent the next hour washing dishes and cleaning up the kitchen. As she worked, she hummed or sung quietly her favorite hymns. This was her own workplace, her kitchen, her home, where she must display all the good qualities her mother ever taught her. Her thoughts were good and meaningful. She was not obliged to give account for whatever acts or words had been spoken or acted out before in this house. But now, it was her turn. She wished, yes planned, to let the love of God permeate every lifestyle to His glory and honor. Timothy would agree, she knew, that to make this home an example for Jesus would take the commitment of both. It would be a task worthy of their energies.

She quietly entered the living room where Timothy sat near a reading lamp. His Bible was open and held in his left hand.

His hand was resting on his knee, and his head was bowed. Betty heard him quietly talking to the Lord, just above a whisper. She knew his mind was deep in thought. Quietly, she sat on the sofa and began praying for her husband, that Jesus would reveal His message to him tonight, and to the people of Spring Hollow tomorrow. A moment later, Timothy raised his head and saw his lovely wife praying.

"Hi, sweet. Are you finished with all the kitchen chores?"

"Yes, dear. There was not much to do tonight. But, I'm tired. I'm sure you are tired too. You drove all that distance without letting me help. Are all your thoughts about the message ready?"

"I think so. But, you know, my love, that I'm not a polished preacher. It is all a new experience with me. I'm growing, but slowly. Please be patient with me. Both of us must grow together, don't you agree?"

"I surely do. Timothy, you can always count on me to pray for you during sermon preparations and delivery. We are a team with Jesus as our Master and the Holy Spirit as our encourager."

The rain came down furiously all day Sunday. It was one of those days where the sky was dark gray and the sun seemed not to exist. A day like this is only good for indoor chores and a cozy nap. Children are restless to be cooped up inside. Mothers are not sure if her home will be intact when the rain is over. Her home becomes all things to all the family, including loud noises. However, it is her children and home. It does not happen too often, and she hopes to live through the ordeal.

Several old folk did not venture out into the weather to attend church. On a day like this, it was best they stay indoors. But, many families did. They counted any opportunity to attend Bible Study and Worship a joy. Even though their Sunday bests got a little damp, it did not dampen their spirit. As usual, attendance was high, and expectations that Jesus was going to bless them proved to be true. They had come to worship God. Their belief held true that He would.

Everybody was pleased to see Brother Timothy and his new bride, Betty. To Timothy and Betty, it was sheer joy to see all ages greeting them. Betty was in tears most of the morning. What was happening to her was unprecedented. Through it all, she loved Spring Hollow folk, and she let them love her. Timothy was already in the auditorium and speaking with someone on the front pew. Betty came by, touched his ear, and as he turned, she whispered;

"If heaven is better than this, I am anxious to get there. Whatever you preach this morning can't be any better than what I've already experienced from these good people."

"Aren't they wonderful? And, It's all because Jesus provided for us for this hour."

The church filled as the rain kept coming down. People laughed about it as if it was something special and might not happen again.

Brother Dick raised his voice somewhat higher than usual, because of the rain noise, and people enjoying their fellowship.

"Now folks, It's time to begin our singing. Please turn to the hymn "There Shall Be Showers of Blessings." The people roared about the hymn selection. But, they sang as they never had before.

Brother Jim Tilley led the congregation in prayer. He wept as he thanked Jesus for the great number attending Bible Study. His heart was humble, and his faith was strong as he talked to Jesus about the future of Spring Hollow. The people responded by amens and praises.

Brother Timothy announced the activities of the coming week and month.

"We are back from our vacation and living in our new home. Betty and I rejoice that we are living among the best of God's people. If you pass our way and smell an unusual odor, don't get alarmed, it will only be our cooking. After all, we do need to learn how. It's going to be years before we can catch up to you folk. Our home is your home. Come see us and stay awhile. We love you dearly."

The congregation applauded approval.

Chapter 29

Timothy and Betty Visit the Stewarts

Immediately after the worship service, Timothy found Millie. Howdy, Mrs. Millie. Timothy gave her a long hug as Frank gave them both a hug. I'm going to miss coming to your house as I've made it my home for nearly two years."

"It's going to be worse on us, Timothy, because we have loved every minute of our son living with us. You can never know what it has meant having you with us and so many times to prepare your meals."

"Well, as you can see, I've come off the better. I've gained about fifteen pounds since coming to Spring Hollow."

"Oh shucks, son. You are not a bit overweight. My cooking didn't help much."

"Mr. Frank, I haven't been too much help to you. When I came to live with you, my plans were to pitch in and help, as you would say, carry your weight. I didn't know that our church responsibilities would be so great. But, I know you understand. You two dear friend have been far too good to me."

"Not so, Timothy, the blessings have been ours. I've never in my whole life witnessed the love of Jesus working in our community, and for Millie and me to know His will. We are both old, but we have grown spiritually in the last two years, more than all the rest of our lives. Now, we are not losing you and Betty. We will always be your second home as long as we live. You can count on that. And, if I may say, I hope we will see some grandchildren before we go to be with the Lord. Does that sound a bit too far fetched?"

"Thanks, for all your love and care, Brother Frank. You and Mrs. Millie are indeed one of a kind. About the grandchildren, we hope to see you blessed with their presence." Betty had joined with them and was chatting with Millie.

"Brother Frank, I need to come over tomorrow morning and clean out my stuff and give you back your room. Betty will help me clean everything up. Will tomorrow morning be OK with you?"

239

"Why, yes, Timothy But don't be in too much of a rush to leave. Millie would love having you all for lunch, eh, Millie?"

"For sure we will. Betty, my child, I have some good recipes to share with you. I'm sure you will be pleased to get them."

"Oh, I will, Mrs. Millie. Any help will be appreciated toward me becoming a better cook. We'll see you folk tomorrow morning. After this, we want you to come visit our home that will be affectionately blessed with your presence. Will you all promise?"

"Sure thing. But, it won't just be one time. I intend to bring cooking over quite often, that is, if it is alright with Betty."

"Mrs. Millie, you are a darling. Come any time."

About 9:00 a.m., Timothy and Betty drove over to the Stewart home. Frank was sitting in the swing enjoying the breeze gently blowing from the west. Millie was busy about other matters of importance, like getting dinner ready. She had spent about an hour thumbing through her many recipes and selecting the best ones for Betty. She knew that her time to cook all these goodies again was short. Those thoughts didn't bother her anyway. Most were new in her mind, and cooking was done from scratch, meaning she needed no reading material to guide her actions. She heard Frank welcome his children, and she put off her apron as she left the kitchen and met Betty in the hallway.

"Good morning, my dear child. How are you today? You look just lovely."

"Thanks, Mrs. Millie. How are you? I hope you are not going to a lot of trouble for us."

"It's no trouble at all, child. Anything for my children is a pleasure. I hope you don't think I'm too motherly, Betty. I love you two so much."

"We are really indebted to you and Mr. Frank. I've never had anyone to express love to me as have you folk in Spring Hollow, and especially you and Mr. Frank."

"We don't know the future, what God has in store for us here. Whatever it is, I hope He will include Betty and Timothy Karr for a very long time. I feel someone someday will write our history how God worked His wonders of salvation and change in

Spring Hollow. You children will be listed as His special servants of this glorious change. We've only witnessed the beginning. You, dear, will see far greater wonders of God's grace. These wonders will not happen here in Spring Hollow only; but around the world in His Kingdom."

"Betty, I believe Jesus is preparing, and will call, youth and young couples to Himself for His cause. They will answer. The many scholarships already in place for our youth's Christian higher education are going to play a big role in God's preparing our people. It's amazing how strong the response has been toward this glorious work. We are being given privilege to overcome much ignorance about how God works when a people are committed to Him. Even within the past two and a half years, our minds have greatly enlarged toward Biblical knowledge and God's purpose among us through His Holy Spirit. I'm old, Betty, but oh, how thankful I am that Jesus has permitted me to see this vision, and be a helpmate toward its realization. I'm happy, so happy!"

"Oh, my! Thank you Jesus! What a vision! What hope! What praises to God's glory! I feel like I'm floating on clouds of glory. I really am. I've never heard before such a visionary testimony, Mrs. Millie. Surely, God has allowed me to hear it for my own need and call. I promise Jesus, now, that I will abide in Him; that He might fulfill, in me, His will in this vision for Spring Hollow."

So, it was to be; God sent Betty all over the world through her strong Christian mission education, teaching, and Godly example. She never doubted her call, or how God would work it out. Betty was required to be faithful, wherever she was in His service. It was her belief that God would send her into some foreign country. He chose to send her through the children, youth, and young couples of the Spring Hollow Baptist church. Later years, two of her own children would be called into God's world mission service.

The End

241